# WHEN SHE WAS GOOD

## BEST LESBIAN EROTICA

*Edited by*

TRISTAN TAORMINO

*Introduced by*

ALI LIEBEGOTT

CLEiS
PRESS

Published in the United States by Cleis Press, Inc., 2246 Sixth St., Berkeley, CA 94710.

Printed in the United States.
Cover design: Scott Idleman/Blink
Cover photograph: Celesta Danger
Text design: Frank Wiedemann

First Edition.
10 9 8 7 6 5 4 3 2 1

Trade paper ISBN: 978-1-62778-069-8
E-book ISBN: 978-1-62778-081-0

"X-Rated Exes" © 2006 by L. Elise Bland first appeared in *Naughty Spanking Stories from A to Z: 2* edited by Rachel Kramer Bussel (Pretty Things Press, 2006); "Domme's Games" © 2007 by Rachel Kramer Bussel was previously published in *Fantasy: Untrue Stories of Lesbian Passion* edited by Barbara Johnson and Therese Szymanski (Bella Books, 2007); "Native Tongue" © 2007 by Shanna Germain first appeared in *E Is for Exotic* edited by Alison Tyler (Cleis Press, 2007); "The Ant Queen" © 2006 by Roxy Katt first appeared on the Erotica Readers and Writers Association website (October 2006); "*Spoonbridge and Cherry*" © 2007 by Catherine Lundoff is from her book *Crave: Tales of Lust, Love, and Longing* (Lethe Press, 2007); "Sweet No More" © 2007 by Radclyffe first appeared in *H Is for Hardcore* edited by Alison Tyler (Cleis Press, 2007).

# CONTENTS

# FOREWORD

Tristan Taormino

Transgression can be a powerful aphrodisiac.
As queer people, we have already challenged
one powerful norm by claiming our queerness.
So when we tell stories of longing, desire, love,
affection and sex, those stories are, by defini-
tion, outside of dominant mainstream culture.
But the college kid, upper-crust society lady,
pro-domme, bootblack boi, female cop, butch
Daddy, grocery store clerk, and others who
inhabit the twenty-two stories in this book go
way past the point of queer lust and fucking.
They push even further beyond what's "normal," expected and acceptable.

For example, people in stories like Chandra
S. Clark's "The Waiting Is the Hardest Part"
and Anna Watson's "Chronic" eroticize emotions we're not supposed to think of as sexy,

like anger, jealousy and revenge. Others find pleasure in ordinarily nonsexual objects and activities, like the boi who shines shoes and also fucks dildos strapped to them in "Shine" by Jacqueline Applebee.

In some cases, transgression is embodied in the boundaries characters cross with the objects of their desire. It may take the form of seducing a woman under the guise of protecting her from the paparazzi in Missy Leach's "And the Stars Never Rise" or hitting on a friend's mom, then taking it one step further into delicious dominance and submission in "The Ant Queen" by Roxy Katt. Miel Rose's narrator travels a similar path to Katt's as she finds herself in the stockroom with a coworker who says, "Damn, girl, I'm old enough to be your mother."

In other stories, the traditional form of the couple is rejected as women explore their sexuality with more than one person at a time, played out in various configurations in "Playing with Toys" by D. Alexandria, "The Bridge" by Isa Coffey, "*Spoonbridge and Cherry*" by Catherine Lundoff, "The Storm Chasers" by Peggy Munson and "Angie's Daddy" by A. Lizbeth Babcock.

Sometimes, it's not the *who* but the *where* that embodies the boundary crossing, when someone literally steps outside the confines of the bedroom into public places, places we shouldn't have sex in or aren't allowed to, like downtown London, the Coronado Bay Bridge in San Diego, a San Francisco back alley, or in a famous Minneapolis sculpture garden.

In Rachel Kramer Bussel's story, a professional dominatrix begins to play with her date at a restaurant. When they eventually go somewhere private, the domme dishes out skills her male clients normally pay for. It's one illustration of how we can and do insert our selves and our queerness into traditionally heterosexual sex spaces. This theme is echoed in scenes set in a strip club in L. Elise Bland's "X-Rated Exes" and at a high-end escort agency in Nan Rogue's "Top Girl."

Another form of transgression can be about the connections we form that defy societal expectations, like the pair in Shanna Germain's "Native Tongue," who find their common language is not one of words. Or Valerie Alexander's lovers, who become so focused on one another that the rest of the world just melts away in their own version of "Paradise." Two stories take it to another level, toying with the lines between life and death: Alicia Goranson's vampire story and D. L. King's modern-day lesbian ghost story.

Like the woman headed to a sex club who wants to shed her sweet image in Radclyffe's story "Sweet No More," some of these characters' transgressions are entirely deliberate. Likewise, in "The Storm Chasers," Peggy Munson's narrator knows what she's doing when she says of the Amish girl she's fucking, "We want to make Ellie so dirty she can't go back." Some transgressions are more circumstantial, but the difference of what these women are doing is known, as with the two girls exploring their newfound desire at summer camp in Tamai Kobayashi's "Different Girls." Others are almost accidental, like one character's revelation of her bisexuality and its unexpected (and unresolved) consequences in "When She Was Good" by Betty Blue.

Ultimately, what ties all these stories together is the desire to push something perhaps a little too far, to give the middle finger to "polite society." These writers have given us vibrant characters who defy roles and expectations and challenge traditions and norms. These characters don't just go against the grain—they rub their leather-clad thighs, cum-soaked fingers, drenched pussies and saliva-coated cocks right up against the grain, leaving a mark so you know they were there.

Tristan Taormino
The Hudson Valley, New York

# INTRODUCTION:
# DUMPSTER DIVING

Ali Liebegott

I spent the summer I turned nine riding my bi-
cycle in circles in the small streets of an indus-
trial park behind my house with all the kids in
my neighborhood. My best friend Natalie, a
huge daredevil and troublemaker, had the idea
one day to look for lost treasures in the indus-
trial park Dumpsters. I don't even know what
we were expecting to find. Maybe beer. Or
some type of portal to a universe that didn't
have divorce or molestation or loneliness. Natalie climbed into the Dumpsters, one at a time,
while the rest of us waited in clusters, watching her head dip up and down over the green
metal side as she sifted through garbage.

  After climbing in and out of three or four
Dumpsters Natalie cried, "No way."

  Her head disappeared and she sat down in

the Dumpster. We all waited and listened to her rustle through what sounded like trash.

"What's in there, what?" we begged to know.

Then one at a time, Natalie started hurling what she had found over the side of the Dumpster to us. Each magazine landed with a slap on the pavement and featured a close-up cover of some disembodied female mouth sprayed with a face full of come.

"There's like hundreds in here," she cried. "They must make the magazines in one of these offices."

I'd never seen hard-core porn before and stood quietly next to the other kids as they flipped the pages. I remember being astounded at how glossy the pictures were. The pages were thick and the paper seemed really expensive.

"Let's get out of here before we get busted," I said.

Natalie climbed out of the Dumpster and we all divvied up the magazines and crammed them in our pockets. Then we rode our bicycles to a nearby park to further examine our literal booty. There were pages of huge pink pussies spread open and spilling pussy innards and giant veiny cocks and huge pancake-sized nipples dripping with buckets of milky come. In other words, the pages were filled with what seemed to be exercises on how to use a zoom lens. When I think about that day I can distinctly remember how the sun felt on my arms as we sat in the park flipping through those magazines, our bicycles scattered on the grass around us.

So this was sex. Giant floating body parts. I felt confused.

Natalie instructed us to bury the magazines in the park so we could come back and look at them whenever we wanted, so we all started burrowing tunnels into the hillside like gophers. Then we rolled up the magazines and shoved them into the holes we'd made. The next day when we came back, we couldn't find them.

"Someone probably stole them," Natalie complained.

I loved the idea of someone randomly coming to the park and digging up the landscape to pull out our porn stash. My father had spent my entire childhood walking across parks and beaches with a metal detector, finding thousands of pulltabs and a few nickels. I could understand the desire to find things. Except for my confusing yet long-standing crushes on Bob Barker, Gumby and Aquaman, even at nine I had a sinking feeling that I might be something weird like a lesbian. I wanted to find lesbians in the way that a nine-year-old could want that. I wanted to find something that felt true like the smell of dirt on my fingers after we'd dug the holes for the porn. Or something real like the amazing sun on my arms as we sat in the park, or the honesty of how concrete smells when it gets hot and wet and we all lay down on it after swimming at the public pool. Truth and realness and honesty. What can I say: I still had a tiny fire of hope at nine.

The next few years solidified each demon in our varied neighborhood kid souls. The future alcoholics made sure to start drinking every day. The eating disorder girls started looking at food as an enemy. The runaways got really good at packing their duffel bags and the future wife beaters and rapists practiced tying girls up in toolsheds and shooting the heads off lizards with BB guns. Natalie's older brother was a future wife beater. One day he promised to show us his porn magazines if we agreed to lock him in a lay down freezer in the garage and sit on the top of it while he tried to get out. He was thinking about becoming a Marine and this was his version of physical fitness training. Everyone knew locking a person in a freezer was stupid, but Walter was convincing when he insisted he was strong enough to get out of it. So we sat on top of the freezer, feeling afraid, as Walter scrambled on top of bags of frozen vegetables inside the freezer beneath us. As long as we could hear the bags of frozen vegetables shuffling around then he must still be alive, I reasoned. It was a miracle when Natalie's older sister came into the garage to get a soda. She'd been inside the house watching soap operas while we were about to kill her brother, if you can even imagine that.

"Where's Walter?" she said.

We sat stunned for a second and then thank god we pointed to the shuffling sound of vegetable medley bags beneath us. We were big-time busted, but Walter was alive and not brain damaged, and he did keep his promise and showed us his porn collection. The "lesbians" in his *Playboy*s sat naked across from each other and touched each other's nipples with their snowcone-pink acrylic nails. I remember pages of women with really round asses. I wanted real women. I wanted women with dark sunken eyes who would sit despondently with me on a curb and understand the beauty of fingertips that smelled like the earth after digging holes in the park to bury found porn. I wanted the obvious signs of fucked-up train-wreck women. But it seemed the train wreck in every woman I found in porn magazines was airbrushed out.

When I was eighteen I got the courage to buy my first bit of lesbian erotica. I was nervous so I just darted into A Different Light Bookstore in Santa Monica and then darted out. Unfortunately, I ended up with lesbian erotica poems. Tons of dolphin and mango imagery. Dolphins simultaneously leaping and diving into waves. Couples creepily, catatonically sucking on mangoes in front of each other. I remember trying to jerk off as I was driving home with my new book, but I was unable to find anything stimulating as I turned page after page. I thought that drive home had marred the words *lesbian erotica* in my brain forever...until I started reading the submissions for this anthology and that idea was smashed. When I got the email from Tristan asking me to be a guest editor I was a little skeptical of my ability to do the job, as I haven't read much erotica in my life. I expected to find hundreds of pages of leaping dolphins in my mailbox. Maybe the dolphins will eat mangoes, I thought hopefully.

But it turned out even better than that—the stories were filled with the real lesbians I'd been looking for my whole life. Peggy Munson makes me want to push my tongue into each of Ellie's cigarette burns in her brilliant story "The Storm Chasers." Roxy Katt makes me wonder why I'm not congregating more often with spoiled upper-class poolside mothers in giant ant costumes. Reading Anna Watson's "Chronic," I remember the gift of health and desire. Shanna Germain reinforces the sexiness of wordless affairs. It was an honor to read and select the stories in this anthology. I feel like I've waited my whole life to see the many sides of my lesbian self reflected like this in literature.

Happy reading!

Ali Liebegott
Los Angeles, California

# DIFFERENT GIRLS

Tamai Kobayashi

It is on the third day at Japanese language summer camp that Susie meets Yoshi, one of the
tough girls who smoke behind the equipment
shack by the lakeside. They are counselors
from the city school but from different sides.
Sues is Westside cardigans and saddle shoes,
Yoshi railway denim and sneakers. Sues has always fancied the tough girls, feared them, their
careless mockeries; uncertain of their loyalty,
as if in a high stakes game of angel/devil. Yoshi
has muscles, and a scar on her shoulder, like a
gladiator or some kind of ancient warrior. She's
not like the girls who squeal at tadpoles, who
shriek and shrivel at cobwebs floating on the
ceiling of the dorms. Yosh plays chicken with
her jackknife by the canoe shed. Yosh plays
chicken but Sues is afraid.

Sues is not a tough girl. She steels herself against the lake scum that squishes between her toes and tries not to flinch at the spiders floating down from the rafters. Her skirts are pleated and her pencils are always sharp. Sues knows all of the rules but watches with envy the tough girls' swagger, their fearlessness and pride. Sues is afraid. Sues is afraid of Yosh. She tries not to notice as Yoshi swings the canoe easily onto her solid tanned shoulders. She glances away as the soap suds bubble down the groove in Yoshi's back. Yoshi is two months older, her breasts blossoming out; the hairs dark between her legs, under her armpits. Sues at seventeen feels the shifting time. The Beatles sing *Yeah yeah yeah* on the flickering television and *She's got a ticket to ride.* At seventeen, Sues is lost and far from home.

The fourth day at camp, Sues asks Yosh for a cigarette behind the equipment shack. The other tough girls laugh but Yosh holds out the cigarette, lights it with a wooden match struck from the tread of her shoe. Sues sputters with her first puff, the girls scoffing, but Yosh just smiles.

Yosh has the most beautiful smile.

After that day Sues follows Yoshi everywhere. *Shadow,* the other girls snicker but Sues pays it no mind. Yosh teaches her about the curl of the canoe paddle, pull of water and motion, the art of steering and the nature of currents. Sues is lost in the ripple of muscle, the curve of Yoshi's shoulders, the quirk in Yoshi's eyes.

Yosh carries Sues's lunch tray, holds her a place in line. The other girls growl and mutter; one of them has left the fold.

That night the storm blows in, midsummer heavy, the air humid and burdened with the strain. Thunderclouds towering but Sues can only see the darkness; the sky cracks open in a blinding, slashing wrench. The lake is dark and the lights in the cabins wink off, on, then off. Black night. Even the sky has fallen.

Sues shivers. She can't see the palm of her hand and the air quakes and rumbles. Too dark, then flashing, too bright, ghost sheet white, her eyes cannot leap between the extremes. Sues has never liked the thunderstorms, fears nature out of control, she feels like crying and she wants to go home.

An arm slips over her shoulders, Yoshi's arm. Warm and strong and muscled. The scent of cedar and cigarettes. Sues's heart is pounding, over the clouds that clash above, her nerves jump and scatter as Yoshi stands and holds and leans. Sues can feel the swell of Yoshi's left breast pressing along her arm, the cup of her hand against her shoulder. *She is touching me, she is touching me,* Sues repeats, her mind flooded with the miracle, and she wonders at such fearlessness.

Yoshi is tough, Sues thinks, and needs nobody.

At least not until the day they set the snare traps.

Tough girls need each other. To be tough against each other, to be tough against the world. Tough girls are their own measure, bitter enemies, bosom friends. Tough girls know their weaknesses and their strengths are never enough.

They set snare traps in the meadow and the next day they catch a baby raccoon. The snare twists around the hind leg, breaks it, and the tough girls gather around. Sues, no tough girl, starts crying, and the girls jeer, *Baby, going soft.* Yosh takes in Sues, the girls, the cry of the small, furry animal and sees no way out of it. She takes a rock and smashes in the raccoon's head. Yosh feels her stomach pitch into her mouth but she masks it with a snarl.

Sues runs.

The tough girls sneer after her but Yosh only stares at the

creature she has killed. Blood speckles the rock and she throws it into the river. Later Yosh tracks down every snare trap, smashes it in two. She gets a welt from the guide wire, her fist bloody from the bark.

That night, Yosh sits in the canoe shed, playing with her knife. Sues comes in.

Chicken—

Its leg was broke—

Can't do anything without your gang—

It was gonna die—

Coward—

But Sues begins to cry and hates herself for it. Tough girls never cry. But Yosh's arm is around her shoulder, her hands wipe away tears, Yosh's lips brush lightly against Sues's cheeks, her closed eyelids, her mouth, and deeper, kisses deeper, a tongue shivering ache into belly, their clothes are off, an awkward shedding, off and on the floor, their bodies slide, playing chicken without knives, this game all broken rules and Yosh's mouth kisses Sues's breasts, kisses nipples standing out, afraid but sucking harder. Sues's whimper is caged in her ribs, watching Yoshi come up for air, Sues still afraid but chicken chicken, smoke in Yosh's hair. Yosh's eyes, asking as her fingers trace down to those fine forbidden hairs, circling, afraid but it feels so good, dampness faster, fingers deeper, wetter inside the cleft, circling the hard little bud round and round and round, Sues's hot, she's burning, her shivers not from tears, a sudden shudder, rising, rising, that ripple-shock from there—

Sues, Sues—are you all right?

Sues holds her, clinging, braces her coming in Yoshi's clasp. She's still fearful of this newness, this game she does not understand but she trusts so completely that Yoshi is undone. Sues doesn't know that tough girls bruise easily but hide under a thin-skinned bravado, under tough girl bluster and pride. But Yoshi still holds her, rocking comfort, soothing caress, a silent appeal for forgiveness, for tough girls, who blunder, even as they win.

Shy girls excel as they try not to be noticed. They know the square root of three thousand and three. Sometimes they know Latin or French and their good shoes have buckles, or eyelets or some kind of fancy strap. They blossom in shadow, waiting for the world to come to them. They try and they try, however awkward and painful it is, but when they come forward, they seem to retreat. Shy girls are forever hopeful, skirting anger and a vague sense of dread. They seethe and they smolder, on the cusp of forever, unaware of the heat they give off.

Sues lies in the canoe shed, her head on Yoshi's shoulder. Her thoughts spin in darkness, her stomach in a knot. "It" has happened. "It" has occurred. Sues has no words for the lightness in her chest. But her body still hums from that burst between her legs, the tingles in her breasts. Sues is all open and she wants to know how.

Yosh, on her elbow, whispers, Are you cold Sues? Are you okay?

But Sues's heart is exploding and she kisses Yoshi, pushes her back, her mouth, taking her own time now, traveling over lips, tongue, teeth and Yosh cannot say a thing. Sues slips lower, feels Yosh tremble beneath her. Sues presses hard but can't keep herself still. Yoshi's breasts, Yoshi's breasts, and Sues exploring every bump, every curve, every slope, every dip. Sues kisses, caresses, her tongue on a quest, ever lower, ever lower, until her lips—

Yoshi sits up on her elbows.

Sues?

Sues opens Yoshi's legs, pushes wide her shaking thighs. Light kisses below the tangled hair and Yoshi almost cries. Sues remember Yosh's fingers but she wants to kiss some more. She kisses and she kisses and she kisses, her face, wetter, tasting deeper, she wants to crawl inside. But Yosh's jerking, helpless now, her legs don't know what to do. Her chest is bursting, her lungs are gasping and her hot palms smack the floor. Sues thinks of her own building rush, and she wants to ride Yosh into that center, to ripple out this storm. Her mouth latches on to that little bud rising and she begins to lick and suck. Sues loves this taste, this feeling, like holding candies in her mouth, her lips pouring out, Yosh beneath her; Sues sucks her in as well, how can this be, but no time to think, Yosh's breath faster now, hips rising, legs wide as Sues presses her mouth down, tongue swirling and Yoshi comes, Yoshi comes.

The morning light begins to sneak through the cracks of the canoe shed. In the shadows Sues can see what she has done. Wet curls back from Yosh's vulva, pink lips waving, spiraling down. Sues knows the words for this place but the name is just the beginning. Shy girls know their Latin, shy girls know their French, but Sues, still shy, wants to know more. The square root of three thousand and three will never be enough. Sues's finger slides into vagina, rippled muscle, contracting space and Yoshi arches, a choking surrender, as Sues begins all over again.

Shy girls aren't so shy now and tough girls aren't so tough. But what they need they will find in each other, as they imagine themselves as different girls.

# PARADISE

Valerie Alexander

Our mouths were rubbed raw where we kissed. Nights were sleepless aches of devouring each other, tumbles of animalism and grief. We didn't eat, we were too anxious, and we could not sleep except for exhausted afternoon slumbers in each other's arms. There was little differentiation in time. Streetlights came on and went off, different degrees of light filtered through the apartment blinds. She sobbed when she came; I came all the time. I loved her.

We barely went to class. Always I was rubbing my eyes, bleary, dizzy, I did not hear if spoken to. The sheets went dirty and cartons of takeout piled up in the kitchen. Sleepless and dazed, my hands shook too much to grasp a pen. There was much to say, years to cram in nights. We had no idea how long we had together. Every second was vital.

We could not even shower apart. Rubbing shampoo into her hair, bare of makeup, she looked so innocent. Our kisses tasted of soap and water. I shaved her legs for her, pulling them around my waist from behind and lathering them up well. Her pussy was also my domain and I sculpted it with the obsession of a lesbian Rodin. Her briny sweetness graced my tongue like nirvana. The tang of her walls clung to my fingers. Like a love-struck dog I couldn't stop licking her, until her screams bounded off the walls and drowned out the rushing water.

The first time with her was awkward but potent. It was after class and I was facedown in her mattress. She was unhooking my bra from behind. Then taking it off. A CD was playing; it emphasized the silence between us. I stared straight into the black of the sheet but I was seeing her room in my mind, the bamboo blinds and framed poster of Virginia Woolf. Her hands, smooth and cool, slid down my hips. My throat was tight with anticipation. She pushed at me and I turned over to see her long dark hair hanging in her face. Her perfect, inscrutable face.

My dress was crumpled in the corner. She hooked two fingers under the elastic of my panties and pulled them down my thighs. My navel looked brand new, like someone else's, under her gaze. She leaned over me and paused. Then she unsnapped her dark blue lace bra. I looked at the ceiling, closed my eyes. Quick, harsh breathing sounded in my ears. It was mine. She crawled over me on all fours. We were naked now, both of us. Her cool soft breasts melted against me like heaven descending to earth. Our mouths met like two halves locking together in a delirious whole. We rolled over and over, kissing, her knee slowly rubbing my pussy until I moaned in her mouth.

Earth ascended to heaven. Everything was pink and brown and like silk. It was ice-cream sex, vanilla and sweet, but I held her shaking body tight when she came and in her honey I tasted the venom of our potential.

At night we'd go into the club like angels, pretty and glittery and messy. We would enter into the humid darkness criss-crossed with neon laser beams; would pause to take in the pleasurable scandal of hundreds of girls dancing with girls, kissing girls against the wall; then quickly we would scan the crowd, taking in who was and was not there. We were superior and haughty, but interested in the crowded female heat. And both of us enjoyed the gossip.

(Girlworld gossip can eat your romance alive. We learned that on our second night. Her roommate told my ex who told her roommate who told her lab partner who told her ex; and that night when we met at a Mexican restaurant as arranged, our ears were ringing with untrue and hostile rumors. We were casual and distant with each other until the truth emerged. Then we realized how tight, together and impregnable we had to be. We got drunk on margaritas and kissed sloppily in front of the restaurant and then we went out and fucked in the alley, in the falling snow. It was November and the first snow of the season. I pushed her jeans down and backed her bare ass against the brick building, her pussy burning against my hand in the cold night. My fingers teased her clit, circling lazily, lightly pulling at her delicate hood, until she stood with her legs strained apart in her jeans, wordlessly begging to be fucked. Finally I slid my fingers deep inside her as her pussy sucked at me like a feverish animal, and more than anything I wanted to taste her but instead I watched the snow melt over her flushed cheekbones and closed eyelids as she groaned with her first orgasm of the night. I knew as I held her snow-flaked hair that I was on to something.)

In the club:

Topless girls gyrated and shook on three platforms. Huge projection screens were suspended from the ceiling, offering a film of two naked girls kissing in a shower, black-and-white stills of famous models, a photo of two perfectly round breasts, then one of a pale-eyed beauty with a vacant stare. Hundreds of women filled the club, exchanging the contagion of kisses and laughter and lit cigarettes, and back in the dark recesses, anonymous hands. Where before her, I had sometimes given myself over to sadness, dazed by the alien coo of computerized music booming through the speakers.

"Are you hot?—Are you okay?—Do you want a drink?"

We would dance until we were wet. We liked to sway to the tacky slow songs, our damp faces rosy-blue in the electric bath of light. I would feel her hot skin through her damp T-shirt. She would gather up my long blonde hair in her hands and blow on my neck. And on the sidelines, women would watch us.

"You are blessed," an older woman said once when I went to the bar for ice water. I looked at her, stunned, and realized a deity of love was communicating to me through her voice. I wanted to ask her for more wisdom but then something fever-ish hurtled at me—my girlfriend, hugging me like we hadn't seen each other in days. When I turned around, the oracle had moved off.

The bathroom was always the usual holding pen of competitors smearing on lipstick, struggling with their hair, slipping on wet toilet paper and screaming out gossip. Ears rang with deafness. Bloodshot eyes squinted in drunkenness and nausea. *Bang, bang,* the stall doors opened and closed and girls went in and out. I would empty my bladder, wipe off my smeared raccoon eyeliner and reapply it, powdering my skin. Then I'd drop my magic tools in my leather bag and reenter the dazzling multileveled game board of the club. Even when I could not find her, I would sense my beloved, batlike, in the sweltering darkness. I would pause and revel in that anonymous crush of love, that ancient desire of girl for girl; and then I would see her making her way toward me, swaggering in her ripped fishnet stockings and tight shorts and high heels.

We were femmes but we liked to put on jeans and combat boots and dress like boys, our long hair escaping from baseball caps. It was some *Playboy* parody of butch that turned us on, much like ignoring or taunting the males who tried for our attention. Sometimes we wiggled into long gowns and hiked up our bustiers and painted our faces, officially "beautiful." We couldn't stop admiring each other. We were monsters and we were in love.

In a girly shop, where French pop music played inanely from hidden speakers and I reclined exhausted on a velvet couch, we looked like all the other girls. The eyes of coiffured salesgirls seemed to flirt and promise. I couldn't tell if I was lucky, beautiful or misinformed about the nature of women. To me, it was obvious we were tired from fucking all night and were unwashed and smelling of sex, but the straight girls critiqued the dresses we tried on, they gushed over our lingerie and our hair.

"It's like we turn invisible when we're together," she said, walking home with shopping bags one night.

"Yes," I said. "It's like our superpower."

We rarely left the apartment. There was no need to. I forgot the outside world existed. The first time one of us got her period, it was her, and I went out late on a Friday night to buy tampons and candy and ibuprofen. We had been in bed all afternoon and evening and she had been sluggish and cramped but content in my arms. Leaving for the store, I was surprised to see the city crawling with students and bar-hoppers. In the harsh fluorescent glare of the convenience store, I saw it was only ten o'clock.

I was paying at the counter when a friend walked in and squealed: "Where have you been?"

"Well," I wanted to say, "I fell in love—I got married—I left this earth—" but I felt she would understand none of that.

"I've been seeing someone," I said.

Walking home through the social plans and chatter of others, I felt invisible again, like a ghost. So irrelevant the rest of the world seemed, with my one real flame burning in a basement apartment at the end of the street.

Her body haunted mine. Every idiosyncratic trick of her skin, from her seashell ears to the crooks of her knees, dominated my cosmos. I was Marco Polo, intent on mapping her planet. Bored in class, I'd begin my mental inventory at her toes and by homecoming would have a list of several questions to test and resolve, from the ridge of her hip bones under my tongue to the taste of the bottom of her ass. I was eating the apple in the Garden of Eden. Knowledge was the key to Paradise and not the key to expulsion. Or so I believed.

It was her pussy that obsessed me, its perfect tang of brine and honey, its soft throbs around my tongue when she came, so in contrast to the fire of her temper. Each come was a surrender, a succumbing to my persuasion. I liked her unperfect: a roughness on her thighs abrading my cheeks, a sleepy dormancy in her wet pink cunt that was my job to awaken and rouse. Never did I want morning sex until it was with her. Her black hair fanned over the pillow, her mouth slack, I'd trail my fingernails over her ass until she awoke just enough for me to slide my thumb into her cunt. Then she would sleepily roll over and open her legs before me as if inviting me to feast on the heavenly spread of her body.

Sometimes we infiltrated each other's dreams and then waking and rolling over on top of her and kissing was just an extension of where we had been. It was as if our sleep had been transformed into an adventure and our bed into a ship, as when we were children and sailing into dreamlands unknown.

Her father came to town on business and took us both to dinner. We were listless in the candlelight. We answered lamely his questions about school and our futures. We'd been fucking all afternoon, one nonstop somnambulistic raw and gritty dream, and nothing in the restaurant, not the white tablecloth or water glasses or the violin music, seemed real. In the bathroom we clutched each other and kissed just to stay awake. Then we stepped out of the stall and blinked in the harsh sterile pink and white brilliance. "I'm so tired," she whispered and she started to cry. I held her dark head as she gripped the sink and said, "Just another hour..." Matrons frowned at us and I remembered in their eyes we were criminals.

The next day her mother took us shopping. On a whim we made her stop at the toy store and buy us, with a bemused but tolerant smile, a Barbie doll. In the car we took her out of the box and touched her long flaxen hair and plastic legs.

That evening we napped and awoke and dressed together before meeting her parents for the symphony. I lay naked on the couch, one leg up and one leg dangling off while she rolled up sheer black thigh-high stockings on me, then slipped my feet into high heels. I spread my legs wider for her, feeling my lips swell and unfurl. My cunt ached to be filled, so wet my inner thighs glistened with it. She slipped Barbie into me, feet-first, the cool plastic of her legs feeling so alien in my heat. I leaned up on my elbows and watched my own pussy as the Barbie doll slid in up to her waist. In and out, in and out... I gripped the sofa cushions, biting my lip as Barbie fucked me.... A storm was building between my legs, a carnivorous tornado that wanted to suck up everything inside me until I came. My girlfriend circled the doll's legs inside me, her black eyes gazing at me with an odd light, and then she pressed Barbie up into my G-spot and I clamped my legs shut as lightning struck and I screamed. I twisted to the side, my throbs breaking through me like a seizure, as she pulled Barbie out and sucked off her legs. Then she put the doll on top of the couch, where it smiled dazzlingly.

"I love you," I said. "I love you I love you" and I devoured her mouth.

We had sex all the time. Night and day blended. Lying under her, after my sixth orgasm, I would open my eyes and not be able to tell if her face floated in the dimness of daybreak or dusk. We kissed in cabs, in theater lobbies, on the street. There was no assumption we could not pervert. I dressed her in pearls and gloves and lipstick in the Lord & Taylor dressing room, then lifted her skirt and exalted her. To feel closer, we wore each other's underwear to class. We slipped into an empty history classroom once and fingered each other silently on a back desk as students streamed by outside. What I loved in her was her ability to be raw, turbulent and dreamy all at once.... She was perfect and I loved her totally.

Men and women both fell in love with us, our fever was so gorgeous. We got used to it. We thought we were born that way and that it would last forever.

Sunday night was sex night; it was then the local girl-girl elite held candlelit play parties at an expensive downtown hotel. Wet and gleaming we were the first time I looked in the mirror and saw us, newly risen from a foamy bathtub, other wet naked girls squirming around us. She slid her hands over my breasts to play with my nipples as her white grin cracked across her face in the mirror. The suite bathroom was too hot, too feminine, smelling of bath gel, lipsticks and sex. I tugged her out to the living room and hand in hand we walked barefoot through the orgy of girls naked, girls in their underwear, girls in Saran Wrap and Astroglide pawing and grunting and kissing each other.

"I want to get fucked out of my mind tonight," she said and she did. On her ass, her head thrown back on my shoulder while a girl in a black Lone Ranger mask fucked her with a leather phallus. She moaned and tossed her head around in feverish half circles, her dark hair sticking to my damp face. The girl leaned over her with a satanic smile, working the leather cock inside her harder, while everyone watched the tender flesh of my girlfriend's pussy stretch wider. I held her steady, felt her trembling build and shake until her body seemed too fragile to house such chaos. Almost sobbing with need, she jerked her hips in wordless supplication for more, her fingernails digging into my knees. I cupped her breasts and thumbed her hard pink nipples as the Lone Ranger long-dicked her like a pro. She moaned and thrashed in my lap and then her tempest blew with a scream so hard her throat went raw. Then she collapsed, sliding down into my lap, and looked up at me, breathing hard. I kissed her wet forehead and she squeezed my hand.

Before then, everything up to that point, was just killing time until I got to her. Straight girls I seduced, gay boys I dressed up and played with, married women who wanted me secretly and on schedule, none of them could begin to compare. The entire world had once seemed a carnal banquet but she was not an entrée but another guest.

We were sure of our Promethean brilliance and we could see the future shining ahead of us.

We would write, direct and produce lesbian films, all kinds. I favored a pretty porno flick revolving around a Catholic girls' school. She imagined a forbidden romance between a repressed middle-aged executive and a young club-girl slut. We would make lots of money. Girls everywhere would long to be recruited.

We would have eccentric children, at least three, and two adorable dogs. We would hire young and nubile help to wash the car and scrub the floors. We'd own a secluded estate in the islands where we would hold famous A-list orgies. We would fund shelters and feminist politicians, be active in our community.

We would dedicate our lives to penetrating the glorious mysteries of the skin.

We would see each other through mastectomies, menopause, old age, lost teeth. One would keep her hearing when the other lost her sight. We would blaze long into the century like beacons.

"What if you die?" she whispered, when I was in her arms late one night. "What if I die?"

Paradise was melting; everything was sliding around, skin and words and time. "We're not going to die," I said with my mind or my mouth. "We're perfect."

One spring night we stayed awake until dawn, drinking champagne and snorting coke and playing games. We drew on the walls with colored chalk and listened to loud opera all night long. I was so dazzled to be conscious with her. Around four we were wet and serious and naked on the floor. She wrapped her legs around my face, grinding her wetness against my mouth. My tongue writhed inside her like a snake, making her come until she rolled moaning onto her side, holding her sides as if she hurt. But then she pinned me against the carpet and fucked me slowly and deliriously over and over, the strap-on between her legs so big I felt stretched impossibly wide. With each thrust of her cock, the floor burned my tailbone until the pain and the heat were one. My cunt was incandescent, every nerve ending alight with fire where she touched me, until I rolled her over and rode her hard, stoking that fire up into a blaze of wet and throbbing glory. We were wet with sweat when I collapsed on her, and we kissed over and over until daybreak showed through the windows. Then it was time to go.

The fresh sky was a dark slate as we walked down the road. Birds hopped after us, branch to branch. A convoy of squirrels began to follow us, pausing to salute us with one paw over their hearts. The breeze of morning picked up, lifting our damp hair off our necks. My thighs were wet and shaking and I could still taste her in my mouth.

The sun was rising at the end of the road like a promise. We looked into each other. She was as flushed and alive as the dawn.

"This is it," she said. "This is the moment."

Her face was lucent. Looking into her black gaze I feared my heart would burst with happiness. I started to speak but then we were struck with a numinous lightning of an epiphany. And in that moment we knew that we were in Paradise.

And as it has turned out so many years later, you were right. That was it. That was the one crucial moment I could never come back from. No other moment has ever been able to compare. Every other lover, other knowledge, has been a dull placebo even though it's been well over a decade since that dawn in which you and I understood everything. How fast it was gone, eight months in which we saw each other as royalty and our hopes spread before us like a shining promise—hopes that didn't foresee the arguments and the fade into mundanity that came so soon. Friends would say now that it wasn't so perfect, they would speak in clichés of narcissism and the idealization of lost youth, but what I am describing is a truth—that perfection does exist and once you've tasted it, the rest of your life turns a little gray.

An Internet source of some dubiety reports the average age for the onset of gray hair is thirty-four. I was two years past that the morning I found a white hair in my darkening blonde. Strangely it was you I thought of, wondering if you'd also been tapped by that first sign of mortal obsolescence. You were just seven months younger than me and it was inevitable that you had changed from my perfect beloved of the flawless skin and firm body I was once so privileged to worship. For a moment I tried to imagine you as her tired, older version, another mother I might not recognize immediately at my son's day care. But that image was a blasphemy so I quickly retreated into the past, the preferred immortality of memory. It's the one perfection you left me with ultimately—the perfection of never seeing you again.

# WHEN SHE WAS GOOD

Betty Blue

Tib was a master of misdirection. While you were watching her left hand, the right was stealing your heart straight through your rib cage. But you didn't notice it then. Only later, when you needed it for something, you'd go fishing through your pockets, patting down your jacket, trying to remember when you had it last. And there you'd find instead a hollow thud beneath your left breast pocket: your empty pericardium.

But that was all later. Before that, there were wet, sticky days and nights of being rolled by her. And Tib, make no mistake, played you like a virtuoso cellist, fingers drawing out notes you didn't think you had in you, slipping and sliding along your taut strings until smoke was coming from her fingers, and she had you, thoroughly and expertly played.

The first time I saw Tib, she was playing someone else. It was hotter than hellfire in the trapped bowl of the town below us, driving us up into the foothills and over desert trails into a canyon that hid in the belly of a mountain. Perched on a rock beside the falls with a leg over each side of the stone like she was sitting on a horse, Tib was dressed in a black, pinstriped suit, barely breaking a sweat. The long jacket was open to reveal a crisp, white shirt, its neatness marred only by the sleeves, rolled up to give her room to pluck her instrument. I found out later that she'd ridden her motorcycle up into the canyon. That she remained so unaffected could only be a bona fide miracle.

The object of Tib's attention as I crested the path before the rain-filled pool was a petite, white-bleached blonde with a 1940s flip. She was bent over the horn of the rock "saddle" with her legs spread wide, and buck naked. Tib, with two fingers in the blonde's cunt, and two in her mouth, was bringing her composition to a rousing crescendo. The fingers in her mouth that she was sucking on feverishly were clearly to keep her mouth shut as Tib fucked her. She was moaning against them, tits and ass bouncing as Tib gave her what-for, and whimpering with regret as Tib slowed down at last.

Tib gave me a smirk beneath her shades as the piece came to an end, patted the blonde on her ass, and stuck out her hand.

"Hey, there. I'm Tib."

I stared with my mouth open for a beat and then stammered, "Sadie," without taking the offered hand.

The blonde shook out her hair and sat up, giving me a cursory glance before leaning back to kiss Tib. She took her time, letting me know I was of no consequence before she slipped down from the rock and dove into the pool.

"And that," said Tib, hooking the heels of her boots against the rock, "was Bethany." She leaned back and smoothed her hands through her slicked-back hair to interlock her fingers behind her head, an effortless gesture that spoke of powerful abs.

The arrival of my friend Greg at the top of the trail saved me from spontaneous muteness. He stopped and took a long swig from his water bottle, snapping the sport-top back into place. "Someone should have told me the Cherry-Popping Daddies were playing here today," he said. "I'd have worn a better hat."

"At least you brought your cherry," said Tib.

My mouth dropped open again, and Greg rolled his eyes. "Keep it in your zoot suit, sweetie. I've already got a boyfriend." He turned back to the trail and gestured ahead. "That picnic site you were looking for is down the road, sweetheart. Say good-bye to the nice man and come on."

Tib's laughter followed us out of the canyon.

Barely six hours later, I found myself toe to toe with Tib once more as Greg and his boyfriend Pete and I hit The Club—part of the revitalized downtown hotel where Dillinger was once famously apprehended—to get out of the stifling desert evening. I was at the bar waiting for my drink when I spotted the unmistakable suit in the hotel lobby. The Gwen Stefani blonde was on her arm, white crop top showing off a perfect tan and a perfect torso over a pair of jeans slung just below her hips. The top of a pair of red boxers peeked out over the belt, with matching suspenders stretched over her breasts.

Tib gave no indication that she saw me and I looked away, intent on calculating the tip as the bartender scooted the drink and change in front of me. When I looked up, Tib was sliding onto the stool beside me. Bethany had disappeared into the crowd.

"Long Island iced tea," she said to the bartender, and I laughed out loud. Tib gave me a sidelong glance. "It's not for me."

"Sorry," I said, trying to swallow my drink. "None of my business."

"And what the hell is that? Grapefruit juice?"

I breathed in at the wrong moment, trying to be cool, and choked, sputtering into my glass. Tib pounded me on the back and I knocked the drink across the bar.

"Well, that was charming," said Tib, and nodded to the bartender with a ten tucked between her fingers like a smoke. "Another juice for my friend, here."

"Salty dog," I corrected, coughing.

Tib raised an eyebrow. "And that's the story you're sticking with."

Bethany appeared at her elbow and plucked the tall glass of Long Island iced tea off the bar, sipping from the swizzle stick. Tib dropped the ten on the counter. "Try not to spill that one," she said as she turned and steered Bethany through the crowd.

The last time I saw her that night, she was leading a tipsy Bethany up the stairs across the hotel lobby.

Greg, Pete, and I closed the place down, straggling out to the street when the temperature finally dropped below ninety. I had ridden over on my Vespa, but I was in no shape to drive home, so we left it in the parking lot looking like a shabby cousin beside a shiny Valkyrie, to be picked up in the morning.

When Greg dropped me back at the lot several hours later, the owner of the Valkyrie was stepping into the heat shimmering off the tarmac: Tib, in a pair of leather pants and a white ribbed tank.

"Nice ride," she said, slipping her sunglasses down her nose.

"Yeah," I sighed. "You got me. I ride a scooter and drink grapefruit juice, and don't fuck in public." The night's festivities had left me a little cranky.

"I could remedy one of those," said Tib.

I blushed to my roots, not sure if I was more angry or hot.

Tib smiled, mounting the bike. "Come on, Sadie. Why don't you hop on, let me give you a ride?"

"Where's Bethany?" I blurted, unreasonably pleased that she'd remembered my name.

"There's only room for two," said Tib. "But if you want a ride with Bethany, I'm sure she'll be awake by sundown."

"I don't want a ride with Bethany."

"Then hop on, sweetie. Let me show you what you're missing on that scooter of yours." Tib patted the seat behind her. "I've got an errand to run over on the east side and I could use the company. I'll have you back in an hour."

Maybe it was the heat. Maybe it was my muddy head from the night before. But God help me, a minute later I was behind Tib with my arms wrapped around her hard waist, heading into the white blur of the desert midday. With my thighs hugging Tib's hips and the vibration of the bike between them, I was oblivious to how far we were going or how long we'd been doing it until the bike slowed and Tib turned onto a dirt road between two brick columns.

The road wound through a field of scattered stones, and as Tib brought the bike to a stop, I realized they were grave markers, small white crosses poking up between them like wildflowers. Tib switched off the engine and kicked the stand into place, swinging her leg over the seat. Her boots crunched on the gravel as she crossed to one of the markers and dropped down in front of it, arms resting over her thighs as she balanced her weight on her heels. I slipped off of the bike and waited, not sure whether I should follow. She stayed where she was, so I moved forward, hands in my jean pockets.

"I come here every year," she said. "I head home once a year to visit Mom. I think she appreciates the company." I had no idea what to say, so I said nothing. Tib stood up, wiping her palms on her pant legs, and turned around. "It's not really the kind of place I could bring Bethany."

"But she makes the trip home with you."

Tib laughed. "Bethany? I just met her yesterday." She started back toward the bike. "Anyway, it's hotter than fuck out here, so maybe the public sex will have to wait. Leather may not have been the wisest choice."

It really was hotter than fuck, and I was too sweaty and flushed to bother with prim outrage at her assumption that I'd come along for sex. I held onto her belt loops on the ride back, not because I was embarrassed to hold on any closer, but because at that point, with my head encased in the steamy helmet, I might have passed out from the heat and fallen off. At any rate, Tib didn't seem worried about my body language.

We pulled into the parking lot beside Nellie, my Vespa, and I stared at the vinyl seat and shining metal. I had parked at night, no need to look for shade. At three in the afternoon, Nellie was a potential human griddle. Maybe I'd go inside for a soda.

Tib followed my glance. "They don't open until five." Most of downtown was closed on Sunday afternoon, making my chances of getting even a bottle of water slim. "I've got a refrigerator in my room," said Tib.

"Isn't Bethany sleeping?"

"She's not even here," said Tib, grinning. "Crawled out sometime before eight a.m. and took a cab. She had church."

"Church?" I made a face and Tib laughed. "Do they still have those?"

"Oh, indeed they do, Little Miss Sin." She flashed her wide smile and put an arm around my waist. "All over the Southwest. I hear they even have some in California."

"Yeah, they're weird there," I said.

The room was furnished in deserty art deco, a Sonoran blanket thrown over a sleigh bed, and a lamp on the 1930s waterfall table beside it with a stand covered in stamped leather and a rawhide shade painted with cowboys and steer.

"I've always wondered what these rooms were like," I said. "Kind of appalling and fascinating at the same time."

"You a townie or a sorority girl?" Tib was pulling off her sweat-damp leather pants.

"A sorority girl?" I laughed. "Yeah, that's me, how could you tell?"

"You never know. Appearances can be deceiving."

"I know I'm no Gwen Stefani," I said, folding my arms across my waist, aware of my belly. "And if you must know, yes, I'm a 'townie.' I'm not even a college student, actually," I added, feeling even more defensive. "I was, but I had to quit. I'm a working girl." Tib raised an eyebrow. "I mean I have a nine-to-five job."

Tib left her pants where they fell, crouching down to get two sparkling water bottles from the fridge, a white thong separating her muscular ass. "So who needs another Gwen Stefani?"

She stood up and handed me a bottle. "I wasn't comparing you to Bethany."

"I should probably go," I said.

"Jesus, Sadie. It's a million degrees out there. Just take the water and sit your ass on the bed. I wouldn't have asked you up if I didn't think you were cute."

I uncrossed my arms and opened my mouth to say something indignant, I wasn't sure what, but Tib pushed the bottle into my hand and steered me to the bed.

"It's a drink of water," Tib said, twisting the top off her bottle. "It's hot out, you're thirsty, we're both hungover, and I happen to think your little tummy is adorable." She took a sip and grinned. "The water's free, by the way. You don't have to pay for it with sex."

I nearly choked on my water, and the carbonation stung my nose.

"You clearly have a drinking problem," said Tib. I tried to take another sip, but I was laughing too hard. Tib climbed onto the bed and took my drink, setting it on the end table. "No more of this for you. You're out of control." She pushed me back against the pillow and climbed over me, shutting me up.

She was still wearing her sunglasses and I pulled them off, revealing steel-blue eyes. Tib pulled her shirt over her head and pressed her bare skin against me, soft breasts and hard nipples pressing against my T-shirt. She kissed me, hard, and I was reaching up for more when she pulled away and closed her mouth over my breast through my shirt. She bit, and I squirmed, as she yanked the buttons on my fly open one by one. Sweat was rolling off of both of us, and the temperature was rising.

After a moment, Tib slipped off of me onto the bed,

flopping back beneath a ceiling fan that did little besides stir the hot air.

"Jesus. I think it may actually be too hot to fuck," she laughed, closing her eyes.

I let mine close, too, just for a minute, and when I opened them again, the light from the window had grown long and low and Tib was curled beside me, fast asleep. I spooned against her, and she drew my hand over her shoulder, tucking it against her breasts.

I woke after dark to find Tib coming out of the bathroom, dressed in her leather pants and white shirt and rubbing a towel through damp hair that hung in curls around her face.

"Hey," she smiled, tossing the towel onto the bed. She grabbed a pot of pomade from the dresser, smoothing her hair flat. One little curl hung down in the middle of her forehead. "I'm starving," she said. "Feel like getting a bite in the bar?"

I had other ideas, but my stomach growled audibly, joining the thumping bass from the club below that meant it was already after nine. We headed down and Tib ordered burgers and fries. We were just finishing up when I heard tongue-clucking behind me.

"I saw Nellie still outside and I was worried about you," said Greg as I swiveled around. He gave me his best disapproving look. "Thought you'd been kidnapped out of the parking lot."

"She was," said Tib. "But I brought her back."

Pete reached around Greg's shoulder and grabbed a Frenchfry. "Is that anything like throwing a fish back if it's too small?" He laughed and dodged the fry I threw at him.

"Oh, I don't know," said Tib, winking at me. "She looks like a keeper to me."

Greg gave a dramatic sigh. "Ohhh-kay, then. We'll be over here," he said as he dragged Pete off to the dance floor.

Tib popped the last fry in her mouth and grinned, hopping off of her stool and dragging me after them. We danced until closing, dripping with sweat and out of breath. There was no sign of Bethany.

"You're good," shouted Tib over the music as we pushed toward the lobby. "I have this theory that people fuck—" She laughed, realizing that her voice was suddenly much louder away from the dance floor. She pulled me close and I looked up into her storm-blue eyes. "I have this theory," she repeated. "That people fuck like they dance."

I was feeling pretty bold after a few drinks and a dance buzz. "I'd be happy to help you test that," I said. "For science."

Tib pressed me up against the side of the banister and put her palms against the wood, her leather-clad knee rubbing hard between my legs. "I'm very dedicated to science," she said, kissing my throat. "But didn't you say you worked in the morning?"

I sighed, playing with her belt buckle. "Yeah, I do."

"What time do you get off? You know what I mean," she laughed.

"Six," I said.

"What if I meet you for dinner? Or will you be too tired?"

I smiled. "I think I can manage."

My shift at the bowling alley seemed interminable after only a few hours of sleep. Days weren't so bad: leagues in the morning wanting breakfast at the snack bar, a small lunch crowd, and a few beer drinkers in the afternoon. But at 4:00, the manager called. Her two-year-old had an ear infection and she couldn't leave him with the sitter.

Tib was understanding when I called. "Why don't I come by and keep you company?"

"Are you sure?" I asked. "It's pretty boring."

"As long as I don't have to wear somebody else's smelly shoes."

"Not unless you plan to bowl."

"There is almost zero chance of that happening," said Tib.

She came by around eight and spent the evening entertaining me by mimicking the bowlers and reading explicit personals from the men-seeking-men section. Her favorite game was "anything you can do, I can do better," taking the ads as a personal challenge. She dragged me to the bathroom periodically to try "Looking to get my holes worked over—no chitchat" and "Sit on my lap—I jerk you off."

With Tib's distraction, my shift was over in no time, but the alley was open until midnight, and by the time I was done with the cleanup and the cash drawer, it was after 1:00 a.m.

"Who bowls until midnight on a Monday?" I moaned as I closed up. "Who does that?"

"And you have to come back in seven hours," said Tib, kissing my neck as I locked the doors.

I looked up at her, silhouetted against the bright moon. "And I just got a text message from Donna saying her kid has a fever of a hundred and three and she needs me to cover her shift again tomorrow night."

"So I'll just come and bother you some more."

"You don't have to do that."

"What else am I going to do? I've been here since Friday, and I've pretty much exhausted everything there is to do here in three days. There's a reason I left home in the first place.

That, and the people bowling until midnight." She hooked her finger through my belt loop and pulled me close. "Besides," she smirked. "I have a feeling it'll pay off."

Tib ended up spending three nights keeping me company at the bowling alley, until little Jared had finally gotten some antibiotics. Mercifully, Donna took over my next two shifts, and I slept for over twelve hours, with the promise of spending Friday with Tib. I was beginning to get used to her company.

Tib announced she was taking me somewhere out of town. I told her that at no point during the day would I be perching naked on her lap on a rock. Tib assured me that she had other plans for me. We got on her bike and Tib headed north, and up into the mountains. The trip took a few hours over twisting roads, and I was glad to be off of the bike by the time we reached the top.

"Ever been skiing up here?" asked Tib as she pulled a thick, fleece blanket from her saddle bag.

"Skiing," I said. "In the middle of summer."

Tib grinned. "Something like that." She took my hand and half-dragged me up the last quarter mile from the parking lot to the lodges I had assumed were closed.

"What are we doing?" I protested. "There's nothing up here."

"Wait here." Tib darted into the one open café, returning after a moment with two rectangles of paper. "Lift tickets," she grinned.

Twenty minutes later, we were rising over the mountain, the only ones on the lift. I laughed as Tib tucked the blanket over our laps. "I'm surprised you didn't bring a parka."

"It's windy," she said. "I don't want you to catch a cold." There was little danger of that; under the blanket, she was making me quite warm.

Tib had unbuttoned my jeans and slipped her hand down my panties, first just cupping her firm hand around me, and then teasing me open.

"Stop it," I protested, wanting her to do nothing of the kind. Thankfully, Tib ignored me.

She rubbed her middle finger against my clit and then kissed me to keep me quiet as she buried the finger slowly inside me. I was wriggling forward to meet her, heedless of the fact that we were suspended hundreds of feet above the ground, clenching my pussy tight around her finger with a jolt when I realized it. We reached the apex, twofold, and I twisted against her thrusting finger with a shout as my cunt throbbed and shuddered, no longer caring if anyone heard. She pulled out and sucked the juice off her finger as I relaxed against her while the lift rounded the corner and headed back down.

"It's actually a really nice view, if you'd been paying attention," Tib teased. "I drag a girl all the way up to the top of the world and shell out money for a ride, and all she does is close her eyes and moan."

When we headed back down the mountain, Tib turned off onto a private drive after less than half a mile. I had to wait until we wound to the end and arrived in a small village of summer homes and cabins before I found out what Tib was up to.

"My family's place," she said as we dismounted in front of a two-story cabin nearly hidden from the road by pine and wildflowers.

Inside, I barely had time to take in the surroundings before

Tib had pulled me over to the thick rug and started pulling clothes off of me. I helped her in her mission, unbuttoning her shirt as she yanked at my pants, and pulling her pants down just far enough to get my hand inside them as I closed my mouth over a nipple as hard as a diamond. Tib rolled me over and tilted her pelvis against my mouth and I sucked her clit between my teeth with my fingers inside her powerful cunt, warm and damp and piquant as mulled cider.

I buried my face in her gingery scent, moaning as she moaned, wetter as she got wetter, and almost came as she came. Tib arched back and tightened her muscles as she let out a howl, fucking my mouth with her pussy while I held on to her ass, and whispering, "Sadie, Sadie," as she softened and collapsed into an exhausted heap beside me.

After we'd curled up before the empty fireplace, stroking and kissing and nuzzling together, Tib divested herself of the rest of her clothing and then dragged herself away from me laughing though I tried to hold her down. After a quick trip to the bathroom, she disappeared into the kitchen and made us sandwiches, and I pulled a blanket around me and checked out the place while she was busy.

"Is this your mom and dad?" I asked, picking up a picture of a couple on the mantel.

Tib popped her head around the doorway. "Oh. Yeah. Don't look at those. I look awful."

"Where are you?" I asked, surveying the other pictures. I saw a family shot with a boy and a much younger version of a long-haired Tib before she came up behind me and got my attention off of pictures and onto the real, live Tib before me.

Tib scrounged up a paper from somewhere and we lay on the rug eating our sandwiches and reading men's personals.

"'Discreet, masculine boy seeks stern daddy for discipline,'" read Tib as I played footsie with her, legs crossed in the air behind us. "Well, discreet, I don't know about," she laughed. "But what about it, little boy? I bet you're naughty."

I stuck out my tongue.

"Keep that up," said Tib, "and I'll find a use for it." She glanced at the paper as if she was ignoring me. "Hmm, this one would make an excellent complement. 'Your cock, my mouth. Bisexual bottom looking for a fuckbuddy.'" Tib pushed me over on my back and climbed over me. "Yeah, I think this is a good one, little boy. You want this, don't you?" She stroked an invisible cock above my face. "Not bisexual, of course. But cocksucking fuckbuddy I can do."

My stomach twisted into a sudden, sick knot. *I shouldn't push it now*, I thought. *Leave it alone.* But out of my mouth came, "I'm bi."

Tib froze in midstroke. "Wow. You sure know how to kill a mood." She swung her leg off of me and sat down hard on the rug, hugging her knees in a tight, impassable gesture.

"I'm sorry," I said, sitting up. "I didn't want to hide anything from you. Why is it such a big deal? I'm not seeing anyone else."

Tib laughed harshly. "It's not who you're seeing now, it's who you could see."

"I didn't say I wasn't monogamous—"

"I don't give a fuck about monogamy, Sadie. You could walk away at any moment and disappear into the safe, acceptable world of being straight."

"No, I couldn't," I said, feeling tears on my cheeks, though I hadn't realized I was crying. "You don't just get up one day and decide to be straight. That's not how it works. That's called lying."

"It's called bisexual."

I felt liked she'd punched me.

"Pete is bi," I said. "He and Greg have been together for ten years. I've seen plenty of people leave each other for the same sex while they've been together."

"That doesn't mean he won't tomorrow," said Tib. "I couldn't trust someone who might leave for the opportunity to live a straight life. It would be like a kick in the teeth. You can't understand what it is to be a real dyke. He can't understand what it is to be gay."

I thought of the time I'd rushed to Greg's side at the hospital to make sure Pete was still alive after a drunken frat boy had beaten him unconscious for being a fag. I thought of my parents throwing me out for loving a girl and telling me they were ashamed of me and I was no longer their family. It sure seemed to me like we understood.

"I'm sorry, Sadie," said Tib, watching me cry with her arms folded as if I were a leper she was afraid to touch. "I can't do this. You're not family."

The ride down the mountain was like dying. I could feel her leaning away from my touch as I held on to her. It was dark by the time we reached downtown and the lights of The Club were brilliant pink letters against a black sky over the hotel. I climbed off the bike and Tib sat idling for a moment, staring at her boots while people lined up around us at the door, laughing, kissing, ready to have a good time.

"Tib—"

"It's like you stabbed me in the gut, Sadie," she said behind her dark glasses. "And that's what you'll never understand. Maybe you should figure out who you are. At least I know who I am."

Tib rode off into the hot desert night, no sunset to give her exit the finality it needed.

I drove to Greg and Pete's place and fell sobbing into Greg's arms when he opened the door. There was nothing I had to say. Greg held me while I cried long into the night, curled on his couch, and Pete brought me Kleenex and chamomile tea. I envied Pete with a bottomless ache.

The boys surprised me at the bowling alley on Monday and came by for lunch to cheer me up. Pete pointed out girls for me on the lanes until I had to laugh.

"Check out that one," said Pete between his teeth, nodding his head at a redhead coming in, bare arms glistening from the heat. "*Very* hot."

"You're not supposed to notice girls," said Greg, elbowing Pete as he read the paper at the counter beside him.

"Right. No. She's absolutely hideous." Pete winked at me.

"I'm going have to kick you two out if you don't order something," I said, smiling in spite of myself.

Greg leaned over the counter. "I'll have a vodka and tonic."

"Okay, that's one Diet Coke."

Greg sighed as I filled a cup with soda from the dispenser. "I rue the day I told you I was giving up drinking." He took the soda anyway, punching a straw into the lid and turning back to his paper. He turned a page as he was taking a sip and nearly spit out his drink.

Pete glanced over at the paper. "Holy shit," he said. "And I mean that."

"What?" I demanded, leaning over the counter as Pete tried to move the paper away from my view.

I slapped my hand on it and spun it around to face me. It was a local interest piece in the Lifestyles section about the megachurch in the metro area an hour and a half north.

And there, in living color, was Tib—or rather, Thelma Thompkins and the entire Thompkins family: little brother David, the Reverend "Tex" Thompkins, and...Tib's mom, Alice. Tib might not have been recognizable except for the eyes. She was dressed in a conservative suit dress, loose curls framing her face just below the chin, with a demure smile on her lips. Lips that had been anything but demure with me.

Beside them, a large, billboard-sized sign proudly proclaimed: GRACE CHRISTIAN CHAPEL. WHERE FAMILY IS FIRST.

# CHRONIC

Anna Watson

Shara can do it today, I can tell. Lately, she's been hurting a lot, and when she hurts, she hides behind the swing of her straight black hair and just hangs on until she can lower herself into a hot bath at the end of the ordeal that living through a day can be. But sometimes, like today, the strong pulse that keeps her going wins out, and she tucks her hair behind her ears and I can feel her eyes on me as I get dressed. She's been up for an hour or so, stretching, listening to her tapes.

"Stop," she whispers, and I freeze, catch my breath. I carefully fold my jeans, put them back in the drawer and turn to face her. I'm wearing my muscle shirt and my boxers—not even a soft pack, since I have to go to work later. The way her gaze rakes me up and down, though, I know she sees my dick, my dick that's always with me, beating right next to my heart, and I'm hard in an instant. This is how it is, this is how it has to be: when Shara can, I must, and when I must, I get hard.

"Down." I'm on my knees beside the bed before she's even finished saying the word. Her painted toenails—drops of cerise—appear next to my right knee. I have a hard-on that won't stop just from looking at them, wondering what she has in mind. I have to go to work. I don't care.

"Andy," she murmurs. "Where were you last night?"

An icy chill lodges itself in my belly. She was sleeping when I got in, must have been sleeping for hours. It had been a bad day. I left her drowsy after her bath. I massaged her aching legs and feet. I clear my throat.

"No, don't." She strokes my shaved head very lightly, and I shiver, goose bumps breaking out on my arms and legs. "Don't even try."

I keep my eyes on her toes—those lollipop toes—and I know she will do what has to be done.

"Stay." She leaves the room.

It's cold on the floor. We cracked our window during the night to let in some fresh air; a late autumn breeze snakes across my body and lifts the minute hairs on the back of my neck. My nipples are hard and painful, cold; my nose begins to run. I stretch across to the nightstand for a tissue—she hasn't told me I couldn't move. I try to slow my breathing, but my cock is too hard and I'm too afraid of what Shara is going to find out about last night.

Last night was so good. I feel tears, a tangled mess of tears right behind my eyes, stuck there, waiting.

Last night's girl was someone from my support group—what

a cliché, right? There we were, straight, queer, old, young, of color and not, slouched on plastic chairs in the community center meeting room. Our guilt and anger and frustration filled the room, made the windows weep with condensation. The facilitator is Noelle, a whip-thin lesbian with graying dreads and a no-nonsense attitude. She talked for fifteen minutes about the book we were all supposed to have read, *Loving Someone Chronically Ill*, then asked us to share our thoughts. This girl, the one I ended up fucking, had been crying the whole time. When Noelle asked who wanted to begin, this girl, this cute, chubby little redhead, her mascara coming down her cheeks and her lipstick bitten off, sobbed out her story. I've been in the group a long time. I know her story.

When I met Shara, she didn't seem sick. She was bright and energetic on our dates, practically edible in her short skirt and low-cut tops, tripping along beside me with her small hand tucked inside my elbow, looking up at me like a sparrow. She wore her hair short back then, which I don't usually go for in a femme, but on her it was ultrafeminine, cute as hell in an Audrey Hepburn way. Dangly earrings brushed the creamy skin of her neck, and as we walked, when we danced, as we ate close together in romantic restaurants, the scent of her perfume would come and go, wafting sexily into my nostrils. She can't wear perfume anymore—it gives her a headache. And I know now how much effort it cost her to go out with me those nights, how she needed to spend the days after our dates recovering in bed, gathering strength so she could access that bubbly, healthy place in herself and present it to me like a gift. Recently, she said, on one of those days she couldn't make it out of bed, when she was hurting and crying, "You never would have dated me if you'd known I was sick," and the look on my face must have betrayed me, because she ordered me out and wouldn't speak to me for the rest of the day.

*Maybe I wouldn't have,* I say to myself, *but I did and here we are and I love her. I love her.*

The girl finished talking and stopped crying. There was a flush on her face and a look of fierce triumph—she had said it, said that she feels guilty for being healthy, feels horrible about the anger and despair she sometimes can't help screaming out at her lover, at the frustrations she feels when they can't do the things they used to do so easily: go hiking, spend time at a museum or shopping, or even head out on a whim to catch a movie in the evening. Now it's all food restrictions, medications, endless visits to the doctor. She hates it. After her confession, she was purged and we comforted her with our soothing words, yes, yes, it's like that, it's true, it's really true.

She was waiting for me outside, standing nervously next to her little yellow VW bug. I smiled at her. She was adorable. She'd fixed her makeup and her eyes were big and pleading. I have never looked for solace here in the group, so I hesitated. When I go out, I want to forget all of it, and I find girls who have never heard of fibromyalgia and who don't know the first thing about environmental sensitivity or celiac disease. With those girls, I talk about music and television and movies, and when I fuck them, there is nothing, just bodies, and perhaps the memory, later, of the way they cried out or didn't when they came.

"You're Andy, right?" She moved away from the bug and held out her hand to me. I touched it and it was warm and I knew when I shook it I wouldn't be hurting her fingers. I took her hand and squeezed until she made a small gasp, but she didn't pull away.

"Can we go somewhere and talk?" she asked when I finally let go. I had to get home to Shara, make sure she was settled for the night, but we made a date to meet later at the Lounge. When we got there, we never made it out of the parking lot. I put her in the cab of my pickup and was under skirt and all over her tits in an instant. She wanted it, I wanted it, we pushed into each other and the smell of her sweat and the way her pussy melted under my tongue, I couldn't get enough. I made her come hundreds of times—can that be right? The windows were completely steamed up, the air thick and salty, and her hands on my dick felt like a blessing. Her name is Melissa. I let her touch my chest. She sat on my lap riding my dick and I came and I never come. I never come unless I'm with Shara.

What can I tell my wife? She is standing over me again, her toes, her tender ankles. I hear the *swish swish* of the switch as she tests it in the air, and then she's touching me all over with the tip. It's been a long time since she's felt strong enough to hit me, and I am trembling with anticipation, fumbling my hands toward my dick. She notices and switches the backs until I stop. It hurts. I can feel the tears—they are standing at attention, but nowhere near ready to fall.

"You were out fucking a girl last night," she says, all the time prodding and flicking me with the switch, forcing me to squirm and flinch away. Sometimes she makes little sounds of satisfaction when she gets me somewhere particularly nasty, like one of my frozen nipples.

"You may speak."

"Shara, Ma'am." I don't know what to say. Melissa begged me to call her. I don't call my tricks. I fuck them and I don't come and I don't call them and if I see them again at a bar or a coffee shop, I nod politely and turn away.

"You fucked her," Shara says.

"Ma'am, I fucked her." Shara waits. She wants details. She wants to know exactly what she's punishing me for. Finally she says, "Her name."

"Melissa, Ma'am."

"Up." I rise as gracefully as I can and follow her to the doorway. She nods at the rings and I scramble to pull out restraints from the bureau. When I am secured to her satisfaction, she begins.

"*M.*" She traces the letter softly on my back, naked now that she's stripped me of everything, even my boxers. She knows how I hate being completely naked in front of her.

"You will say the alphabet," she orders, and I start. A lash for every letter until we get to *M*. I can hear the joy in her as she beats me, the strength that has come to her this morning from who-knows-where. I can hear her turn-on in the healthy grunts she makes as she brings the switch down on my reddening shoulders and ass, in her sharp, excited indrawn breaths. When I have spelled out Melissa's name, I am on fire, and the tears are closer. My nose is running again, but I know she won't let me wipe it. My cock is hard, and when she checks between my legs with a nonchalant swipe of her hand, I can see how much that pleases her.

She puts the switch away and gets out nipple clamps—the pink ones, the girly ones she knows I can't stand. They have little bows and bells and they hurt my pride. She arranges them and begins to play with my chest, humiliating me with her words, calling me stacked and pretty and womanly. The tears are even closer now. I close my eyes.

"Open," she commands, and when I do, I see she has dropped her robe and is wearing nothing but her lacy red bra and her—

oh god, I can't bear it—her femme dick, the one shaped like a dolphin, the glittery purple one. You're probably laughing, but that thing is an instrument of torture for me, a twisted obscenity of everything that's right and good, and she knows it. "Open," she says again, releasing my hands and ankles from the restraints, not even giving me time to rub sensation back into them. She has me on my hands and knees, ass in the air. She pushes inside me, hard, angry, demanding, and I am shaking and begging her not to, but she doesn't stop.

"You bitch," she says over and over, slamming me, sticking that thing so deep I feel it piercing my heart. "You fucking bitch."

Some sound—a howl, a scream—tears out of me, shredding my throat. Still I don't cry. She slumps against me, sweaty, furious, then pulls out. She hasn't come, and a small part of my brain thinks that her knees have probably given out—she hasn't even put down pillows—but the rest of me just falls to the floor and waits. She kicks me, herding me back to the bed, where she makes me lie on my back, spread-eagled.

"Exam," she snaps, pulling off the nipple clamps with one vicious yank. I cry out but know better than to try and rub my chest. All my muscles tighten when I think about what she is going to do next. I am boiling mad for a moment—isn't it enough that she fucked me like a girl with that abomination, that she adorned me with the clamps, isn't that enough? But I know it's not, that perhaps nothing is enough for what life has brought us.

Shara puts her robe back on—white terry cloth; it looks a little like a lab coat. She quickly braids her hair into one plait, pulls on latex gloves, and assumes a professional demeanor. She moves briskly toward me and takes my hand.

"I'll be doing your exam today," she says in a neutral but friendly voice. "I'm going to start with your breasts." I cringe as she leads me through the familiar routine, possessing my chest—my tits—moving them around, squeezing the aching nipples, running her long fingernails sharply up under my arms.

"They seem fine," she says at last. "We do recommend you get a mammogram this year, however." She waits until I nod and say that I will, I will get a fucking mammogram. I don't say fucking.

"Now I'm just going to touch your vulva lightly with my fingers," she continues, moving down to my crotch. I tremble from the desperate need to pull my legs together, roll over, protect myself from her soft touches, but she has me pinned as much as if she'd tied me down. I am so ashamed.

When she is done, the speculum and KY back in the drawer, I am drenched with nervous sweat and the tears hover close, close. She sighs and sits still for a moment, holding the slimy gloves in one hand. I watch her fight to regain some of the energy that was driving her earlier. She gives me a burning glance.

"Get up. Get ready."

Oh yes, oh praise Jesus, she's going to let me fuck her. I roll off the bed and hurry into the bathroom. The relief of settling my equipment where it should be—of pulling on my boxers, getting back into my muscle tee—is exquisite. She's lying on the bed waiting for me, naked now, spread out, her fingers toying with her juicy cunt. I can see shadows of fatigue, of pain, behind her eyes, but we both ignore them. She won't let me kiss her, but she beckons and I lower myself onto her, sink into her, my wife, my femme, my true love. Her pussy wraps around me and I burrow my face between her warm, fragrant breasts. Letting her set the rhythm, guide me, tell me how it's going to be, I move inside her, fucking her like the precious angel she is.

She is close—I know she's been ready for a long time. Her breathing quickens and she scrapes her nails down my sore back, pinching, drawing blood. "Who do you belong to?" she whispers in my ear. "Whose boy are you?"

She is coming and as she clutches and grinds against me, tears finally burst out of me.

"Whose *boy* are you?" she asks again, but I am sobbing so hard I can't speak. She knows the answer though, and she holds me, lets me pour myself into her, forgiven, welcomed home, and I come.

# THE BRIDGE

Isa Coffey

It's dark. We're driving fast. The Coronado Bay
Bridge sweeps lights like diamonds overhead.
I'm drunk, baby, but not on booze. I'm drunk
on you. I don't know your name, but it's good.
You're good, and I'm falling, fast. You're hot;
your suited self just right, behind the wheel. My
wheel. Take over, baby. Drive this car of mine
right up to heaven. The ocean's dark, taking
off below us, all rocking waves tumbling like
crazy. Shit. Throw me overboard; I'm heading
there already.

Your fist is tight between my legs; the stars
are shooting licks between my earlobes and my
naked ribs. You've got me, tied between this
bridge and the fucking sea below. I'm full. The
moon is too. She's up there, competing with diamonds, competing with stars, competing with

you. You've got one hand on the wheel of my black, coal black, cool black, shining black, '69 VW convertible, top way down. The other's opening from fist into hard, fat, dark fingers, figuring me out. Yeah, baby, that's all of me, and I'm gonna slide myself right onto you so you can fill me fast. You do.

Slick, your fingers are your dick. I'm riding, we're riding, the bridge is flying quick. I wanna be on this bridge all night. The wind is blowing out my brain. I gotta pull my tits up to the sky and moan and groan real loud, but—fuck—down's the only way for me. Pull my lever, baby, and there's no way, there's no other way, but down. You're on it, in it, and I'm losing now. Pull this fucking car over to the side, right here, right now, on top, the very tip, of this damn bridge. Fucking pull it fast. You do.

Suddenly balanced between now and then, midnight and dawn, I can't remember who you are, or who I am, but I am falling, fucking, in love with you. You can do your thing to me. Right now. You do. You come down, quick, across the stick, all dark skin, dark suit, dark hair. A huge sex sweep across the lit-up sky. You're heavy on me; you've got me pressed down deep into leather, deep into this fast-moving bridge, deep into you. Push me into the sea, baby. Take my breath. Take it away. Who needs it now?

It's tight; my knees are splayed against metal doors, and rods. My pink silk, soaked panties lost somewhere down there, to lust. And bust.

You got some kinda crazy ass dick burning hard right down my inner thigh. Long and thick and ready to go; you're a breathless femme's idea of heaven.

Your juicy lips are licking, nibbling, my nose, my lobes, my brows, my lashes. Wherever they can get. I'm biting back, real hard. You better eat me fast, baby, or I'll devour you.

Your bound-up chest rests thick on mine. I like the feel. I want some more. My nipples rub up hard against your bind. Pressing tits and nipples up, they're begging, I'm begging, "Suck them off. Suck them the fuck off." We're too crammed up in here for that. You moan, "Baby, you wait. When we've got enough room, I'm gonna suck your nipples off so bad, you're gonna die from cumming."

It's tight, and you're groaning, low, and I'm sweating; getting whatever kinda movement I can get going, going, 'cuz I'm ready to move big against your fucking fingers. You're turning two to four, all wet and fat and kind in me. You're going, baby, right into high gear, pushing it in with your weight, pushing it up with thrusts, suddenly moving faster than those cars speeding by, speeding right over the peak of this sky-scraping bridge. Oh yeah, baby, you've got speed. Run me over. Fuck me with your fingers, then your fist, while I shoot myself, and you, right up into lights, into the goddamn moon.

And yeah, you're curling it up, just right. You know your way around, just right. Rolling your fingers, balling me now, up into where I don't let anyone go. It's deep. You're deep. I'm shooting us into that moon, baby. And I'm falling right off of this bridge.

Falling, whispering, "You're pushing up against my heart, baby."

Falling, whispering, "You've taken my heart, baby."

You murmur back, low and slow, right down into the center of my done-in heart, "I'm all yours, baby; I'm all yours."

I can tell you're gonna cry, but don't. You are one fucking butch.

Then I'm cumming, and I'm cumming, and it's loud, and you're with me.

It's loud, and you're with me. It's loud, and you're with me. I'm finding that I want you more. I'm fucking crying. For you.

"Hey baby," you say. You hold me real tight. I know you're gonna stay right here, no matter what the fuck you need, no matter how uncomfortable you get, no matter how worried about cops, or cold, or how much you need to pee. You're gonna stay right here, with some femme you hardly know, until I stop crying and say I'm okay; until I'm ready to get dressed and drive off this bridge, for burgers or coffee or my house or yours, because that's what butches do. It's why I started falling for you as soon as we got into my car and I was looking up at the lights and the stars, feeling a little too drunk on you, pulling off my blouse, and bra.

The cop does come, right after my cum. We—we're a we now, that's where my cum's led us, at least while we're still way up high on this bridge—see him first as taillights, heading the other direction, just as we're peeling ourselves up off the seat, back into the land of the bridge and the cars and the rocking ocean waves far down below metal rails by our side. Fuck.

You climb over to your seat, straighten your suit. I gather my bra, my frilly peach blouse, the remains of my panties, stretched out and soaked; then snap, button, draw on in time for the cop, who's turned right around and is coming our way. We knew he would; they always do. They sniff us out. Our scent makes them mad, makes them feral, makes them want to scratch and claw, or shoot and skin.

He pulls up behind us; his head's to our ass. Headlights are blazing, blinkers are pulsing, strobe lights are like a fucking carnival night. He's out of his cop car, strutting our way. Fucking pig. This won't be easy. Not in this town, home to a million studs in uniform. Not with a white cop. Not with a black butch driving a shiny black convertible, owned by the white woman sitting all femme in the passenger seat. Not with two women, any colors, alone in a car on the top of the Coronado Bay Bridge, lit up by cum. Not a chance.

My butch is sweating. Acting tough, for both of us, but scared. It's always harder for butches. I lean over, touch her hand, "You okay?" She says, of course, "Yeah, baby, no problem." I go ahead and ask, now that we're here, close and scared, sitting on top of the chopping dark sea, waiting for harm that's heading our way, "So, baby, what's your name? Tell me quick, before that prick tries to break us with his dick."

"My name's Sun, and baby, I wanna be *your* Sun."

Fucking full Moon on one side of my heart, way up here, way up high, and now Sun's on the other. Damn, what a night. I kiss her lips. Deep down inside I'm thinking, "Yeah, baby, you can sure be my Sun. I'm fucking gonna be your Moon."

The cop doesn't ask for Sun's ID, just tells her to get out of the car. Fuck. He tells her to walk over to his flashing cop car, lean up against the warm metal door, spread her legs, arms up, wide. It's bad. We knew it would be. He can smell dyke dick. Damn if he's gonna let some black butch fuck his white girl. He for sure thinks he owns me, and that he's gonna get me, after he takes Sun out. I'm watching out the window, feeling Sun's fear, knowing she's not going to show it, not to him, not now. Only to me, later, and only after I show her mine.

He starts at the top: bending Sun's arm in toward her head, he holds Sun's fingers, stiff with cum. Looks like he's maybe gonna break them back. Then, one by one, he slides them into his mouth instead, and starts to lick each one. Huh? Placing her hands back on top of his cop car, he pats down the sides of her body, treating that suit like it's worth a million dollars. A cop? He slides his hands, slowly, around to her tight bound breasts, but gently, like there's some kind of respect going on, then draws his body into hers, leaning long against her back, arms still wrapped around her binding. Looks like he's thinking of getting off.

But on a butch? What's happening here? I lean out further, look more closely. This isn't a man with facial hair. I slide out of my side of the car, make my way slowly up toward them. The cop allows me to; he's clearly gone by now, into his search...for what? Sun wonders too, of course, and turns, to see Cop's eyes, glazed over. Hunting for his hidden world, his secret self, I grab his cop cap, pull it off, and down come waves of copper hair. Well, my. Surprise. A babe.

This he's a She. My she's a He. All up on this crazy ass bridge. Some night.

I push Cop into Sun, real hard. My body's into Cop's, especially down low. Cop seems to come alive, to find that hard-ass copper drive. We're sharing, and it's Sun's turn to get off with that long-ass cock. The three of us are panting now, cars whizzing by. They can't see much beyond the flashing police lights, bridge lights, starlight and that fucking juicy, full-assed moon. Just a little of us, getting off, spreading heat right out, right out, into light.

Cop's hot but acting like she hasn't a clue what to do when faced with the real thing. I reach around, take her hand, slide it down into Sun's pants, tight boxers, and along the full length of that sexy cock. Cop starts to rub, soft, gets the hang and goes on, hard. Turns out this copper's got some style. Sun's breathing is loud grunting; he's gazing heavy in my eyes. He's with me strong. We're in it, deep. We're in it way up to that sky that's dark behind the stringing, singing lights of this vast stretched-out bridge.

While she's on him, I do my own, unbuckle Cop's thick silver belt, let it drop, then slide her zipper down as well. She's sweating now. I want to make her cum; to give her power up to Sun. This doll's one bundle of surprise. She's willing, more than willing, *easy*, to slide in low; her belly breathes me right down deep; her hair is soft, seems sweet. A cop? How did she make it through? But damn is she ready: pearly, slippery, dripping, silky panties glide my hand, easy as can be, right over tiny curls I imagine share the copper of her head. My fingers spread her lips so I can fondle that tender clit, rising and falling as her rhythm decides to join mine. Oh yeah, baby Cop, oh yeah, here we go.

She's busy, too, trying to figure out how to pull Sun's cock out of his pants, and get it inside her. Clearly a virgin dyke. Sun's breathing so hard, he's totally gone, humping that cop's hand like he's gonna explode, not getting that Cop hasn't a clue what to do, except trying to figure out how to handle not falling apart with being about to cum herself, my hand moving that clit so swift now she's breathing like a teenager. Fuck—maybe she is one.

I got it now, I take control, of two way-out-of-it queers stuck in the middle of a great big bridge over a great big sea with a great big moon fucking with everything they got.

I reach around, slap Cop's hands, her fricking hands, out of my way, and shove them down her own, now swollen, chick dick, to keep the rhythm going. I grab Sun's dick—man, that dick's huge—a giant among dicks, out of his pants, pull a rubber from my skirt, rip it with my teeth and pray the bloody thing will fit his thing. It does. I spit some polish onto it, pull the copper's pants down low, the silken panties with them. She's lovely copper underneath, just as I'd supposed. I turn her round and push her back, the first time I've ever shoved a cop. I am into this. I'm turned on, and thrust her onto her warm cop-hood; it's ready for a good hot fuck. Then pull those uniform pants off her kick-ass boots, toss my fingers into her. No way to resist that cop's pussy naked on her machine.

Sun's right here, dick so high, so hard, he's clearly gonna pop if he doesn't get inside that copper's pussy. I wouldn't stand between that urgency, not after what he's given me. I pull out, and in he goes. Slow at first, letting her get used to him, then fuck-ass hard. Cop, wow, she hollers, and just as suddenly, she moans. No doubt it's her first time being butched. Lucky her, to have Sun break her in, and bring her out. Doesn't get much better. And, cool. Right here, with us. We're now a sudden secret sexy team, a sudden secret sexy us. It's cool.

Sun's driving her, Cop on her car; he's pumping it. Up and down and all around. Cop's clearly into it. All she's saying now is "Mmmmm," or "Yeah," or "More, please, more," or "Aaaaaahhhhhh," or "Oooooohhhhh." She's one damn polite cop fuck.

The cars blaze by. A couple cars, they're in the know; they slow. They watch. Uh-huh. They see. They see, and now they're humping fast in their own cars, whipping out whatever stuff they've got: their toys, their gear, their fists, mouths, sticks and whips. On their way to their own play. Lucky to cross this bridge tonight.

I'm hungry. I want him too. Not Cop. Well, maybe Cop, but I want Sun. I need him now. I got my stuff, right here with me. I reach into my girly skirt, grab another see-through wrap, and some slick-dick lube; stretch my sexy self along his suited side; nibble on his dark, shell ear, and whisper, "Can I rub your butt, slap your ass, slide inside your tender hole? I promise to be true."

Sun's so gone, mesmerized by his thick dick in that soft copper pussy, he isn't thinking much about his butt, or me. He turns his face; he looks at me, remembers me, grabs me with his mouth to suck my face, my lips, my brow, and looks down at my tits. I lift one up, pull back my bra, and press it in his mouth. God, how much I've wanted it inside, ever since we drove onto this smoothly swinging bridge.

Sun sucks. He bites. He licks it light; he licks delight. And all the while pumping copper pussy. This He is Herculean. For the second time this mighty night, I cum, then cum. His eyes light up: a tit-clit dyke. And yeah, he wants me inside that hole of his. My butch.

He turns back to Cop, who's groaning now for Sun to take her life away, right now. Sun's moving different now, slowing it all down and deep. Cop's cumming; that's sure. Now it's all, "FFFFFFFFFFUUUUUCCCCCCCKKKKKKKKK!" and "SSSS-SUUUUUUUCCCCCCKKKKKKKKK!" Sweet girl transformed to dyke. Sun surely has just saved her life, in this one night.

I snap my wrap on my fuck finger, bite open my smoothest lube and slip my hand right down his shorts. I feel him whisper to himself, to me. I hear the sound I knew I would. I know it well. Hurt and desire: both. While Sun gentles into Cop's post-cumming melt, right on her hood, I rub my hand just light at first, all over Sun's big butt. He starts to roll, he starts to groan, he starts to have faith in me. He gazes back, and fills my eyes. "You got my heart, baby," he moans, 'cuz I'm right here, real close, about to get closer.

Sun pulls out of Cop, leans over her, unbuttons her uniform

shirt. I hear Cop suck in breath as Sun starts to lick, so I lean over to see. Cop's got some fucking big breasts. Her eyes are closed; her breath's coming all strong again, and so is Sun's. He's licking, but he's thinking, he's feeling, he's breathing: ass. Hole. But you're not getting it, baby, not yet, not 'til I'm ready. And I'm not ready. I'm into this big ass of yours. Into it enough to pull down these sharp wool trousers of yours. Into it enough to pull down these black, tight-ass boxers of yours. Pull them down just enough to see your strap, just enough to see your hot double-moon ass, right under the tails of your fine, black-ass jacket.

Rubbing is heading right into slapping, right into licking, right into whacking, and kissing. I'm settling at your butt-hole, baby, for the gentlest of tender strokes. Looks like you've caught on fire, baby. I'm rubbing; you're groaning; you're pushing back on me. You want me in. No way, baby. No way. Not yet. I know you can handle it with me at the wheel, baby. You drove us already tonight; it's my turn now.

This night was growing long. The bridge was way more empty. Fewer people heading out to the beach to make out. Fewer people heading back into the city to do it in someone's bed. It was starting to feel like it was just us way up here, flying high. Just us and a couple of random cars, too much in their own trip now to get what was going on under our bright, spinning lights.

There was just this one car, some kinda sedan, that had decided to stop, totally stop, and hang: two dykes in their car, checking us out. There they were, poised on the thin inner meridian, close enough to take in what was going on, far enough to do their own fucking in private. I looked up at Car, giving Sun more time to want me moving down and in while I teased that sexy butt of his. I could see a sweet Honey ass in some pretty pink lace panties, big breasts hanging low, falling out of matching pink lace cups, clearly making someone I couldn't catch real happy. Mmmmm. A moment later some high-class wool pants, pulled down far enough to see a black strap tight over a deep Chocolate butt, come up. They'd sure brought the right size car. Was this their second, third or fourth time round tonight?

The two of them, the three of us: clearly Dyke Night now on the Coronado Bay Bridge.

Sun's so ready now he's practically shoving his ass onto my hand, my arm. His groaning is loud enough that Honey and Chocolate have looked up at me: am I fucking with this butch? Sun's taking it out on Cop, as well, and she's liking it, kicking her hips up and down so hard that hood of hers has gotta be denting. I guess those tits of hers are driving her wild. Sounds like she's cumming. Again. Can't keep track, but I'm sure it's a record for her.

Okay, Sun, here we go, baby. I slide right down over your hole, circling like you're my golden crown. And baby do you grow quiet and still. The pause. Like the bridge, the wind, the midnight doves, the shooting stars all decided to inhale and wait, for you. I hold still too, my finger pressing and waiting right at your gate. The shift comes. You open, so far, I slip one finger easily in. Oh man, I forgot. No matter how many asses I've been in, I never remember this moment. You are damn sweet inside, you big tender butch. All soft and smooth and nothing but sugar. But wow do you go, no damn pause anymore. You're pumping on me like heat, like fire, like there's never going to be tomorrow. You need way more than I've given you yet.

I've gotta work fast. No one-finger covers are gonna do this right; you're clearly a full-fisted job. My left hand pulls a purple glove out of my pocket, dangles it from my mouth, while my right finger fucks your butt, your heart, your everything. I grab the lube, squeezing it over those dangling purple fingers, as well as down my clothes. Anything for you. I dip my face down low, to lick your back, while I change gear, then press two, and quickly three, fingers into you. Wow, baby, are you full. And wanting it. You're licking Cop, down to her twat. She's grabbing cock; she needs more now, and so do you. I move from three to four. Your cock's in her, my cock's in you.

I glance back to that Honey-Chocolate car, to see if they approve of what I'm up to. Clearly I'm off the hook, 'cause that car's rocking now. Someone in there's cumming, loud. It's Chocolate's ass that's up and pounding, so Honey's surely ejecting herself right off this planet. And from the sound of it, she's gonna make her way to Mars.

Cop, Sun and me, we're rocking, we're socking, we've got it in sync. You're pumping Cop and I'm pumping you; our rhythm is hot. Our bodies are sweating it out; we're setting it up; we're wanting it now: all Cum.

I'm looking down, right into your butt. And I'm looking up, right into the stars and the lights and the moon. It's all right together; it's shooting us out: your butt and Cop's heart and my mind and the moon and her cunt and my heart and the stars and your heart and the lights and those strangers just over the lines, that aren't really lines.

Then POW comes the wave and FUCK is it high: a twister, a quaker, a hip-hopping TSUNAMI.

Sun's cumming, Cop's cumming, Chocolate-Honey's cumming, every single fucking star's cumming, every single fucking light on the multi-thousand-foot strands of the bridge's cumming, the moon for sure is cumming, and if I don't cum within the next twenty seconds, I'm going to throw myself off this damn bridge, into the frigid waters of the salt-laden Pacific Ocean, to die.

Of course, Sun gets this, and turns around. Cop and Chocolate-Honey seem to get it too, because Cop sits up, moves off her hood, Chocolate-Honey slide out of their slick sedan and head across the lunar lanes. Suddenly they have rope, lube, gloves, cuffs, belts; everything except blindfolds, because they're gonna let me see the stars, the swaying lights, the moon that never changes course tonight. And them.

They strap me to the bridge, arms spread, legs wide, wind up between my legs, my thighs. They rip off my skirt, my soaked panties beneath, my thin little blouse and my bra just below. I'm naked right here on the Coronado Bay Bridge. It's me and the seagulls, the doves flying by.

The moon that seems bigger, that's filling my heart.

Then these dykes take their turns. They hold and caress me. They sing me love songs. They strap on fresh dildos, don black leather vests, frilly gold panties, with matching gold bras. They start rubbing my titties 'til they're rising, real tight; start licking and sucking, real gentle and tough. 'Til I'm crying and laughing and moaning and groaning. They're caressing my belly, ooh baby, that's nice. They're stroking my hair, all of it, and it's good. They're saying my name, over and over. They're stroking my feet, and sucking my toes.

Songs are coming, and they're going. The stars are sharp; they fill the sky; they fill my eyes. Oh yeah. They're really singing now. My name. My love. Their love for me. It's good. The bridge is holding me. The wind is strong. It's blowing all of us, into each other's arms. Sun's right here, right in my face. He's kissing me, right on my lips, so light, so hard, so everything. Right now, just now, all the slapping I could want, over my entire body, starts. My hands, my feet, my tits, my thighs. And in they go, my holes get filled, and pumped, and I want more. Sun's kissing me, real light. And calling out my name. The singing is so loud by now, up to the stars. It's all I want. I'm filled, I'm fed, I'm held, I'm slapped, I'm loved, I'm high, I'm bright, I'm dark, I'm gone, I'm here, I'm swelled, I'm wet, I'm hot, I am, I'm not.

And I am fucking cumming.

Cumming into everything. Cumming into Sun and Cop,

Chocolate-Honey, Moon and Stars, Light and Me. And Not-Me.

Cumming, and cumming. Cumming, and cumming, and cumming.

Now we're all laughing,
and I'm crying.
We're all laughing,
and I'm crying.
We're all laughing,
and I'm crying.
Way up on the bridge.
Way up high on the bridge.
Way fucking up high on the Coronado Bay Bridge.

# SPOONBRIDGE AND CHERRY

Catherine Lundoff

I'd say that I'd never had sex for money but that would mean forgetting about last winter. But that wasn't about the money, not really. It was about her. Or maybe them. I think.

I was broke, down to my last dime with no job leads on the horizon. It was my own damn fault for a change. I knew the manager at Carol's Coffee was going to fire me and I just didn't bother finding something else to jump to and scrambling for it before the axe fell. Sometimes you gotta play the hand you're dealt. This time I had bad cards and a worse strategy.

It still might have been okay if Michelle hadn't dumped me and kicked me out that same week but they say these things come in threes. I'd say meeting them in the bar a few days later was the third thing; but if I hadn't met them then none of it ever would have happened. That would've really sucked, at least looking back on it all now.

That night I was out drinking with my remaining friends, the ones who'd stand you a cheap beer when you were out of work. We were at some dive up in the Northeast, but since it was Minneapolis, none of us could ever really say what it was "northeast" of. Not that it mattered.

What did matter was that it was the hellish midwinter freeze that we get up here, long about February or so. I was killing time before I had to hike the ice-covered blocks back to Kelly's place, where I was crashing on the sofa. I was also hoping to find someone to replace Michelle, which meant I was leaning up against the bar looking as butch and broody as I was capable of in hopes that somebody would buy it.

But the woman who showed up wasn't exactly what I had in mind. For one thing she was older, like old enough to be my grandma kind of old. For another, she didn't look right. Even in the flickering neon, her blues eyes had that junkie stare going on, the kind where they look right through you and never blink. She was dressed nice though. Good watch, good shoes, so she must've had some cash, at least before she got hooked on whatever it was.

Just then those eyes were fixed on me and I was trying not to back away. Finally she said, "Hello," in the most normal voice in the world. I nodded, then turned back to watch the pool game while the space between my shoulders got all prickly. She kept talking like she knew I wasn't ignoring her. "I'm looking for someone to do something for me. Something I'm willing to pay for. And I overheard you saying that you were out of work."

I whipped around to stare down at her, my mood bouncing between seriously creeped out and crazy pissed off. She smiled then, a thin-lipped, twisted scary smile that didn't make anything look any better to me. Pissed off won. "I don't know who the hell you think you are—"

"My apologies. I'm a rude old woman and I don't have much time left. Not enough to play social games anyway. So for your information, you were whining about being broke and getting fired and dumped loud enough for them to hear you down at the Mall of America." She gave me a once-over and I finally saw her blink. Except now she looked like I wasn't worth her time.

I opened my mouth to snarl something back at her and what came out was "Yeah, so what? Not like it's any of your business. Whyncha' just leave me alone to get drunk in peace?" I turned to walk away and she grabbed my arm. Not tight, but just enough to slow me down from storming off.

When I stopped, she let go. "It's about her. That's why it's my business." She nodded over at a table in the corner. "Normally, I could care less. But now...well, you look a bit like me when I was younger, back before I got sick. I think that might make her happy. And that's all that matters to me right now." I followed her nod over to the table.

There were three old dykes sitting around it drinking their beers and trading war stories. I ignored them. But the fourth one, she made my heart stop. I used to think that was pure b.s. but man, was I wrong. She had blonde hair and blue eyes, standard Nordic goddess for these parts. Except that she was the most beautiful woman I'd ever seen. She smiled and the rest of the room went away, even though she wasn't smiling at me. No, that smile was being thrown away on the scary old junkie standing next to me. There is no justice in this world.

The scary junkie smiled back and I started to change my

opinion. Maybe she wasn't hopped up after all. Sometimes they kept the stare up for years after they went clean. Whatever. Not my problem. For a minute, I considered making a play for the blonde, the notion sending a hot wave up my thighs.

"So I take it you're interested?" Those weird blue eyes were fixed on me again. "It's a worth a couple of hundred if you're in."

"Wha—say, what is your deal? You looking for a third or something?" For a moment, I seriously considered it. Beauty and the Beast. Yeah, that'd be one to share with my buddies, probably worth a couple of beers. I imagined the blonde minus that bulky sweater, her sweet curves under my expert hands. I started getting wet, forgetting for the moment that there'd be a third party participating. The crazy woman inched closer and my little fantasy went up in smoke. No way. Not even for the goddess.

"Not what you've got in mind?" She gave me a wicked smile, one that made me madder and hotter all at the same time.

"I can handle anything you can dish out." I growled the words, wishing a moment later that I hadn't. This one could be into just about anything. But it was too late now and I was too down and out to take it back.

"Good. Let's go before you chicken out." And she turned and walked away, not bothering to look back to see if I was following her.

I wasn't. I leaned against the bar and watched her walk over to the blonde, saw the blonde smile up at her again, and winced. Then the blonde looked at me and I had to catch my breath. She didn't look too thrilled as far as I could tell. But maybe she frowned like that every time her crazy girlfriend picked up a third. I pulled myself together and gave her my best cool smile, the one that says I'm every girl's dream, especially at bar closing time.

The maniac with her waved me over and I sauntered across the room, my eyes never leaving the blonde's. "Hi. I'm—"

But the nut job cut me off. "We don't need to know your name. And you don't need to know ours. It's not important for what I've got in mind."

I glared at her but she wasn't paying attention. Instead the blonde shrugged, then got up to help the other one into her jacket. From the way she was looking at the old bat, it was obvious they'd been together for a while. *Why?!* a little voice wailed in the back of my head. I told it to shut up and followed them out, ignoring the whispers behind me. Maybe they did this every week. Who knew?

The other two led the way to a small SUV in the parking lot. I think it was green but I couldn't be sure. I didn't bother to get the plates either, stupid me, not that I cared until later. Then we were off, headed across town. Crazy woman cut me off every time I tried to talk so after a few tries, I just sat in the back and looked at the blonde's profile. You could tell she had her doubts about whatever her partner had planned but she was going along with it anyway.

For the life of me, I couldn't figure out why. The other one just seemed like a nut to me, and a sick nut to boot. I wondered what was wrong with her and guessed the Big C, just because. Not like I could ask anyway. Then I tried to picture myself in bed with them. That helped, for some weird reason. At least it helped when I saw myself going down on the goddess and burying my face in her sweet pussy.

I could almost feel her start to come when we got to Loring Park. Then Crazy Eyes slowed down like she was going to stop. Then it hit me: she was figuring on some kind of outdoor scene. I started to panic. A couple of hundred bucks wouldn't help me if I died from exposure. The SUV followed the curve around the park while I looked for a way to turn down whatever they had planned. By the time I'd gotten to "Thanks, but no thanks," she'd crossed the street and parked up past the Walker and the sculpture garden.

"So...we're headed back to your place, right? Wherever that is?"

They ignored me in favor of their own conversation. "You sure you want to go through with this?" the blonde asked.

"Long as you're okay with it, love. You know I've wanted to bring you back here to do this for a long time. This looks like it's as close as we're going to get." Then they stared at each other forever and smooched like I wasn't there.

"Ummm...hello? When do I get a piece of the action?" I was getting tired of being ignored and pissed off was better than nothing.

Blondie broke off the kiss and turned around at that. She reached out and pulled me forward so my face was right in front of hers. She stared at me for so long I lost some feeling in my toes. Then she kissed me. Hard. My lips opened under her tongue and I kissed her back with everything I had. Didn't even hear the other one get out of the truck.

When we stopped for air, I had to ask, "So where'd she go?"

"She had something to take care of. Don't worry about it." The goddess was a woman of few words, just the way I like them. I smiled as she kissed me again. The touch of her lips was sending a hot wave of pure lust through everything from my rib cage on down. I wondered if she was getting half as wet as I was and if I could stick my hand between her legs to find out.

Crazy Eyes came back right about then. "We're all set. You ready?" This was to her girlfriend of course; guess I always looked ready or something.

"You sure?" the goddess asked, like she already knew the answer to that question.

Crazy Eyes jerked her head in a nod, then pulled my door open. "Let's go." I got out, moving kinda slow like I thought I could delay whatever they had in mind. But I was aching for the blonde, all hot and empty, and I knew I wouldn't say no to anything that wasn't really scary. The goddess grabbed my arm and started towing me back down the hill toward the museum and the sculpture garden.

We went down the hill past the condos and mansions and our breath was a frozen white cloud around us, which probably meant I was panting. Downtown was crystal clear in the frigid air, all the little lights on the skyscrapers twinkling their hearts out. The snow cover was just right, fresh and white and sparkling in front of us as we got to the greenhouse with its big glass fish.

They'd found a way into the greenhouse after hours? That must be it. Well, I figured that'd be okay, or warm at least. But the goddess kept going, pulling me along in her wake. What the hell did she have in mind? Lights went off all over the snow as we hit the motion detectors' sensors and I blinked at the statues and stuff. I hoped to hell the place wasn't alarmed too or we'd be meeting Minneapolis's finest pretty soon.

I was making noises about hotels and the SUV and common sense when I looked up and realized what she was headed for. Oh shit. The sculpture of the big-ass metal spoon with the cherry on top. Probably the only thing the rest of the country recognized about Minneapolis and we were just going to wander up and do what? Take nekkid pictures in front of it until my tits dropped off from the cold?

"*Spoonbridge and Cherry,*" the goddess murmured, like saying the thing's name out loud made the whole thing make more sense.

I was still sputtering when I noticed Crazy Eyes walking over to sit down on one of the benches. She was holding herself like she was in pain or something. The goddess let go of me and started over to her but stopped when she shook her head. I decided the time had come to take off, gorgeous woman or no gorgeous woman. But the goddess turned out to be in better shape than me and I went down on my face in the snow when she tackled me.

Nothing like a snoot full of snow to get a girl in the mood. I twisted around so I was faceup and tried to flip the blonde over. She locked her legs around one of mine and moved to pin my arms down. I twisted my hand loose and grabbed one of her arms and that was about the time I noticed that her perfect face was an inch away from mine. Her lips were set in a line and she was frowning so I kissed her.

This time, I took her by surprise and was able to flip her onto her back in the snow. She opened her legs and wrapped them around my waist so I decided to stay put for a few minutes. Her lips were icy on mine but it was warm, not hot, inside her mouth. Her tongue shoved its way past my teeth and I sucked on it, wrestling it with mine.

Once I was distracted, she raised her hips up and twisted out from under me. Next thing I knew, she had me by the collar and was dragging me through the snow toward that damned sculpture. I grabbed some snow, then some frozen grass under it but I only managed to get my gloveless hands wet and cold.

I had a fuzzy memory of there being water under the spoon, that being what made it a "bridge," but it was my lucky night and Hell had frozen over.

I slipped and slid along behind her until we got right up to the stupid thing, but no lights or alarms went off. I finally realized that they had a buddy in the Walker, which meant someone else was watching our little production. I wasn't sure if I felt better or worse about that. The blonde snapped snow-covered fingers in front of my nose. "Hey, wake up. Remember me? Climb on up here, tiger and show me what you've got. We have a show to put on."

I stared at her as she climbed up into the spoon just below the cherry. She stared back at me, her expression shifting from Norse love goddess to Valkyrie. I followed her up into the thing, shivering the whole time. Nothing says fun like balancing in a giant metal spoon in the middle of a Minnesota winter. The blonde took a deep breath and grabbed my hand. Then she shoved it up under her coat and sweater, up to where the nipples of her big soft breasts were trying to turn themselves to stone under my frozen fingers.

That did it. I pulled her close, my tongue wrapped in hers and my hands getting warmer by the second. I imagined what she looked like without eighteen layers of clothes, maybe in a nice soft bed. Indoors. But I needed to work with what I had. I broke away from the kiss and dropped to my knees in front of her so I could suck on her hard little nipples.

The goddess moaned deep in her throat, possibly from impending frostbite, and I slipped a hand between her legs and started rubbing through her pants and all. I decided not to think about the woman on the bench and whoever else was watching through the security cameras. Or maybe I just decided it was hotter this way, playing to an audience. I tongued one icy nipple against my teeth and she yanked my hat off and buried her fingers in my hair.

I could feel the crotch of my jeans getting damper but I couldn't spare a hand to get between my own legs, not with the way the goddess was gasping for air now. Instead, I concentrated on standing up and getting my thigh between hers. I started unsnapping her pants as I kissed her, licking my way over her ear and neck. She bit me then, sinking her teeth into my earlobe until I yelped. Her icy fingers were under my jacket and sweater now, working their way up. I was mumbling some bs about how hot she was as I got my own hand down into her hot moist fur and her soaking wet slit.

She sucked my earlobe harder and groaned into my ear, almost a growl. I shoved my leg against her, driving a couple of my fingers into her pussy. She got even wetter and I kept going, setting up a rhythm that was getting both of us warmed up more by the second. I could tell she was getting close from the way she was breathing and it made me grin.

From the corner of my eye, I saw her girlfriend make some movement that looked like she was getting happy in her own pants. Always good to know your work is appreciated. I bared my teeth and bit the goddess's neck, working on one of those huge high school type hickeys that no turtleneck will ever completely cover up. Normally I'm classier than that but I wanted to mark her, make her mine even for a little while.

Her pussy walls closed on my fingers then and she wailed into the frozen air, legs shaking around mine as she came.

She grabbed my face and kissed me again, eyes closed, and I guessed that she was imagining being there with the girlfriend. To hell with that. I shoved her hand down my pants, startling her enough that her eyes shot open. If she was hot before, she was smoking now: big blue eyes all cloudy from sex, white teeth chewing on pink lips. She found my clit so fast I thought it must be about three feet long by now, then she flipped me around so I was in the spoon.

Her hand forced my legs apart so she could get just about all her fingers inside me. I was plenty warm enough now, even when she yanked up my sweater and bit my tit. Then she pulled some snow from the cherry and rubbed it into my nipple. She warmed my nipple back up with her mouth, then she did it again until I thought I'd pass out from being roasting hot then freezing cold.

All the while her fingers were rubbing and pinching my clit until I couldn't take it anymore. I came hard, with only her hand inside me still holding me up, I was shaking so much. Some lights flickered on in one of the condos nearby and I realized I'd been making a hell of a lot of noise.

That was when Crazy Eyes showed up next to us, making me jump. "Time to go," she growled. The goddess didn't argue, just zipped up her pants and tapped me on the cheek and jumped down. Her girlfriend stuffed a couple of bills in my pocket and the next thing I knew, I was standing around freezing my ass off watching them walk away. I zipped up my pants and pulled my shirt down, shivering now from being completely frozen. I followed them out but when I got to the street, they were nowhere to be seen and there was a cab idling in front of the museum.

I looked around, hoping for one last glimpse, but my bad luck still held. Figuring the cab was for me, I hopped in and headed back to Kelly's. Everything was all sticky and achy and even the crinkle of new bills in my pocket didn't make it all better. I wanted the goddess for my very own and it wasn't going to happen and that depressed the hell out of me. Even getting a job a few days later didn't help that much, at least not at first. The blonde was the only thing I saw when I closed my eyes. Plus I couldn't figure out whether it was hotter that I got paid for the best sex I've ever had, or not.

But eventually I stopped looking for them in the local dives and got myself a new girlfriend: blonde hair, blue eyes, standard Nordic goddess for these parts. Maybe someday soon, I'll take her by the sculpture garden and see how she likes art.

# THE WAITING IS
# THE HARDEST PART

Chandra S. Clark

I wonder what you are thinking as you wander home, walking the blocks from the train
station to your apartment. Do you hum to
yourself the song in your headphones? Do you
stop at the corner store for milk? You do sometimes, I've seen you. Only milk or beer and the
rest of your groceries you buy elsewhere, usually Trader Joe's or Jewel, only four bags or so
at a time. Practical single girl. Never more than
you can carry. Never more than you can use.
Are you thinking about what you'll have for
dinner? Whether you've enough goods to make
something, whether you're too tired to bother
and will just order in instead? Do you know
what you want, what you have a taste for?

I do. And I'm waiting here, in the dark of
your room.

You won't see me. You'll come through the door, turn on the living room light, hang your jacket in the hall, then make your way into the bedroom by the dim glow of the streetlamp. You'll start to take off your shoes, leave your jewelry on the dresser. Like you always do. But not tonight.

Tonight I am waiting for you, between the head of your bed and the closet door, where the shadow falls deepest, a knot of twisted cloth in my hands.

I hear your keys jingle in the lock, the soft sound of fabric being removed. The click of the light switch and your heels, your quiet singing. I know the melody but can't quite catch the tune. The fabric is growing damp in my hands. I can feel the sweat making its way slowly down my ribs, catching in the waistband of my jeans. Every muscle taut. Waiting. It seems I've been waiting all my life, just for this. Just for you.

The sound of your footsteps grows louder, then quiet as you reach the edge of the living room, moving toward me.

One earring is off and the other almost in your hand, one foot is bare and as you balance on your left I am upon you, swift and silent in the carpeted hush of your bedroom. The torn sheet is between your teeth in an instant and I use it like a handle, use your imbalance to yank you backward and almost into me, dragging you to the bed. I push you, facedown, pin your arms behind you with my knees and tie the sheet tight into your mouth. You're screaming. I can hear it, muffled beneath the cotton, but no one else would. No one else can. My knees are on top of your back as you thrash and kick at me without effect, trying to roll over, fighting for leverage. It's not easy to hold you down. The click of the knife near your ear stops you, that and my whisper after—just behave and I won't have to hurt you—and it's then you know it's me.

You manage to swing your head wildly to one side, just enough to see my face. I imagine you must've hurt your neck doing that. We lock eyes and for an instant, I see a flash of relief that it's okay. Everything's going to be okay. It's only me and this isn't really happening. But when I don't move, when I merely hold you there, our gazes locked, my expression unchanged, you realize, yes, this *is* really happening.

To you. Right now.

And it's then that I watch ten different expressions roll across your face like storm clouds.

You asked me for this—don't you remember? Of course that was months ago, back when we were still together, when you told me stuff like that. Before you decided things "weren't working out" quite the way you had hoped. Which basically translated into you still wanting me to fuck you, just me plus a handful of other unnamed people. Not that I said no. It was just that neither of us said I love you at any point during sex anymore, no one spent the night, no one cried after. Well, at least I never did in front of you. I saved that until I got home.

So now here we are, pretty. When you wondered where your desires might take you, is this what you imagined? Am I spoiling you for a date you had planned tonight? When you made your way to work today, was this how you pictured your evening: your face a mask of panic and total helplessness, a fury you're unable to vent?

But I know you, my sweet. There is something else there, something you're trying to conceal in your expression. But it's all spelled out for me by the heaviness of your breathing and the wetness I feel as I reach my hand up your skirt.

You were always so lovely when we fucked. Your eye make-up smeared, your hair a luxuriant mess around you. I felt so proud after, that I had ruined your carefully composed image, the face you showed the rest of the world. As though another woman waited under your skin, alive and magnetic, and only I had the power to free her, free you from yourself. Like Aladdin I rubbed you, waiting for magic to happen. But just like every clichéd genie story, wishes come true only in their most literal sense, a backhanded blessing. As I stirred what lay dormant in you, it was not only me that reaped the benefit. I woke you, my beauty, and you made me pay the price by sharing your love. What do you think of wishes now?

I pull the length of rope from my pocket and tie your hands behind you. I keep the knife near your throat, the soft hollow just beneath the jaw, near your ear. I think of slasher movies. I think of high school, and cutting my arm with a broken ash-tray when my heart had been shattered and the only way to cause him pain was by hurting myself. The only sound in the room is your breath mingled with mine. Both of us panting.

I tell you to stay still as I lift my knees from your back, slowly, gauging your reaction and how hard you're willing to fight. I ease one knee between your thighs, press the knife into your neck a bit more, for effect, before I trace its edge down past your shoulder, let you feel its presence near your ribs as I use my other hand to unbutton my jeans. I wonder about your choice of stockings versus panty hose, and what that might say about your plans for the evening. No matter. You only make it easier for me. The knife slips through the black mesh of your underwear and you breathe in, sharply, followed by that rasp you make when you're almost beside yourself, and I'm quite sure bringing the knife back to your ribs makes you hotter. You're so wet your panties slip right through my hand, and I rub the soaked edges against my cock, tell you how good it feels, how hard you make me.

Did I buy you these panties? Certainly a possibility. A couple weeks' wages in lingerie was nothing to complain about. Not spent on you. I check your face again—nah, they're new. Correction: were new. I can tell by the look you try to shoot me over your shoulder. As though you have a fucking thing to say about it. I smile to myself and smack your ass one good time, hard enough to see my hand in red relief. I ask you who you were gonna fuck tonight, who was scheduled to be the conquest of the evening. I ask you because you have a knot of sheet in your sweet, lying little mouth, so you can't answer me. I don't really want to know.

What I want is you—possession, revenge, something I can't quite name as I stroke my cock, teasing your pussy with the tip of it, watching you slide around the edges, trying like hell to get me inside while I call you names, while I name what you have become to me. Bitch, whore, slut, fuckhole. You were my fucking goddess. What pisses me off extra is that you still are, I still want you as much as I ever have. I still want you to want me like that. And right now, you do.

It's the red one, baby, the big silicone fucker we laughed about and called devil dick, the one you asked for when you wanted me deep and hard. My extrabutch dick, I used to joke, the one I couldn't pack unless the goal was to be obvious. Am I obvious now? Can you feel me hitting the edge of your cervix as I give you all of it, all at once moving from tip to hilt in one fluid motion? I have you by the hair, push your face down into the bed harder as my hips meet your ass with every stroke. I'm channeling good dick tonight and I swear I can feel you pull me in deeper, the contractions of your cunt begging for more, for less, I don't even give a fuck. I can feel you slick and firm and moving around me, in you like this, grinding and slapping against each other until I think one of us might tear in two. I'm sweating, you're sweating and we slip until you land flat on the bed, struggling to get on your knees for balance, to get your ass aimed back at me so I can hit you harder, drive it in further, but the press between me and the bed is too much for you and you come, the sheet finally slipping from your mouth as I yank your head back hard, your neck turned at an odd angle and you screaming, screaming from a guttural place deep in your throat, a dark, animal sound.

I keep pounding into you after, squeezing my thighs and hips together as I ride high up on the soft swell of your asscheeks, letting the dildo bump against my clit again and again and I am breathing raggedly, my fist still in your hair, yanking you back with every thrust forward. You are a thing, a thing to be filled and defiled and I am worried about the knife but I've dropped it on the bed next to you, and I think about drowning in red, about your throat slit wide open and I'm coming hard in you, against you, and you surprise me when you buck against me and do the same. No screams this time, just hard grunts and moans into your bedspread, soaked with the both of us.

I lie there for a while, letting the sweat dry to a chilled film under my shirt, drifting off somewhere. Somewhere away from here, away from you. It's only when you begin to squirm beneath me that I remember where I am, what has transpired between us. Your arms must be sore, roped behind you like that all this time. I try to untie you, but my joints feel weak, my hands and the rope slippery with sweat and sex, so I cut through them instead. You lie there, your face half-turned toward me, but not looking. Not seeing. As perfect and unreachable as always.

Neither of us says a thing as I pull up my jeans and make my way to the door. I knew what I was doing when I showed up tonight, the lines I was crossing and cutting in the process. I turn back one more time to look at you, waiting for my heart to tell me something, to whisper your name in the cave of my chest. But instead I notice the blank look on your face, as though you're merely waiting for me to leave. And I realize you have been, right from the very start.

# WHERE THE RUBBER MEETS THE ROAD

Aimee Pearl

We're walking down the street and he's fucking me. Everything's slippery and delicious. This is all true.

We're at the Folsom Street Fair—the annual BDSM outdoor playground event—and it's a hot San Francisco September day. Hot in a way that only San Francisco can be, and only in September. They call it Indian summer. There's a monsoon swelling between my legs. He's going to make me gush.

We're walking in broad daylight. The crowd is thick around us. He rubs a wet thumb against my clit. We move side by side in stride, no pauses. I wonder...

*If people looked down toward my crotch, they might see his right hand sneaking around the edge of my bright cherry-red latex micromini. They might realize that he's got a finger sliding between my lower lips. What would they think? What would they say?*

My skirt is so short that it doesn't cover the full curve of my ass. You can see my cheeks peeking out from the bottom of the shiny rubber coating. I can't wear panties in this, and I can't sit. Can only stand. Can only keep on walking. While he fucks me.

He's devilishly handsome, this one. His skin is the color of a toasted hazelnut, and twice as tasty. We've fucked many times before, but never like this. Never outdoors, in the middle of the street, digits stretching wet rubber wide...

The red of my skirt is polished to a gleam, and I love the way the color looks metallic against my velvet-soft brown skin. This was the first piece of latex I ever bought, the first one I ever tried on. Its tightness around my narrow waist, rounded hips, and plump ass makes me look and feel space-alien exotic, and draws attention to the fullest part of my body. Yes, my butt has stopped traffic. Who doesn't like to look at a black diva in red rubber?

For now, though, we're blending in, seeping into the throng around us. He's giving me a teasing fuck and my cunt is starting to ache with desire. Pretty soon, I'll want more fingers, I'll want to swallow his fist whole. We've got to find a doorway to lean into. I can't cum while walking. I'm perched on spike heels and might fall over.

The orgasms he gives me have been known to cause great commotion.

We find an alley and he pounds me quick and hard, leaves me wet and feeling dirty. This boy has a way with those hands of his. He once made me cum while I prepared a cup of tea.

Holding kettle, boiling hot and full, precarious. He came behind me at the stove and rammed four fingers into me. Undid me. Unraveled me. I don't know how I managed to pour steadily after that.

But I did.

We're discovered in our crevice by onlookers, dykes from around town, smiling at the queer couple that is us. I wish he was packing, so that we could give 'em a real show. Unfortunately, he left his dick at home today. Who needs it, I guess, when you've got hands like his?

Still and all, I do crave his cock sometimes. For a moment, as he fucks me roughly one more time for our audience, I imagine him, silicone in hand, rubbing his rubber-covered rubber dick against my rubber-covered rear. Rolling up latex for greater access. Sliding toy into tightness. A fetishistic ass fuck on a city street, sweaty.

I do it again. Cum.

Later, we leave our latex-alley love nest and slide back into the crowded thoroughfare. He runs into a friend, a gorgeous high-femme white girl with a buzz cut. Six-two in heels, she works as a pro-domme at a local house. Today is her day off, and she and her girlfriend/submissive are strolling through the fair. She's wearing an ankle-length latex dress, and she's drenched in sweat. She squats down and lifts her skirt to circulate air around her sweet blonde pussy. I want to swoon, but not from the heat. She complains about the weather, and about the clients who keep spotting her in the crowd and begging to be dominated.

Beside me, he chats casually with her and smiles. He knows I'm a sucker for a pissed-off femme domme, not to mention one wearing even more latex than I am. From my angle above her, I can see down into her cleavage and admire the beads of wetness on her full breasts. I'm starting to feel wet again myself. He knows. He knows it's time to fuck me again. He knows it's time to go for a walk....

On our next date, we meet at midnight, this time in another alley, in a different part of town. He's hanging out in a club up the street; I've been instructed to drive into the alley and wait for him in the backseat. I send him a text message to let him know I've arrived, and arrange myself to be ready for him. He leaves the club and approaches my car.

I'm wearing a cream-colored knee-length A-line leather skirt. The material is so soft and buttery that most admirers don't even recognize that it's made out of leather—at first glance anyway. This skirt always gets a second glance. It's not short, it's not tight, and it's not an eye-catching color. But it manages to exude a subtle yet no-nonsense sexiness. It's a great skirt for a dominant woman to wear, because of its strict lines. But I'm a submissive, and I like to wear it to feel encased in it, bound by the leather, however loosely, as it falls around my thighs.

There's a rap at the window, and I reach over to unlock the door and let him in. Let him come in and fuck me.

As requested, I'm not wearing any panties. Although this time it's not because of the length of my skirt, of course, but because of other constraints of the scene. Namely, he wants quick and easy access to my cunt; he wants to fuck me quickly and then leave me to go back to his friends at the club. It's all been prearranged. We move like we're dancing. Only there's no music. Just the sound of leather rubbing against vinyl, and breathing. His breath and mine. Mostly mine as he's fucking me hard and I'm struggling to endure it.

To take it all in. He's packing this time, all right, using one of his biggest cocks.

The day was hot but the night is cold. The windows steam over, and as I'm parked illegally in a one-way, dimly lit alley, I'm beginning to worry if we'll attract any unwanted attention. He doesn't seem to be concerned. He was cavalier from the moment he entered the car. He hasn't said a word to me, in fact. Just leapt in, closed and locked the door behind him, shoved me down onto my stomach, and used one hand to pull his cock out while the other pushed my skirt up.

He's gripping my skirt, the thin leather bunched into his fist. One of my arms is pinned under me, but with the other I start to reach out and run my hand along his pant leg. I discover he's wearing leather chaps over his jeans, and that they fit nice and snug. I try to reach far enough to get to the edge of the leather, so I can stroke his crotch, feel his real cock, the one that's slowly been getting bigger as he's been transitioning and taking testosterone. But he's not having any of this, doesn't want me to move. He rams his cock into me to the hilt and uses both his arms to hold me down, immobilizing me. My face is buried in the vinyl of the seat, my legs spread wide with one on the seat and the other leaning over the side toward the floor, and all else is sound and heat and motion and fullness. His chaps are rubbing the vinyl, my skirt is rubbing the vinyl, and there's no room to breathe. I'm gasping for air, wondering which one of us will come first, when suddenly, without warning, he pulls out.

He pulls out, and pulls back, and I can finally catch my breath. But I'm confused. I shift around to see what's going on, and witness him pulling two things out of his pockets. My eyes go wide as I see that one is a rubber ball gag with leather straps, and the other is a small packet of my favorite anal sex lube. He lays the lube packet on my bare ass and speaks for the first time all night.

"Open up."

I open my mouth to receive the gag, and then he secures the straps in place at the back of my head. Now he twists the tab off the lubricant, and dribbles it onto his dick. His second sentence comes at me:

"Get ready."

The head of his cock is already pressing against my asshole. When we talked about meeting in the alley, he said he wanted things to go quickly. But if he's seriously thinking of fucking my ass with that big toy, this is going to take a while.

Or so I think.

He works it in with surprising speed. Behind the gag, I'm grunting and half-screaming, but he knows I can take it, and I know he's going to make me. The perverse thrill of submitting to this sadistic "forced" ass fuck actually causes me to open a little more, which eases his way inside. He's one step ahead of me, and pushes as I acquiesce.

When his cock is completely in my ass, he pauses for a moment, to give me a chance to feel the extent to which he's stretched me out, to confirm my own surrender. One moment, and then it's over. That's all I get. After that, it's his turn.

He pounds me hard, fucking me for all it's worth. He's determined to come and he knows how to use my ass for his own pleasure. My job is to endure. Gagged, held down, plowed, I am a thing to him. An object. A leather-clad fuck-hole. He slams into my ass, over and over, until he shoots his orgasm into me. It's not liquid, of course; it's an energy, and thus, twice as potent. I take every drop, deep into my ass, for him.

And when he's done, he pulls out gently, undoes my gag gently, slides me over onto my back gently, smoothes down my skirt gently, and gently, very gently, reaches under my skirt and flicks one slick finger against my clit.

I explode.

I come against his hand with a roar, violent waves of pleasure crashing through me. He holds me as I come, body to body, leather to leather, gripping me tightly until my moans subside.

Then, just as quickly as he entered, he puts his silicone dick back in his pants, zips up, and leaves.

Next time we'll play in PVC.

# SHINE

Jacqueline Applebee

I see her every morning; she's a late starter, always turns up after nine. She walks leisurely down the length of Liverpool Street Station, trying not to be obvious, but I know her sort. She's got all the signs that say she's more than interested in the shy chubby boi-dyke who shines shoes. She always glances at me one too many times, as she floats by in an unhurried way, smiles and looks down shyly as she passes. And that is the thing that really gives her away; everyone is going to his or her lifeless office job and everyone is in a frantic rush. Everyone that is, except her.

Still, she has never sat, never spoken. She has never let me shine her shoes.

She always buys a peanut butter bagel from the snack bar at my side, checking me out discreetly. I know I'm a novelty—my difference makes me a definite attraction. As she walks by once more, I spy the small smudged white paper bag she holds, already weeping with the sweet brown melting ooze, but all too soon she disappears up the escalators and outside into the financial center of London.

There have been others more bold than she, though they always try to appear subtle and dignified. I see their feet beat a determined path to the newsagents, the food stalls or the open plan pub that surrounds me, but as they get closer, the heady scent of waxy polish catches them, makes them visibly falter on their way and they turn on their heels. They turn toward me.

At these times, I say nothing; I don't even look up at their faces. I just quietly smile to myself and kneel before them, already laying out my simple supplies before they inquire about price.

Money is important to me; I've got bills to pay, but it's not the sole reason why I shine. I do this because I love my job, I love to serve and if I can have some fun at the same time, then who am I to argue?

This is what I sense from the woman stuttering in her gait as she walks hesitantly toward my stall the next day: that she has the same sensual need as me. Sometimes it's too easy to spot a kindred spirit. I instantly picture her squatting at my side, spit-shining like a pro, as we polish the shoes of strangers together. We submissives have to stick together, is how I feel.

She wears smart brown knee-high boots with a low solid heel and a classic shape. She has pale knees and long fine fingers. Her manner is polite but a little awkward as I wave away the money she offers me, before I even start.

"Cold day," I say. Small talk, but you have to start somewhere.

"But it's lovely and bright," her voice is nervous and a little quavering. I bet she has dimples when she smiles.

We are both silent now and I am left with the sounds of a thousand different footsteps ringing out loud and clear, taking over, as I start to work. This is the constant background music in my head and for a while, I am lost in the flowing melody that invades me when I am concentrating.

Her boots are a little dirty, but not much; they really just lack a polished shine. I produce my sponge and saddle soap and set to work, stroking wide and slow, up and down the length of the leather, molding my hands against her boots.

"You're very good at this," she remarks.

This is something that I already know. I learned my trade from one of the best, from a friend of a neighbor, who was an ancient Cockney gent called Mister O'Connor. He had a real pride in his abilities and knowledge and told me how he used to work as a bootblacker back in the days when there was one on every street corner in Central London. He was eager to pass on his skills to someone and glad to know that a part of him would go out into the world, even if he couldn't get out of his flat without breathing apparatus.

He always used to call me "sweet girl," even though I told him several times that I was a boi and that his endearment made me cringe. He never listened, and in the end it didn't matter, because what's important is that he taught me things that I didn't have a clue about. He schooled me in all the extra little tricks you could do to earn a big tip, like how to give a mirror shine so fine that you could see up a Scotsman's kilt, or how to set fire to the polish if you wanted to be really flash.

I think it was O'Connor that made me realize what an honor it was to serve, and I'm sure he knew that some people appreciated that service in a very special way. He was definitely right; some of my regulars get off on the bootblacker thing in a reassuringly erotic manner. It's not a problem for me; I love to serve, they love to be adored. The sight of a young boi kneeling in supplication between their thighs is a big turn on to more people than you might think and it doesn't matter what they look like, or how expensively they're dressed. We perverts are everywhere.

Sometimes I can almost smell my customers' arousal over the licorice scent of the polish. I'll practically see the smoky curling aroma of desire that hits me at the back of my throat, making me swallow deep, gulping for air.

Right now, I put these thoughts away, adjust myself between the woman's ankles and pull on my latex gloves. I smear polish over her uppers, working in the compound with deft, long-practiced movements, using my fingers and then the horsehair brush.

I always work diligently, cleaning and soothing the stressed leather until it's smooth, buffing it until it shines, but sometimes, I'll get a particular customer who'll pay extra if I take my protective gloves off; they want to see the blackened goo ingrained in my short fingernails and maybe they like to know that later I'll be scrubbing away at myself like a good little boi, cleaning my sticky skin after they've soiled me, made me dirty. Either way, it's a special request and I don't do that for just anyone.

The woman above me is still sitting rigidly on the low seat and I smile at her.

"It's okay to relax," I reassure her, and I gaze up into her kindly looking deep-blue eyes, see her own mouth crinkle into an embarrassed smile. She sinks lower into the seat and exhales.

"I could stay here all day," she sighs indulgently and my

bashful smile grows bigger. I wish I had no need for money, and then I would sit here all day too. I would do a job that I love to bits and I would make people happy with my hands.

I often go into a trancelike state when I work, and now as I continue to polish I allow myself to think back to a woman I once knew called Symphony. She was an ultrafemme girlfriend of mine and a top laugh; kinky as hell. With rich chocolate-brown skin, as sweet as you like, squeezable tits and a devious streak a mile wide, she dominated my tiny world and I was eternally grateful. She loved to drag me around the multitude of sleazy sex shops in Soho, spending a small fortune on the latest piece of equipment that would promise us both happy sex lives. She bought me a dildo for my birthday; I thought it was nothing special until she produced the short strap that came with it. It turned out to be a shoe dildo and Symphony fastened it to a pair of her very expensive, thigh-high, spike-heeled boots. I'd always adored those wonderful boots and the way she would transform into a warrior of a woman whenever she wore them.

Symphony stood poised and regal, with her dressed-up foot raised on a small wooden storage chest as she instructed me to sit.

I thought I'd seen a lot in the limited time that I'd been exploring my sexuality, but this sight was so beyond me. I must have been frozen in terrified shock, because she grabbed me by the scruff of my collar and yanked me down.

Back then, I was still getting used to the whole gender-bending thing. It felt good being Symphony's boi-in-training; my intense shyness made her swoon with motherly delight, but at that moment, I was plain petrified. Symphony had made me feel powerless, scared and intimidated like no one else ever had. She also looked about seven feet tall when she was angry and I felt about three inches.

She made me kiss and lick the leather first and I ran my silent tongue up, down and all around her boots. My mouth was already dry from fear, but I did my best to let her know that I was devoted to her; I worshipped her.

I peeled off my already sticky boxers and lowered my ass slowly onto the glistening black dildo, already wet from my saliva even before she had applied any lubricant. I inched myself down and tried to remember how to breathe as I attempted to steady myself while I ground myself against her foot. I felt embarrassed and awkward and thought that I must look like a dog shagging his mistress's leg. I was also worried that I would squash her foot, but Symphony seemed to love having me impaled there. Seeing her proud ecstatic face, all fluttering eyelashes and heaving breasts, I started to get incredibly hot too. The wooden chest began to wobble as I pushed down enthusiastically on the dildo, plastering my burning face to the long, smooth leather of her legs, gripping at the insides of her warm sticky thighs with my hands, grunting, keening and biting at any bit of her flesh that I could reach, panting like an untamed creature. The only thing I didn't do that night was bark like a dog, but everything else was up for negotiation. I behaved like an animal and Symphony seemed to like it. She grasped a handful of my short, spiky brown hair and pulled my head back painfully as I quaked and shook. The dildo was buried deep within me and the raised stitching of her boots rubbed happily up and down the length of my clit, making me curse under my breath with pleasure, so bloody good, so very bloody good...

Suddenly everything flew sideways and I toppled from my

throne of glory, while simultaneously coming in waves of lust mixed with panic. I gushed in spurts as I tumbled to the floor, the dildo painfully popping out of me. I clutched at my pussy, as if I could hold in the burning slamming pulses of satisfaction that tore through me. I remember looking up to see Symphony trying to right herself in time, but she also fell, breaking the thin heel of her boot as she landed heavily on the floor next to me.

To this day I don't know if it was that broken heel, the bruised forehead she ended up with, or the unremovable stains I left in the leather that made her break up with me a week later, but whatever the reason, that episode gave me an appreciation for boots and shoes that has never left.

I bring myself back to the present and realize that the woman above me is looking at me with a perplexed expression. I also realize that I am rocking against her slippery boots and my loose blue trousers are smeared with brown polish at the crotch. I put my game face back on and finish quickly, spraying the leather with a little water before wiping and rubbing with my polishing cloth until a nice sheen appears.

"Don't mind me mate, just reminiscing," I say with ragged breaths, swabbing beads of sweat from my forehead with the back of my wrists.

"You must have had a good time," she says, as if she knows exactly what happened back then. Then I sense something; smell both our growing desires, mixed with the warm odor of peanut butter. We are turned on beyond reason and we both want more.

She hesitates and finally says:

"Do you think I could learn...about shining shoes?" Her voice is a bare whisper. "My partner would appreciate a special treat." She is embarrassed, but I am glad that she asked.

"I'll give you some tips, sure." I smile and I am happier than I've been in ages.

The next day I see her familiar boots walking in my direction and I look up at her, take in the broad smile on her face, the jaunty swing of her wide hips. I know that she hears the special music now, when she is in service, bending over to please someone above her. She plonks herself heavily down on the seat and she lets me shine her boots. I know even before she opens her mouth that she had great sex last night. She leans forward, affording me a nice view of her cleavage, and then she tells me in detail how her first attempt at bootblacking went, how her girlfriend loved her amateurish efforts and how they both want me to come around and give private lessons. The woman presses a card into my hand, then surprises me by dipping down and pressing soft, plush lips to the inside of my wrist, in a single reverent, sticky kiss. She decorates me with the imprint of her dark red lipstick and dimples appear on her face like magic. Then she steps up and away, walking with a spring in her step, almost dancing to the escalator and out into the cold day. I look down to read her address on the card and pocket her very generous tip. When I gaze back up, trying to find her among the commuters heading out into the heart of London, I can't spot her, but I don't worry. I'll see her again tomorrow morning, just after nine.

# SWEET NO MORE

Radclyffe

"Having second thoughts?"

"No," I told Phil, my best friend from work, for the tenth time.

"Okay, then." He said something I couldn't hear to the bouncer on the door and then motioned me inside. We paid our cover at a window in a closet-sized vestibule, and Phil pushed aside the black vinyl curtain blocking the entrance to the club. "Have fun."

The minute we walked into the Ramrod, Phil and his boyfriend melted into the crowd, and I was on my own. I couldn't complain. They said they'd bring me, they never said they'd babysit. I didn't really think places like this existed anymore, post-AIDS—a warehouse-sized room illuminated by black lights, rough brick walls, exposed pipes in the ceiling, pounding bass beat, and wall-to-wall bodies, mostly naked and at first glance, mostly men. Bare chests, pierced nipples, chaps over naked skin, straining cocks beneath codpieces and jocks. I felt overdressed in my leather vest and pants, even though I had nothing on underneath either one. The place smelled like stale beer, acrid poppers, and the musky odor of sex. Lots of sex.

It was exactly the kind of place I fantasized about while I jerked off, picturing what I *thought* might happen so many times it was getting tough to come that way anymore. I needed the real thing—or maybe I needed something I hadn't yet imagined. Trying to look like I belonged, I wended my way toward the bar. I shoehorned into a place at the bar and worked not to stare at the guy standing next to me while another guy knelt in the cramped space and sucked on his cock with gusto.

"Beer," I shouted when the bartender glanced in my direction.

When the guy next to me grunted, I automatically looked over just in time to see him yank his cock out of the other guy's mouth and pump it frantically, his face a twisted mask of concentration. Then he smiled at me half-apologetically and came all over the guy's chest.

"Nice shooting," I observed and reached for my beer. I drank half of it off to steady my nerves.

"Thanks," he gasped after he caught his breath and wiped his hand clean in the other guy's hair. "You alone?"

I kept my gaze on his face but I could hear the guy on the floor whining as he jacked off. From the sounds of things, he was about to unload a gallon so I inched away to keep the stuff off my boots. "Came with friends, but I lost them already."

"I brought a friend too." He looked me over. "You a novice?"

"No," I lied. "Why?"

"Because she's not."

My clit shot out an inch and turned to marble. "Sounds just right."

He didn't look convinced. "What are you looking for?"

"I'm not here to look." Praying he couldn't see my hands tremble, I unbuttoned my vest and uncovered my tits. They were small and round with neat dark areolae, which made the silver rings through the center of each nipple all the more obvious. I gripped the rings and pulled, tenting my nipples until they turned white. "I've done sweet. Now I want something else."

"Like what?"

I twisted both rings until my nipples wouldn't stretch any more without tearing. The pleasure and the pain fused into a fierce ache in my clit and my knees nearly buckled. He watched my face and I knew he knew I was struggling not to moan. "I guess that will be up to her."

"I'm Jerry." He stuffed his limp cock back into his pants and sidled away from the guy slumped on the floor. I hadn't noticed him shoot, but the puddle between his legs and the come splattered on the bottom of Jerry's pants lit up like neon under the lights. "Follow me."

It was the best offer I'd had so far, so I did. I didn't bother to close my vest. I was just another body. Besides, my nipples were engorged after the twisting and so sensitive if they rubbed against the leather vest now, I'd have to go somewhere and jerk off. I wanted to anyway. My clit was pounding like I'd been working it for an hour.

We went through the bar and down a hallway and into another room. The only music now was the grunts and cries and moans of people fucking and coming. Jerry paused for a second, then said, "Over here."

He led me toward the far side where a leather sling hung from the ceiling by chains. A young blond guy with smooth pale skin reclined in the sling with his head thrown back and his legs bent up to his body while a dark-haired guy whose face I couldn't see stood between his legs, a fist up the blond's ass and the other hand jerking the blond's jutting cock. The guy doing the fucking was slender with finely muscled shoulders and a hairless back that tapered into a narrow waist, and he wore nothing but chaps that left his high, round ass exposed. His sweaty skin glowed beneath the lights as he rotated his forearm in the blond's ass and worked his cock like a piston.

The blond raised his head and stared at the hand jerking his cock, his face dazed and his stomach heaving to the beat of the fist in his guts. "I'm gonna blow," he yelled. "I'm going to blow my fucking load."

The guy fisting him never stopped pumping the iron-hard dick as come arced into the air, the first shot hitting the blond in the face, the next couple spurts landing on his chest, and the last few squirts finally dribbling into little puddles on his belly. A third guy leaned over and licked up the blond guy's come, then took two steps back and shot his own load in the blond's face.

"Jesus," I whispered, my clit twitching like crazy. I needed to jerk off now more than ever and wondered if I could just go lean against the wall like a few guys I could see and get a quick shot off.

"That's his lover," Jerry whispered, pointing to the guy who'd just blasted off in the blond's face.

"Who's their friend?" I asked, tipping my chin toward the dark-haired guy who eased his hand out of the blond's ass, stripped off a glove, and tossed it on the floor.

"That's who I want you to meet."

Before I could reply, the fister turned to face us and I was looking at a woman so hot I forgot all about my stiff clit and needing to jerk off. Her eyes were dark like her hair and her expression remote, as if she hadn't just fucked some guy for an audience. She had smallish breasts about like mine and stomach muscles that were etched and pumped from the workout she'd just had. Her mons was trimmed, not shaved, and framed by her chaps, which were all she was wearing. From what I could see of her cunt, it was swollen and shining with come. If she hadn't gotten off during the fisting, she must really need it bad now.

"Ask her if I could please suck her off," I said desperately to Jerry, having no idea what the correct protocol was, but I didn't care. "Ask her please. Anything she wants if I can just suck her clit."

I stood still while Jerry made his way to her and said something. Then she stared at me for a long moment before walking over. I didn't say anything as she held open the edges of my vest and stared at my breasts. She flicked one nipple ring with a long finger.

"Are these for show?"

"No," I croaked.

She unzipped my leathers and slid her hand down my pants. I sucked in a breath as she explored my clit with one finger. After a minute of that I started to sway, but I was afraid to touch her to steady myself.

"What do you want?" she asked, dragging her fingertip up one side of my clit and down the other, over the head and back again.

"I want to suck you off."

She pulled her hand out of my pants and I fought not to whimper. "What about that pretty little hard-on you've got in your pants?"

"I'd like to come for you," I whispered. "I'd like to come for you harder than I've ever come for anyone."

"Any way I want it?"

"Yes."

She gripped my wrist and dragged me through the crowd, past the sling where she'd fucked the guy, to the corner where a padded pole a foot thick ran from the floor to the ceiling. She stripped off my vest and dropped it on the floor, slammed my back up against the pole, and jerked my arms around behind it. I felt her buckle leather shackles on my wrists before she came back to face me. She yanked my pants down to my ankles and kicked my feet as far apart as they would go.

"Is there anything you want me to know?" she said, rubbing her palms in rough circles over my breasts, bringing my nipples screaming back to life again.

"I don't fuck men."

"What else?"

"I'm not sucking anybody's cock."

"That's it?"

"That's it."

She grabbed my face and shoved her tongue into my mouth. I couldn't breathe so I bit her, just hard enough to make her ease back. Then I sucked her tongue until *she* couldn't breathe.

She pulled out and licked my lips like she wanted to eat them off my face, flicking her tongue into my mouth too fast for me to catch it again, although I snapped my teeth and tried. She laughed.

"You think I'd waste these sweet lips on a cock?" She bit my lower lip and twisted my nipple rings. I whimpered. "I'm saving your mouth to come in myself."

Breathing fast, she rubbed her cunt on my leg. She was hot and slippery and her clit was a hard knot in the center. "I'm going to drown you in juice."

She kept at it, rubbing and sliding, until she shivered once, hard, and jerked away without coming. My cunt was spilling and I was drenched to my knees with her come and mine. She forked her fingers, clamped my clit in the V, and squeezed.

"Fuck," I whispered, sagging against the pole.

"You've got a nice fat one, don't you?" she murmured, jacking me slowly. Too slowly to make me come but enough to make me need to so fucking bad tears leaked out of my eyes. She pinched the head with her nails and I did cry. "Poor baby. Let me make that better."

"Please," I begged, all pride washed away in the sea of blood pooled in my cunt. I wondered if I was supposed to resist but I didn't care now. I just wanted to come.

She pulled something off the waistband of her chaps at the same time as she spread my cunt open with one hand. I couldn't see much, but when I looked down my clit was standing up between her fingers. Even in the dim light I could tell it was wet and the dark color it got when I was about to come. If she jacked me now, I'd shoot.

She did and my legs started shaking and my clit got extra hurting-hard the way it did when I was ten seconds from coming.

"I'm coming," I said because I thought I should tell her, but she must have known because she stopped cold. "Uh uh god... I'm about to come...please."

"Breathe, baby," she whispered, and before I knew what she was doing, she replaced her fingers on my clit with a two-inch spring-loaded clamp. It closed onto the shaft of my clit with a snap and the rows of blunt teeth dug in and banished the blossoming orgasm into oblivion.

I screamed.

"Shh, shh, shh," she crooned, her mouth on my neck oddly gentle as she licked the sweat and tears that ran down from my face. She rubbed my lower belly, pressing into me in deep circles that somehow made the profound ache inside almost bearable. "Does it hurt, baby?"

"Yes," I whimpered. My cunt throbbed like someone had kicked me and needles of pain speared through my clit.

"You've got a beautiful clit," she whispered, jiggling the clamp with one finger. "Look how big you are now."

I bent my head and tried to see, but the tears clouded my vision. My clit pulsed between the jaws to the beat of my heart and I felt something else, something even more powerful than the pain. "I need to come."

She flipped the clamp back and forth. The pressure surged in my clit and my cunt opened and closed like a fist.

"Oh fuck that's so fucking good."

She gripped the clamp and twisted.

"I want to come so bad."

"And I want you harder. Harder than you've ever been for anybody." She pulled my nipple ring and jacked my clit with the clamp. The teeth dug into the hood and pulled it back and forth over the head with every tug—pleasure, pain, pleasure, pain, pleasure, pain. "*Now* you might be hard enough to shoot a nice load for me."

"I don't think I can," I moaned. The clit torture made me

harder than I'd ever been but it wasn't hitting me right to get me off. "I really really need to come."

"Watch me do you, baby."

I tightened my stomach and bowed forward, shaking sweat from my face so it wouldn't run into my eyes. My clit was stretched out, impossibly swollen, the head bulging beyond the clamp. Seeing her fingers, slick with my come, tugging the clamp was too much. "Oh god you don't know how bad I need to come. I think my clit's gonna burst."

"Now it might," she said, and pulled off the clamp.

Blood rushed in, my clit doubled in size. The nerves in the head short-circuited from the sudden stimulation. Pain and pleasure blasted up my spine in equal measure. I thrashed and tried to get loose. I had to hold it, rub it, do something, anything, to stop the agony.

"What's the matter?" she whispered, fingering my nipple rings rapidly again.

"I gotta come," I howled. There were more people around us now, most just staring, a couple jerking off. I didn't care about them. I didn't care about anything except coming.

"Let me help you." She fingered the head and, oh god, it hurt. It was so good and it hurt and I wanted to come so much and it hurt and I couldn't and I was fucking dying.

"Oh Jesus, don't touch it!" I moaned. "It's too hard now. It hurts. Oh Jesus. Fuck." I was blubbering, tossing my head around. I thought I might throw up.

She seized my face again and forced me to look into her eyes. "Shut up and breathe." She kissed me, so gently I felt like she was rocking me in her arms. "I'm gonna make you come, baby, so sweet."

She kept kissing me, her tongue delving deeper and deeper

until I was sucking it again. Then I felt her fingers glide over my clit and my body jerked. She rubbed it and it felt so good and I moaned. She backed out of my mouth and straddled my leg, her wet cunt hot enough to burn my skin. She whimpered and I realized how long she'd been holding back.

Some guy close to us groaned and I could hear the frenzied slap of his hand on his cock and she growled, "Shoot on the floor, cocksucker, not on her," and he did.

"Get ready, baby." Then she lowered her head and took my nipple in her mouth, chewing on it and tonguing the ring while she switched her grip on my clit and started to jack me. With so much stimulation happening everywhere at once—her cunt, her fingers, her mouth—the pain in my tortured clit didn't prevent the orgasm from building this time. My clit couldn't get any harder, but it started to throb inside, and the pressure spread into my belly, and I knew nothing was going to stop me.

"I'm gonna come," I cried, and my cunt started to spasm.

She shoved her fingers into me and raised her head to stare at my face. "Give it to me." Her palm thudded against my unyielding clit as she fucked me, and I unloaded into her hand and over her arm, crying and yelling *Oh fucking god it's so good...*

She didn't quit until there wasn't a drop left in me and I was twisting to get away from her fingers, my clit so fucked out I wasn't sure I'd ever need to come again. She reached behind me and released my hands and I fell to my knees, trying to drag air into my lungs. She didn't care if I could breathe or not. She grabbed my head and tilted my face up and jammed her clit into my mouth.

"Now suck me off," she ordered through gritted teeth, her clit like rock and already jumping. She bucked her hips and pumped her clit in and out of the circle of my lips, jerking herself off in my mouth and muttering, "Uh uh uh."

She was starting to come, so I sucked her just hard enough to keep her clit in my mouth. I wanted it to last for her.

"Here it comes, baby," she gasped, her fingers trembling in my hair. "Get ready to swallow. Sweet baby, you're making me come."

I clutched her ass and yanked her hard against my face, sucking her clit in to the root and clamping my teeth around it. She cried out and ejaculated on my face and down my neck and I felt her legs go. I wrapped my arms tightly around her thighs to hold her up because I knew she would hate to go down in front of everybody. When she stopped coming I licked up the juice that clung to her cunt and tongued her clit until she murmured a protest and pulled away.

Somehow I got my legs under me and heaved myself to my feet, hauling my pants up with me. My clit was still so tender I couldn't zip up. She backed me into the pole again and leaned her arms on either side of my head so she could lick her come off my face. Her whole body trembled and I risked putting my arms around her.

"That was sweet, baby," she whispered so no one else could hear.

I kissed her and she let me, and as I played my tongue inside her hot mouth, I realized that I had been wrong about what I had been looking for. What she had given me was sweeter than sweet.

# X-RATED EXES

L. Elise Bland

"Pull his pants down!" the men yelled from the sidelines as I danced around and tormented their friend onstage. His lunch buddies had bought him a special birthday dance. For sixty dollars extra, they treated him to a humiliating fifteen minutes of fame in the "spanking cage" with two rambunctious strippers—Desiree and me. Out of all the dancers, I always had the most fun with Desiree. She was just my age and just kinky enough to make me love my work. We had been flirting for weeks, but we couldn't let ourselves get too distracted onstage. We had spanking to do.

After situating the customer's hands loosely over his head in faux bondage, I slipped the leather belt out of the loops of his starched jeans and got to work on his rear while Desiree rubbed her Texas-sized breasts against his chest. We performed our usual routine of undressing, grinding, slapping, and strapping, much to the delight of the birthday party at our feet.

"Spank him! Harder!" his friends called out. I reared my arm back and slapped his boxers with a flourish of fancy swats. When all was said and done, our birthday boy ended up on his hands and knees, his T-shirt up around his armpits, and his leather belt looped into a leash around his neck. For the grand finale, I led him around by the belt while Desiree sat on his back, waving one arm in the air as if she were riding mechanical bull. Wild applause broke out all across the main floor of the club.

Stage spanking is different from real spanking. First of all, the spankees are usually rowdy and drunk, so the spanking has to be dramatic enough for entertainment, yet light enough for safety. Second, it's just not quite as much fun to spank a stranger. There is no real connection. The guy walks off the stage rubbing his ass to impress his friends, but in the end, it's all for show.

Once the birthday ruckus subsided, Desiree and I went back to our respective stages and a blaring, midafternoon calmness settled in. Between two and four o'clock, the polite cowboys and mild-mannered businessmen clear out and all the perverts creep into the dark, dirty corners of the club. I usually take a break after lunch to avoid the freaks, but, through the flashing lights, I spotted a familiar face heading toward my stage. It was Erin, my ex. Well, she wasn't really my ex, but my ex-fuckbuddy. I had had no idea a female customer was on the premises, much less somebody who had seen me naked far beyond the limits of my thong.

"What are you doing here?" I asked her. I bent down to the

edge of the stage and, in spite of the stale bar stench, I could still detect her familiar "earth-friendly" shampoo. Her shaggy dark hair had grayed around her temples, but she still had the same cocky smile. I remembered her full lips all too well; they were always in a state of motion, sometimes eating me out, and other times telling me good-bye.

Erin was proof that a fuckbuddy relationship just didn't work for me. I am too much of a romantic. Somehow I always ended up getting fucked, and not in the good way. And anybody who has ever been on the receiving end of the "just friends" speech knows how painful it can be. Technically, Erin didn't break my heart because we never had a relationship. Still, I would have taken her back, at least for one night—that was all she could ever promise me anyway.

"I saw you up there spanking that guy," she said in a suspicious tone. "You looked like you were enjoying yourself a little too much. I didn't think you were into guys."

"No, not guys so much as spanking. I'm equal opportunity when it comes to playtime. You trained me well, huh?" Erin had taught me exactly how good a spanking could be, especially when you are getting done doggy-style with a strap-on. Back in the day, I was such a bottom I couldn't get enough of it. But once I got my hands on somebody else's ass, I was hooked. Hearing the slaps ring out and feeling the heat bloom under my palms sent me soaring. Over the years, I had become an expert spanker, even better than my ex.

"Come over when you get a chance," she told me. "I'm in VIP."

"Okay, but only if you'll buy a dance."

"No problem," she said and sauntered back to her seat.

Soon after that I found her in VIP on a leather sofa, her legs spread like a guy's, waiting for me to sit in her lap. With an ex, everything is easier; there's no getting-to-know-you time. After minimal chatter, I started my table dance and took off my bra. Being pressed up against her body once again brought back good memories as well as nasty fantasies. I usually think of other things during a dance—hair appointments, groceries, new tires for my truck—but with her, it was uncomfortably different. As much as I tried to distract myself, I couldn't stop thinking about her muscular fingers, her wicked mouth, and the outrageous collection of medieval-looking sex toys that she kept under her bed. I knew I was getting in over my head, but I didn't care. When I pulled my skirt up to do my infamous butt grind, she gave me a familiar slap on the ass.

"Ouch," I squealed.

"Sorry, I couldn't help myself."

"You'd better not have left a mark! I have to work tomorrow. Kiss it and make it better." She pulled my ass up into her face and caressed my cheeks with her strong tongue and hands. Before I knew it, she had moved my T-back to one side. I felt a sudden, cool breeze of air-conditioning, and then the wet heat of her mouth as it slid all along my pussy. I tried to turn around and stop her so I wouldn't get in trouble with the manager, but she held me still.

"Don't worry," she said in a low voice. "Nobody's looking."

Her fingers reached around and quickly found my clit. I placed my hand over hers so she would let go, but soon found myself guiding her like a trusty vibrator. She swirled and licked my pussy in perfect rhythm with the music. I had forgotten how good she was, and how quickly she could get me off. For a moment, I lost my professional façade and felt a wave of unstoppable pleasure sneaking up on me right there in the club. I really didn't want to get off. After all, I was at work. I tried to shut my mind down, but she kept me at the brink of orgasm until I couldn't take it anymore. I started to let go, but then we were interrupted. Suddenly, at the most awkward time, we had a curious visitor at the table, my friend Desiree.

"Hey, what's going on up here?" she asked, swinging her little purse and jiggling her cocktail. I don't know why she even bothered asking. Wasn't it obvious? I was laid over the table getting tongue-fucked by a female customer.

"Why didn't you invite me?" Desiree seemed intrigued, but also disappointed. We had always tag-teamed with male customers, but this situation was different, especially since the customer was a woman.

"Shut up," I panted. "Just stand there in front of us so nobody can see." As ordered, she turned her beautiful ass around right in front of my face. Desiree always goes for a classic French bustier with stockings and garters, so there is never coverage on her cheeks. The lacy red and black thong ran right up the center of what I had always longed to lick. It was all too much for me to take—Erin's tongue on my pussy and Desiree's very spankable and lickable ass in my face. I reached across the table and grabbed her soft hips to stabilize myself. After one last slap from Erin, I came so hard my ankles nearly lost control of my stilettos.

Erin yanked me back so I wouldn't slide off the table. I sank into the cool, leather sofa in ecstasy. We never even kissed that day, but I didn't care. There is nothing like sex with your ex, especially when you realize you are finally over her. I lay there staring at the flashing colored lights until I was able to speak again.

"Thanks for the cover-up, Desiree," I winked. "This is my

buddy Erin." Without asking, Desiree plopped herself right down on Erin's knee. "Erin is the one who taught me to spank," I added.

"And Elise is the one who taught me," Desiree announced proudly.

"She taught you well," Erin said. "You seemed to be having fun whooping that cowboy's ass earlier."

"I was," Desiree laughed. "But I am more into being spanked, as long as it's light and sexy. Nothing too severe."

I exchanged looks with Erin. My pussy was still throbbing from the crazy orgasm, and the adrenaline in my veins was churning so hard, it had even drowned out the pounding music. I was up for anything. I whispered into Erin's ear and then pulled Desiree across me on the sofa so that her feet were in Erin's lap.

"What are you doing?" Desiree asked, as if she didn't know. I had never given her a real spanking before and wasn't sure how it would go over. Desiree always tipped me on stage and I returned the favor with a public slap, but never a private one.

"You said you liked to be spanked, didn't you?" My hand quivered with nervousness as it ran across her round cheeks. The first time spanking someone is always scary for me, especially somebody like Desiree. I wanted to slap her hard enough to satisfy my own sadistic streak, but I wanted her to like it enough to come back for more.

"You know I have to punish you for spying on us earlier!" I scolded playfully.

"I'm sorry," she said, pretending to pout. "I just got, well, you know, kind of lonely."

"You're such a bad girl," I told her. "But that's why I like you so much."

I laid one hand on her cheek and gave her a pat so delicate, my palm didn't even sting afterward. When Desiree sighed and jumped, I knew I had her number. She wanted more. She said she was a lightweight, but it turned out she could take a decent round. I slapped every inch of her ass—longer-lasting strokes in the center of her cheeks, light circles around the outsides, and sharp stingy pecks on the most tender parts. Spanking Desiree was completely different from spanking our customer onstage earlier. This time it was real.

Between spanks, I ran my fingers up and down the back of her thong, which was hot and wet from the burn of exhibitionism. Desiree writhed against me so that the metal of her garter straps dug into my bare thighs. Once she was completely worked up, I let loose. My hand started moving so fast and feathery, it looked like a bumblebee's wing. Desiree raised her derriere into the air as if she didn't know whether to come closer or escape.

All the while, Erin was watching. "Hey, don't hog her," she called out. "I want to get to know your friend Desiree, too."

"Good idea," I said, playing along. Truth be told, I wanted to secure Desiree for myself. Erin was too much of a player to have total control over my horny new friend. If things worked out, Desiree might even turn into a fuckbuddy, or more. I should have learned my "bad girl" lesson with Erin, but I just can't help myself. In spite of all the spankings I've received in my life, I'm incorrigible.

As I shifted around to let Erin in, I sneaked a first kiss from Desiree. Her lips were even hotter and softer than her asscheeks. She kissed me back and even slipped me a little tongue. It definitely wasn't empty like kissing an ex, and it sure wasn't like kissing a friend.

I pulled Desiree on top of me in missionary position so that she straddled my thigh. As soon as Erin planted her firm hand into Desiree's bottom, she started grinding her pussy into my leg. The brush of her flesh only prolonged the pleasure I had felt before. It was as if my orgasm had never really ended. I held on to Desiree's body from below, making out with her and watching over her shoulder as Erin's hand sent electric jolts into her buttocks. With every blow, Desiree ground harder and harder into my body.

"I'm going to come," she whispered into my ear between smacks and slaps. "Do you mind?"

"Go ahead," I said, kissing her once again. "You earned it." She let out a yelp and I felt her wetness melt into my own pussy juice.

Exhausted yet curious, I reached around and touched Desiree's steamy skin. She had taken a lot—and given a lot. Anyone who has ever been spanked knows that a long, light spanking can be just as intense as a short, heavy one.

Afterward, Desiree and Erin both gave me their numbers. I promised I would call each of them the next weekend, but on my way home in the truck, I was already dialing Desiree's digits. A week was too long to wait.

"All my exes live in Texas," as the old George Strait song goes. "And that's why I hang my hat in Tennessee." Past exes or future exes, I don't care. I'll stay in Texas where the women run wild and the spankings are as hot and nasty as the weather.

# PLAYING WITH TOYS

D. Alexandria

I like to please my Daddy, because he isn't your ordinary butch. He holds his Butch Card in the back of his mental wallet, rarely caring for the rules and roles our community can lay out. He lives for pleasure and expects to receive it in all shapes and forms. Daddy prefers his girls, but isn't above sliding his dick into a boy mouth if it's pretty and inviting. He's rough and unapologetic, his hand tight around my neck while he bucks his cum above me. Yet, he can be soft and vulnerable, allowing himself to part his thighs so I can taste the delicate folds he often dismisses. His word is sovereign and he loves me beyond reason because I can shatter him like no other. But overall, he controls me in a way no other Daddy can; making me unable to refuse the pleasure he so often seeks.

He sits in the armchair about five feet away from the bed. He's relaxed, a cigar fixed between his lips, a Backwood, 'cause he prefers things to be raw and unrefined. The smoke rises and entwines, half-hiding the smirk on his face. He's amused, which is perfect. That means I'm being a good girl.

I'm on the bed, legs spread, the lips of a coworker greedily sucking at my wet cunt, but my eyes are on him. I watch as his long, callused fingers pull the cigar from his lips, and see his tongue briefly dart out to moisten them. I sigh in visual pleasure, my hand reaching down to press her face deeper. She's pretty, almost Daddy's type, but not quite. He prefers his girls bigger, softer, with asses that can jiggle under his heavy hand, and large breasts for him to twist. Still, she's not skinny; thicker than average, with small tits and wide hips. I chose her because she's simple, like me. She's never been demanding, always in and out of bad relationships, because she wants to be ruled, yet doesn't really know it, always finds men who do it well, but not right. I can recognize my own with ease, and I knew she'd only need a little coaxing, because girls like me start shy but are greedier than one might think.

Daddy let me play with her first on my own, so I could see if she was ready. Before the night was over, I had her tied to her bed with scarves, spanking her Irish pale ass 'til it was redder than the hair on her head, and fucking her pouty mouth with her one hot-pink dildo. This is our second night and she's prepared. She knows she's a toy tonight; probably not in the full sense, but for her, pleasure is pleasure. A half bottle of wine for us, a shot of tequila for Daddy, and I lead her to the bedroom, kissing her deeply as I undress her on the way. Daddy lets us roll around for a while before coming in and taking his seat. I know he's enjoying the position he's found us in, because he has full view of her ass which is high in the air as she devours me like the sweet chocolate I am. And I know he'd love to just unzip and fill her, but he doesn't. Daddy likes to torture himself, so he'll sit and wait until the last possible moment, and then he'll tear into her like no one has.

I like the feel of her silky curls as I twine them around my fingers, pulling her in deeper as I lift my hips. I slowly grind and hump her face, and she's moaning, but it's muffled and I can feel the vibrations against my clit. I watch Daddy inhale, the tip of the cigar glowing red hot, and I press my full thighs together, trapping her. She feels good, despite only having college experience when it comes to giving female head. Her tongue is small but firm, and she's wisely fixated on massaging the sides of my clit, which makes my stomach flutter. I like it when the tongue is meticulous, not erratically licking every nook and cranny, and she's working her way up to my possibly returning the favor. Her tongue suddenly drops to my hole, and I gasp loudly.

Daddy softly growls in arousal, his hand slipping down to cup his dick through his jeans, pressing it against him. Even in the dimly lit room, I can see his eyes are fixated on my face, and how I'm responding to her manipulations. I let go of her hair, my fingers traveling up my body to cup my breasts. I squeeze them, and pretend it's his hands twisting them roughly. I see his lips part and I grab hold of each nipple, pulling at them. As her tongue snakes its way into my hole, I'm pinching my nipples tightly, my body tensing as I increase the pressure, Daddy's knowing gaze prompting me to do it as he would. When I bend my fingers and press my nails in, I moan loudly, my legs crossing behind her head as I cum in her mouth.

Daddy winks. I've done well. Like a good girl I watch his

face for any sign telling me what he wants next, but he's still. He takes in the scene before him then looks at me expectantly. I smile. Daddy's going to let me do whatever I want. I'm to show off for him.

I unfold my legs from around her and get to my knees, grabbing hold of her hair. I give her ass a soft slap and she purrs, pushing it out toward me. As I pull her head back so she can see my face, I give her a couple of firmer slaps across each cheek. She's writhing, a contented smile on her face, her eyes locked with mine. I lower my hand, cupping her pussy, and she instantly spreads her legs wider. I'm not ready to go in, but just hold her firmly, watching her rotate her ass in anticipation. She's gasping, her eyes already pleading with me, but I ignore her, pulling my hand away, and resume slapping her ass. I'm twisting her hair in my hand, forcing her to keep her head up as I decorate her. I like the feel of her soft skin and how it warms under my hand, and I'm fascinated by how quickly she starts to redden. I start aiming for her upper thighs, and she whimpers, trying to pull away from me, but I know she's just playing and wanting to spur me on. I grab hold of one cheek, digging my nails into her, and she cries out and moans yes.

My eyes rest on Daddy, my cunt swelling just by the look of him. While I go back to spanking her, I'm taking in his jersey, the loose jeans, the boots that have pressed my face into the floor. I allow my gaze to travel upward, settling on his face, only half-shadowed by the cap that he has pushed back, exposing the white du-rag that's in perfect contrast to his russet skin. At times his eyes can be as dark and foreboding as the scariest abyss, yet they are also quite capable of expressing playful teasing. For a moment I wish she wasn't here, and that I could have him consuming only me the way his eyes are now.

I give her ass a firm slap before trailing my fingers to her dripping folds, and I give him a wink. I then look at her face, pulling her hair back even more.

"Ask my Daddy if I can fuck you."

Her entire body trembles, and as I glide my fingers over her hole, I feel it try to suck me in.

I pull my hand away, giving her another slap. "I said ask."

She turns her head, and for the first time takes in Daddy's presence seated so close. Her voice is soft and almost breaks. "Can she fuck me? Please?"

"No," he says.

I smirk and give her furry lips a tickle before my hand moves back to her ass. I almost feel sorry for her as I feel the heat from her skin before I spank her again, this time even harder. I watch tears well in the corner of her eyes, and she's biting her lips intently, trying not to cry out from the pain. After a few minutes of this, her whole body is glowing from sweat, and I finally slip my hand back to tease her clit, which is so swollen that when I tap it, her entire body jumps.

"Let's try that again." I snap her head back, my eyes boring into hers. "Now, ask my Daddy if I can fuck you—properly."

She quickly turns her head toward Daddy, and I can now see the genuinely imploring look on her face. "Please, Sir, can she fuck me?"

I see the curl of his lip before he chuckles. "Go 'head and fuck the bitch, baby girl."

I sigh and when two of my fingers quickly enter her, she surrenders the cry, grabbing at the bedsheets. I let go of her hair, grabbing her by the shoulder, and dig into her, feeling her slippery walls grab me. She's so damn hot, I have to bite my lips as I twirl my fingers, feeling her flutter along with me.

She's moaning, rotating her hips again, and I like the feel of her grinding against my hand, like hearing the noises her wetness is making as her cunt greedily sucks at my fingers. I pull away from her, letting my fingers tug her clit, and she goes still, pressing her face into the bed.

I bend my head and bite her ass as I flick her clit. She's like me and likes to be teased; wants things to be drawn out so she can earn that cum. But sometimes cums have to be forced to put us in our place. I give her clit a soft pinch, and her hand shoots back to reach for my arm. My other hand slaps it away and I squeeze her clit harder. She's moaning loudly, her arm waving, indicating to me that it's too good, too soon. She's enjoying finally having me in her and doesn't want it to stop. I ignore her, tugging on it, feeling it stiffen even more. She's trying to close her thighs, trying to lock me out, but I just chuckle and push my fingers back inside her, and pump her hard.

I can hear Daddy's breathing increase. He loves a good audio and I know her moaning is definitely music to his ears. I slip a third finger into her and she bucks, trying to twist away from it, but I place my hand on the small of her back to keep her steady, thrusting into her harder. She's pulsating on my fingers, muttering curse words under her breath between moans and sighs, and hearing her so agitated arouses me even more. I'm reaching in as far as I can go but her walls are trying to squeeze me out. She finally caves and starts moving along with me, begging for me to make her cum. Just as I reach around her to pinch her clit, I see her reach for her nipples, tugging at them almost cruelly, and she goes rigid in my arms. She cries out "No," as she wets my hand, her cum pooling in my palm. I nip at her asscheeks with my teeth, still pumping her, forcing her to ride it out before I turn my eyes to look at Daddy. He's almost ready. He's pulling on the cigar, gripping his dick tighter and I can see the almost easily missed tremble in his right leg.

I move to the edge of the bed, and reach for the nightstand, finding the gloves and lube. As soon as she hears the snap of the glove, she whines and tenses. A quick look to Daddy and I see the glint of amusement in his eye at what I'm about to do. I'm liberal with the lube on my gloved hand, and when I touch her asshole, she yelps from the shocking coolness. Her yelps are quickly traded for groans as I coax her ring to relax and one finger slips in. She's tight. Almost too tight. I close my eyes, relaxing in the feel of sliding in and out of her most private orifice, feeling the intense clenching on my fingers. Her groans are coming from somewhere deep; somewhere I'm reaching that hasn't been touched in a long time. I'm almost gentle with her, easing her into it, lulling her into a sense of calmness. My free hand cups her breasts, tenderly squeezing them, hearing her soft gasps of pleasure as she gives in to the invasion.

I feel her ring opening, and a second finger slowly penetrates her, and she's mewing into the sheets like a kitten. I'm slow and steady, careful to keep her relaxed as I push and pull, explore and recede; preparing her while my Daddy looks on with approval. When I slide the third finger in, she's gripping my arm tightly, rocking against me, trying to impale herself. Sluts like us crave this; feeling stretched and filled, knowing nothing else except what is being done to us.

I start to squeeze her breasts more harshly, rolling the nipples between my fingers, and I feel her hole contracting.

"Do you want me to stop?"

"No!" she cries out.

I let go of her breasts, and start raking her asscheeks with my nails. "Why don't you want me to stop?"

She lets out a sob "'Cause I need it."

"Need what?"

She's moving her hips faster, almost gliding on my fingers. "Need this! You, fucking me."

"And why do you need to be fucked?" I give her ass a slap, and my eyes find Daddy's.

She trembles as she cries out, "'Cause I'm a slut!"

Daddy's eyes close briefly at what he hears, and I watch his hand move to his belt. He quickly gets his dick in his hand and my pussy is drooling at the sight of it, watching his hand slide up and down the shaft.

"Tell my Daddy," I prompt her.

"I'm a slut!" She's moving faster on my fingers, her eyes taking in the sight of Daddy jacking off. "I'm a slut, Sir. I need to be fucked!"

I'm pumping her faster now, my hands a blur. She's crying out loudly, throwing her ass back at me, this time ready to let go. And I let her. I let her fuck my fingers till she squeezes on them and I know she's probably wetting the bed. She's gripping me tightly, her body shaking so hard that I hold her as well, telling her she's a good girl. I slowly pull out of her and bend my head, kissing her full on the lips as I shed the glove. I stretch out beside her, pulling her in my arms, my tongue exploring her mouth, as she sniffs and gasps for breath, aftershocks occasionally rocking her body.

We're like that for a few minutes, rolling around on the bed like starved lovers. I like that she's energetic like me. That after a mind-blowing cum, she can bounce back and be ready to play. I maneuver her so that she's lying on top, between my spread legs, and I'm still kissing her, running my fingers through her curly red hair, enjoying the taste of her sweet mouth on mine.

Only I hear the creak from the chair, as I lock my legs around hers, spreading them. Only I feel the slight movement in the bed, as my hands slide down to cup her ass, squeezing the cheeks, and then finally pulling them apart. And only I can see Daddy above her, giving me a wink, just before he groans and she gives a piercing cry into my shoulder. I feel the roughness of his jeans against my fingers as I hold her apart for him. She's gripping me tightly, her nails sweetly digging into my skin as my Daddy fucks her, burrowing into her ass as only he knows how. I know she's completely filled with him when her eyes, wide as saucers, peer into mine, filled with lust. He gives a slight thrust and her eyelids flutter closed, her lips forming an O. I like the feel of her weight on top of me, our breasts smashed together, the sweat from our skins mingling into one.

Daddy's remaining still, enjoying the feel of being deep inside her, the feel of her ass against him. I let go of her cheeks, my fingers trailing up her spine, making her quiver. When my fingers once again find her hair, this time I roughly pull her face down to mine, our lips crashing together. I suck on her lips, nipping at them with my teeth, and her fevered gasps are becoming moans again, so I know that Daddy's moving. His thrusts are slow and deliberate and I can feel the anguish in her body at having it done this way. So often, we sluts want a fast and furious ass-fucking, because the slow ones forces us to deal, to feel each inch, each level of us being peeled away. I know Daddy's giving her his full length on each stroke, pulling out 'til only the head remains, allowing her to remember how terrible it feels to be so empty, before driving back into her so deeply. She's feeling the impalement she's been after all night.

My lips are glued to hers as if I'm using this kiss as a way to meld with her, to feel all that she's feeling. To feel full and stretched, having the very core of you tapped by someone who understands what you are. I raise my legs higher so that I can feel Daddy's denim-clad ones, and let my heels press into his ass. He grunts and gives a hard thrust that makes her moan into my mouth, practically gasping.

"This toy feels good," Daddy says approvingly, as he shifts. I see his hand clasp her shoulder before the hard thrusts come, her body pushing me into the bed with each one. Her face is buried in the curve of my shoulder, and I hear each grunt, each whimper and groan of pleasure. She's whispering to herself how fucking good it feels, her fingers gripping me even harder. My lips seek out her neck, and I lick it before softly nibbling at her skin. She's saying yes over and over again, and I feel her wriggle between my legs, probably trying to get more of him in her. Sometimes we can be too greedy.

I can see the same thought in Daddy's eyes. His hand disappears and I know he's grabbing her hips. I feel her lift from me, just as I hear the soft crash of skin meeting jeans as he slams into her. She screams so loudly, my hand shoots out to cover her mouth, watching as she's being pulled back onto my Daddy's dick, unable to move on her own because of the grip he has on her. Daddy is fucking her like she's a rag doll, her arms flailing about as he bounces her on his dick. He wraps an arm around her waist, holding her close as he continues to jab into her, and I can see her eyes roll back in her head. She suddenly shrieks, biting my hand, and I can feel her juices dripping on me as she cums.

But Daddy doesn't care. He continues fucking her, bent on using her for all she's worth. He releases her, letting her fall back on me. His hand is in her hair, and he shoves her face over my breast. She doesn't have to be told, and quickly sucks my nipple into her warm mouth, and I give a sigh. He lies over her and his lips hungrily meet mine. I push the cap and du-rag off his head, exposing the thin cornrows I braided earlier that day, and grip his head tightly, wanting his mouth against mine forever. His tongue glides over my teeth, teasing me, making me reach for it with my own, and as I catch it, sucking it deeply, he thrusts into her so hard she bites my nipple.

After a few more thrusts, she cums again, sucking harder on my now sore nipple, but I don't care, the only thing that matters is Daddy's mouth on mine. When he finally breaks the kiss, he winks at me, before grabbing her hair and starting to fuck her faster. She's on top of me, in a constant tremble, and I know she's just about fucked out. But we know better. Toys know that it doesn't end until they're all used up, and Daddy's not done playing. I see his hands reach for her nipples, and watch his dark fingers squeeze and pinch the pink nubs until they're almost red and she's hollering. His nails find her skin, and she breaks, unable to scream anymore, her body convulsing.

When Daddy pulls out of her, he leans forward to kiss my forehead.

"Get rid of her," he tells me, before leaving the bed and going into the bathroom.

It takes me a few minutes to get her on her feet and lead her to the guest room. I help her clean up and watch her fall into the big bed. She sleepily kisses my hand, licking each finger, trying to entice me to stay with her. Girls like us are always greedy, always ready to play. But I kiss her forehead and before too long, she's falling asleep. In the morning Daddy will take her home.

When I return to the bedroom Daddy's on the bed, naked

and ready for me. Like a good girl I settle between his spread legs, and kiss his hairy thighs, letting my tongue taste his salty skin. I work my way up, the smell of him leading me to where he wants me most. As my tongue finds him, wet and ready, he groans, his fingers in my hair, loosely playing with the strands. This is my reward. This is what I strive for; to touch Daddy in a way no one else is allowed to.

I part him with my tongue, stroking him slowly. I find his hole, licking across it, toying with it before finding the hard and swollen nubbin that's begging for my lips. As I gently suck it into my mouth, Daddy's legs tense. I flick the tip of it with my tongue as I continue to slowly suck, feeling his hips rise and rotate. He's saying filthy things, things only Daddies should say, his voice gruff and breathless. He's telling me that I'm a filthy whore with whores for friends. He wants to fuck us all and use us all as toys. My hand is between my legs, furiously rubbing my clit; his words make me want to get fucked, to show him how much of a whore I'd be for him.

I lick him slowly 'cause Daddy likes things slow. Daddy likes to cherish every movement his good girl makes. I flatten my tongue and give him one long lick, and he closes his thighs on my head. I fasten my lips around that little nerve and suck him hard, making his hips buck. His fingers in my hair are no longer nice, twisting and turning, pulling my face into him hard.

"You gonna swallow it for Daddy?" he asks.

I moan my approval and slowly bob my head, letting him feel my soft lips glide up and down on him. Daddy's grinding hard into my face, his thighs squeezing tight, blocking out everything but him. All I can do is suck, until I hear the loud growl and feel him shoot, filling my mouth that's so desperate for him, and then I quietly cum. I drink everything he has to give me, my tongue greedy and searching.

After a few moments, Daddy pushes my head away, lovingly calls me his greedy slut and pulls me close. I settle in his arms, relaxing in the smell of sex that surrounds us. And once I feel his large hand finally settled and cupping my cunt, I sigh and allow myself to fall asleep.

# UNDONE

## Miel Rose

There's this woman I work with. She moves around with more confidence and self-possession than anyone I've ever seen. Sometimes I think it's because she's in her late forties, older than most of the people I hang out with. But who knows? Maybe she's always been that way.

She works in the bulk department at the grocery store I cashier for. I love to find excuses to sneak into the back and watch her, the muscles in her arms tensing as she hefts the fifty-pound bags of dry goods. She has this old-school butch feel, and in this town, old-school butches might as well be unicorns.

After she got hired, my work clothes got a lot more interesting. My skirts got shorter, my jeans tighter—and this is really saying something. Plunging became the best adjective to describe the necklines of my tops. If the neckline was too high, I would just cut it lower. I started wearing more makeup to work, but I drew the line at heels after spending most of a shift barefoot when I decided it was more comfortable than standing eight hours in front of a cash register in platform sandals.

I would watch her move around the store, her short graying hair tousled and messy like she'd just rolled out from between some girl's thighs. She drove me crazy. My mind would start running in circles. Did she date femmes? Would she even recognize me as femme? Or would she think I was some young, freaky straight girl trying to fuck with her? She looked like the exact kind of trouble I liked, but outside packaging can be deceiving. How did I even know she was a top? Lord knows she inspired the bottom in me.

I turned on my best flirt.

At first, I don't think she knew what to do with me. Then she started playing along, seeing what I'd do. When I didn't run for the hills, but continued flirting shamelessly with her, she turned up the volume. We'd be alone in the back room and she'd start dirty talking me, nothing too nasty, just enough to make my breath catch, my cheeks burn. The way she looked at me made me want to get down on my knees before her, my wrists held together behind my back, and show her what a good bottom I could be.

It was crazy making, wondering if she was going to make a move, if she would ever ask me out. Maybe she had a wife. Maybe she thought I was too young. Maybe she didn't get hot for chubby girls. Maybe she didn't get hot for femmes. The possibilities for rejection were endless in my head.

Then came the night we were on inventory together and the third person working our shift called in sick. I almost pissed myself when I walked around to the back of the store and saw her sitting on a stack of crates, smoking a cigarette. I always did inventory with the same two people, I hadn't even bothered to check the schedule. I was totally unprepared to see her. She squinted at me through the smoke, looking me over like I was dessert on legs, like she wanted to devour me right there.

Under her stare my aggressive flirty self dissolved like unstable ground out from under me. I said hi, and fumbled around my brain, finally adding something about getting to work, and walked past her into the building. I worked my ass a little extra, hoping she was looking.

I made my way to the office desk in the back, getting my clipboard and inventory list together. I heard the sound of her boots behind me as she entered the building, slow and measured, echoing through the back room. I listened to her steps getting closer and my body started breaking out in goose bumps. She didn't stop until she was right behind me. My hair was pinned up and I could feel her breath on my neck, smell the smoke from her cigarette. This woman had me undone and she hadn't even touched me yet. My heart was beating hard and I was working to control my breathing.

She leaned closer, whispering in my ear, "Well, sweetheart? You've been flirting viciously with me for months. You want to take this to the next level? Or do you want me to back off and we can start working?"

She was being rather gentlemanly about it, not even implying that I was a cock tease. I didn't know what to say, my heart was racing and my breathing wouldn't slow down.

I turned my head and looked at her over my shoulder, trying to let all the built-up want for her show in my eyes. She smiled at that, took hold of my shoulder and turned me around to face her. Her hand came up to stroke my jaw, her thumb tracing my lips. My eyes were locked to hers and I kissed her thumb, opening my mouth and sucking it in as far as it would go. Her eyes blazed and she moved her thumb gently in and out of my mouth. She was working me with kid gloves so far, treating me real soft and gentle, but I could feel the power building inside her, making her body tense.

She took her thumb out of my mouth and spread my saliva back and forth over my lips.

"That looks like consent to me, sugar, but I want to hear you say it."

"I want you," I said. It just slipped out. I wasn't feeling very eloquent.

It seemed like enough though, because she smiled and said, "And what should I do with you, baby girl? Hey, by the way, how old are you anyway?"

It was hard for me to remember my own name at that moment, but I answered her, dazed, "Twenty-five?"

She whistled softly and said, "Damn, girl, I'm old enough to be your mother." And then, "Actually, you're younger than my daughter."

I was thrown off balance. I did not want to be thinking about this woman being my mother...maybe my daddy, but not my mother.

"You have a kid?" I asked, hoping I didn't sound too shocked.

"Yeah, I didn't raise her though. Gave her up for adoption. I was only fourteen when I had her." I could sense everything she wasn't saying in the way her body had pulled away slightly, the way she wouldn't meet my eye. I turned her face toward me and kissed her softly on her mouth, letting her know that her having a kid older than I was didn't stop me wanting her. She ran her hands over my hips, pulled me into her. I moaned into her mouth, I couldn't help it. I was so turned on I felt shaky. I could feel my pussy dripping puddles into the crotch of my jeans.

She broke the kiss and tilted my head back to get at my neck. She kissed me lightly, leaving a trail of moisture on my skin from her parted lips. Then she was at my ear, nuzzling me, whispering, "What do you want, sweetheart? What can I do for you?"

I started blushing furiously. Where was the confident girl who had worked so hard to be able to say what she wanted? I couldn't find her. I managed to whisper, "I want you to rough me up."

"Yeah?" she said. I could hear the edge of tension and excitement in her voice. "What does that mean to you, baby? Give me more."

"Ummmm," was all that would come out of my mouth. My face was still hot and I bit my lip. Why did this woman make me so nervous? I looked down and noticed the wide leather belt she was wearing. I felt my pussy clench as the inspiration hit me.

I slowly raised my eyes to hers.

"What is it, girl? You can tell me."

I took a deep breath and blurted out, "You could hit me with your belt."

I felt like an idiot, but she smiled and leaned back against the wall, crossing her arms over her chest. She said, "Are you going to let me fuck you too, or do you just want me to hurt you?"

I wanted to spread my legs for her right there, show her how wet she was getting me. Instead, I tried to get a hold on myself and said, "No, I definitely want you to fuck me." My voice was still shaky.

"Are you going to be able to tell me if I do something you don't like, or if you want me to stop? You want a special word or something?"

I wanted this so bad and I wasn't in the mood to pretend I didn't. "No, I don't need a safeword," I said. "I'll just tell you if I want you to stop."

"All right. Take off your pants."

My fingers trembled as I undid the fly of my jeans and wiggled them over my hips. I left my panties on, since I hadn't been instructed otherwise, and I was sure there was a huge wet spot spreading up the front.

Arms still across her chest, she looked me up and down. "Lean over that desk and stick your ass out for me." I did as she said, pushing the papers and clipboards to the side. "Spread your legs wider." I spread my legs as wide as they could go, my back arched. The air felt cold on the soaked crotch of my panties.

I heard the leather of her boots creak as she pushed off from the wall to stand behind me. "Damn, this is a pretty picture." She hooked her finger under the crotch of my panties and ran her knuckle up and down my slit. We moaned at the same time, hers a growl, mine a whimper in the back of my throat.

I wanted more, I wanted her whole hand inside me, but she took her finger away. Sliding my panties down over my hips, she whistled again, low under her breath. I imagined what she was seeing, my bare ass up in the air, legs apart; my pussy spread open, exposed.

I could hear her unbuckling her belt and sliding it slowly

from the loops. My legs turned to jelly. I was glad I was lying down across this desk because I probably couldn't have stood if I wanted to. She trailed the belt down my lower back, across the crack of my ass, the tip brushing my pussy lips. She brought it between my legs and rubbed it back and forth, getting the leather wet with my juices. She pulled it back and tapped it lightly against my thighs, making a wet sticky sound on impact.

"All right, sweet thing. We're going to start out slow, a round of five and then we check in. You okay with that?"

I would have rather she waled on me, but the words to explain this escaped me. I nodded my head and said, "Yeah, that sounds good."

She didn't hold out on me though. When the belt came down, it came down hard. The first stroke made my knees buckle. My body shuddered at the pain so sharp it drove me crazy, overwhelming me as it quickly turned to pleasure, making my cunt ache, my clit pulse. She followed the first stroke with another four, crisscrossing my ass.

"You want more?" She ran her hand over my ass, feeling the heat.

"Yes, please? Yes," I said, moving my ass back and forth.

She started really going for it, harder and faster, making me cry out with each hit. She passed the fifth stroke and went on to the sixth, starting in on my thighs, barely missing my pussy. My body rocked forward with each hit. I was wondering if I could take more when she reached ten and stopped.

Her hand felt cool on my ass, tracing the welts. "Your ass looks beautiful all marked up." I could feel her lean closer, scrutinizing the marks. "Damn, girl, you're already starting to bruise! Are you ready to get fucked yet?" Her hand slid down to my pussy, checking how wet I was getting. I pushed myself back at her, trying to get her fingers inside me, but her hand evaded me.

My endorphins were kicking in and I felt more relaxed and more shaky at the same time, and also kind of silly. Little giggles were sneaking in between my moans. I bit my lip trying to stop.

"What are you giggling about?" She slapped my ass with her hand, making me gasp. "Do you want to get fucked or not?"

"Yes! Please..."

"Roll over." She slapped my ass again and I rolled over, trying to arrange my sore cheeks on the cool surface of the desk. She pushed over one of the office chairs, parked it in front of my spread legs and sat in it. She leaned back and looked up at me.

"Take your shirt and your bra off. I want to see your tits."

I pulled my shirt up over my head and unhooked my bra, letting my double Ds down slowly onto my belly.

"You are so beautiful," she said. One of her hands was resting between her thighs, her thumb running back and forth over the seam of her crotch. "Play with your tits for me, baby. Give me a show."

I could feel my face heat up again, if I had ever stopped blushing in the first place. This woman could make things I had done before, of my own volition, seem new, and so dirty. I lifted my tits up and pushed them together, grabbing my nipples between my thumb and forefinger, twisting and pulling them. I watched her watching me, getting hot on getting her hot.

She reached up and stroked my thighs, pulling them further apart, spreading my pussy wider. Leaning back, she said, "Come sit on my lap, sweetheart."

I got up from the desk and straddled her legs. She grabbed my sensitive ass and pulled me down onto her, hard, grinding my pussy into the fly of her jeans.

"Ohh, fuck, fuck, fuck," I said.

"I'm getting there, baby, I'm getting there," she chuckled. She held my tits up to her mouth, pressing them together so she could get both my nipples into her mouth at the same time. I leaned back, bracing myself, holding her knees, and rode her lap for real.

"Don't come yet, girl. I haven't even fucked you yet." She reached down to my pussy and I raised myself up to give her access. She slid two of her big fingers up my cunt and started fucking me with hard, fast strokes.

I lost it, if I had ever had it around her in the first place. I started moaning, loud, my breathing all over the place, too fast. I was losing my war with hyperventilation and I was getting dizzy. She grabbed the back of my neck, forcing me to look into her eyes. "Slow your breath down, honey. Breathe with me." She started breathing real deep and slow, her hand pumping in and out of my pussy slower, but still hard and deep.

I was whining, feeling like a brat but not able to stop. I tried to breathe deeper, slower, drawing the air down to my pussy. It made me even dizzier. I leaned forward, resting my head on her shoulder.

"You okay, sweetheart?" Her fingers stopped moving inside me. I felt embarrassed. She kissed my neck and shoulder, stroked my back with her free hand. "You want to try something else?"

"Like what?" I asked, nuzzling my face into her neck. I could smell her skin and my lips parted to taste it.

"Mmm, that feels good," she said, her hand tangled in my

hair. "I was thinking about how much I would love to eat this dripping pussy of yours." She curled her fingers gently inside me, making me moan into her neck. "Would you like that? You want to sit on my face, darlin'?"

I was still feeling shy. I made an affirmative noise and she guided me to sit up. I angled my hips so she could pull her fingers out of my cunt, leaving me feeling empty. I got off her lap and leaned against the desk, aware of how naked I was.

She went over and grabbed her coat, one of those jean jackets with the fake sheep lining. She laid it on the ground, positioning herself so there was plenty of jacket on either side of her head for my knees to rest on. I smiled at her chivalry.

"Come on down, sugar."

My legs felt shaky, like a newborn colt's. I managed to straddle her face without hurting her or myself. Her hands grabbed my hips, trying to pull me down to her mouth. I giggled and fell forward, catching myself with my hands, raising my ass in the air.

"Come on, give it to me," she said. I lowered myself down to her mouth and felt her tongue part my lips, licking from my pussy hole up to my swollen clit. She sucked my clit into her mouth and swirled her tongue around it in circles. I started humping her face, making her work my clit harder.

It was then that I realized I had to piss. I panicked, not knowing how to stop the action, not wanting to. She stuck her tongue up my pussy and I bounced up and down on her face.

"Oh, fuck, fuck, fuck." I knew I couldn't hold it much longer. I stopped moving and raised myself up off her mouth. "I have to piss, I'm so sorry. I'll be right back, I promise."

Her hands on my hips tightened. "You're not going anywhere." She tried to pull me back down to her tongue.

"I'm serious, I have to piss! I can't hold it!" I felt close to hysteria.

"Don't."

"What?"

"Don't hold it," she said, craning her neck up to get at me, licking my pussy lips. Her tongue went between my clit and my hole, putting pressure on my urethra.

"You want me to piss on your face?"

"Uh-huh."

I was looking down at her, trying to make eye contact. When she looked up at me her eyes were hard, laced with steel. I'd seen that look before during pervy sex. It said, *I dare you to say no, call me a freak, walk out on me.*

I wasn't going to say no. I also wasn't going to think about what we would do after, piss covering my legs, her face, her hair, her jacket, the floor. I rested more of my weight on her face and she went back to working my clit, sucking me into her mouth, grazing me with her teeth.

It was crazy, this building of pressure in my bladder and cunt. I let her build me up more. I wanted to come as I pissed, something I had wanted since before I knew what orgasms were, as a little girl touching my clit while pissing in the woods.

She was lapping at my pussy now, rocking me into her face with her hands, wanting me to let go. Her hands strayed to my ass crack, spreading me open, brushing my asshole with her fingertips.

That was it. I started coming. My piss squirted out of me in spurts, timed with the contractions of my orgasm. I tried to raise myself up, give her the choice not to get it all in her mouth, but she held me down, lapping it up, licking my clit, drawing my orgasm out. It felt like I pissed forever. She kept her face there the whole time, loving every second, rubbing herself into me.

When my waterworks were finally done, I rolled off of her and groaned, finding my legs even weaker than before. "I don't think I can walk after that," I said, lying down beside her, curling my naked body around her fully clothed one.

She laughed and held me tight. "That's okay, baby. You can take the inventory on the bottom shelves and I'll take the top ones."

# THE ANT QUEEN

Roxy Katt

(Inspired by the drawing *Ant* by Osvaldo Greco)

When I got to Katy's spanking big house in the suburbs, no one answered the doorbell. The front door was unlocked, and I was on good enough terms there to walk in. Perhaps everyone was out back by their big pool, I thought.

"Katy? Mrs. Wellington?" I peered into the living room, then made my way to the enormous, shiny kitchen at the back of the two-story house. The house always made me think of sex.

Not because of Katy, my best friend, but because of her mom.

Katy's mom was hot, and she was one of those people who knew it, and who knew she could write her own ticket that way—or not—as she saw fit. Tall, full-bodied and narrow waisted, she possessed a kind of retro domestic complacency about her. But it was strangely coupled with what seemed to me a complete confidence that while she would always be *very* selective, and didn't usually *need* sex that much (not to put too fine a point on it) she had the capacity to satisfy anyone on the planet.

Naturally, as a lesbian, I could say nothing. About my attraction, that is. She had been married, until a year earlier, when she got divorced from her Stan. Powerful and masculine, he was as headstrong as his wife, and that had probably been much of the problem right there.

Who was I anyway, I thought—passing through the expensive house that always made me feel like a loser somehow—but some skinny-assed chick just out of high school? Yeah, I was thin, and I suppose "cute" in a way, dressed today in a floppy T-shirt and cutoffs, but in the presence of Mrs. Wellington, I always felt somehow that I wasn't really a woman yet. God knows I had the desires of one, but it was as if I hadn't grown into their power, if that makes any sense. You might even say that in a general way, I was a little fed up with that lack of power; fed up with a nagging, nameless inadequacy; a vulnerability to whoever was convinced he or she had a right to weigh me in the balance and find me wanting.

I looked through the big sliding glass doors at the pool and its abundant deck. There were trees and fence aplenty, so that it was, all told, a very private backyard.

What I saw then amazed and puzzled me. My mouth fell open and I whispered in awe, "Way cool," like some dipstick valley girl.

Of course—I remembered then—Katy wasn't home. She was

camping for the weekend. And I remembered that her mom was going next week to a fancy costume party, which would explain who that was out there by the pool in the incredible getup, trying it on in advance, checking out how she moved in it.

When I'd heard she was going to go as an ant, I'd thought, yeah, right. Some stupid foam rubber suit, some baggy shit like that, some cutesy version of Barney the Dinosaur, waving and bouncing, with a fixed idiot smile, some Disney-movie sentimentality. But I had underestimated Katy's mom.

There she was in black plastic and latex, all polished to a high shine. She could have stepped right out of a fetish magazine. Since her back was turned to me while she seemed to be surveying her big pool, I had time to stare. With Katy gone and it not being the maid's day to come in no one would have been at home with Katy's mom this morning, so she must have had a devil of a time getting into it. It seemed to be in effect a latex catsuit, thick, tight, replete with corrugated joints at knee, hip, shoulder and elbow for flexibility and equipped with high-heeled PVC boots. A kind of high-waisted, hard plastic panty (two pieces, snapping together at her hips) was part of her ant shell, as was a very large, round-cupped bra, with heavy plastic strapping, forming a hard, short, sleeveless top.

Her helmet was a bug head. Again, hard shiny plastic, and, as she turned, I could see nothing behind the large black bug eyes. She had a pair of vicious-looking snappers at the mouth.

And she had two more pairs of hooks for her hands. Marvelous and frightening constructions, they were part of tubular plastic shells or cuffs that went up to just below the elbow. Within, her hands worked the claws, for I saw one of them open and close, meditatively.

I had always loved her little waist and big ass, but I couldn't believe how much the suit brought out the contrast. And, narrow as the waist was, there was a tummy. Oh yes, a tummy from bearing three children and being over forty. She couldn't get around that; had to have the delightful bulge built right into the mold of the inflexible plastic—a bulge that curved right down between her legs, where there was a sturdy latch, designed, it seemed, to open two doors on sturdy hinges, fore and aft, for visits to the little ants' room.

She turned and saw me, and expressed her delight as well as one could in such gear. I, for my part was as effusive as possible without giving myself away.

"What do you think, dear?" came her voice with a muffled echo. "Do you think I'm ready to start a colony?"

"Oh god, yes. You're a marvel."

Between the hard shell of hips, tummy and ass, on the one hand, and boobs and upper back on the other, the waist was the area of flexible rubber. She was tight, narrow like an ant there, and seemed to like to sashay her ass around and flex it in order to point her tits toward you.

Was she hot for me? I don't think so. It was just that the suit brought out the she-cat in her, the sexual predator, and she pranced, half-consciously, because that was what one did in such a suit, whether anyone eligible was there or not.

She took a sheer delight in her power. And so did I, even though I was intimidated.

"Hey!" I said. "I've got my digital camera with me. Can I take pictures of you?"

"Why not? I'm pretty hot, aren't I?" I could hear the smile through the helmet.

"Can I put them on the Web?"

"I don't see why not. Show your friends."

By "your friends" I wondered if she meant "your lesbian friends." Ah, Mrs. Wellington, you want to tease my friends, too? You want to say, "Look, lezzies, but don't touch"?

I thought about her struggling to get into the suit, and wished I could have watched, secretly, as she sweated and strained. She was cool as a cucumber, as if this were what she wore every day, as if she looked like such a predator all the time. But it couldn't have been easy.

If only, I thought, she were some kind of lesbian Mrs. Robinson. God, how lucky that would be....

She had to have put those claws on last, because with her hands in there, there would be no way she could have wriggled into that tight helmet, her head firmly ensconced in a tough plastic shell.

A thought flitted through my mind and I lost it as she turned to me.

I took pictures while she posed. Standing, sitting, bending over tastefully, then, unexpectedly, she said, "You know, I see how models get bored so often. I can see where this gets repetitive."

"You have a terrific shape, Mrs. Wellington."

"Thank you, dear."

"You look so hot I could, like, just take you right here."

I couldn't believe I'd said that. Oh god, I'd really put my foot in it.

She turned her expressionless ant mask toward me and said coolly, "You could what?"

"I mean..."

"I'm not surprised, dear. I mean, you're a lesbian and I'm to die for. It's not wise to put it quite so presumptuously as you just did though, is it?"

"No," I stammered, "of course not. I'm an idiot, Mrs. Wellington, it just blurted out...."

"Do you have a girlfriend, honey?"

"No."

"Well, maybe you should try to find somebody your own speed."

"I...I'm sorry Mrs. Wellington. I mean, coming on to a het woman was just stupid of me...."

"Oh that's not what I mean, dear. Sure I'm straight, but I wouldn't rule out, especially since I've been quite aloof from sex for a while, I wouldn't rule out being serviced by a woman...."

*Serviced?* I thought.

"But you're practically a girl. I mean, really dear, you're just out of high school. I'm way out of your league. And you are my daughter's best friend. And as for taking, well, with all due respect, dear, if anyone were to take anyone, it would be me taking you, right?" She laughed. "But I think it's cute. Like I could be your bitch or something. Now be a dear and fetch us some Cokes, will you?"

Shamefaced and not knowing what to say, I went to the kitchen as she told me. Setting the drinks on the tray, I glanced out the kitchen window toward the pool.

It seemed she was trying to take her hooks off.

And she couldn't. Fitting first one forearm and then the other beneath its opposing armpit, she tugged mightily, but could not get her forearm out. She would need help. She looked frustrated, then paused, and composed herself.

Shit. Who would have thought?

I pondered a moment. With those hooks, she couldn't take off her tight helmet. She couldn't unsnap the catches on her plastic parts, she couldn't unlace her boots. She was stuck in there. Totally stuck in her bug suit. Unless I or someone got her out of it.

Something came over me. I shuddered—pleasantly—with fear and desire. Weird ideas began to form in my mind and I tried unsuccessfully to ignore them. Oh she was a Mrs. Robinson all right, and I but a humble high school graduate of little interest to her, but...

After standing there and staring I don't know how long, I began to rummage around in the kitchen, and put together— besides the drinks of course—a few other things my imagination had suggested. I glanced out the window, thought, then rushed upstairs to the bathroom. Ah yes, I found exactly what I was looking for.

I put everything on a tray, all under a neatly folded tea towel, except the drinks, which were on the tray beside the towel.

When I was back on the deck, she said, "This suit sure is hot. Be a dear and just pull these claws off for me will you?," complacently holding them out toward me. I took a breath. I must have looked a little scared, and at the same time like the proverbial cat who swallowed the canary. I looked at her.

"Well? Can you pull these hooks off for me please?"

"You can't get out of that suit, can you?"

"Huh?"

"I said," I said, summoning my courage, "you can't get out of that suit, can you?"

"Of course I can. What are you talking about?"

"If I left right now, if I went home and left you here, you couldn't get out."

We looked at each other. Still terrified, I pressed on by the sheer force of selfish horniness, if that's what it was that was making me feel all strange and trembly inside.

"You're a formidable woman, Mrs. Wellington, but you're not as smart as you think you are. You're stuck in there, and you're helpless."

She seemed to stammer, just a little. "Why, of course I'm not stuck, dear...."

I smiled. "I don't want to sound mean, but potentially you could have turned into some amusing human interest item on the six o'clock news: *Woman Trapped in Bug Suit Seeks Help.* I picture you tottering down the streets on those heels, scaring children and old people, begging for help from surly, indifferent teenagers, and everyone too suspicious to listen to you."

"Don't be ridiculous. That could never have happened under any circumstances. Besides, I'm not stuck in here."

"Then prove it."

"Why should I? It's just hard work. Why should I? Just get me out of here."

I popped the tab on my Coke and settled into my deck chair, trying to hide the fact that I was shaking a little. "I'm going to watch you struggle out of that gear, lady. That is, if you can. But it's going to be fun watching you try."

"Oh I see," she said, recovering herself a little, stepping forward, her hooks on her hips, "this is about my saying I'm out of your league, isn't it? Or is it some titillating game you young lesbians play?"

"Yes. Actually, we do this all the time. One of us gets trapped in a bug suit quite by accident and the others laugh at her. You'd be surprised at how often it happens."

"And are you laughing at me? Well, you're not going to get the best of me, young lady...."

It both angered and turned me on that she should give me

that "young lady" stuff. I don't know what I was thinking at that point—maybe my arousal had made me impulsive by then. I reached out between her legs and twisted the latch. It groaned and then burst open with a *boing* sound. The two doors, with springs on their hinges apparently, sprung open and stayed that way.

She gasped, and tottered backward, hooks flailing...

Abundant ass and pussy bulged and burgeoned stupidly from their confines. Yes, some women have neat-looking labia majora below a flat tummy with a dainty bit of inner lip demurely poking out. But she had a delightfully fat cunt.

And the fur! Damn, she was a beast! Involuntarily, I licked my lips.

She gasped and tottered backward, as I said, hooks scrabbling ineffectually at the hatches, pushing first one, then the other down, but unable to get them to latch together. Then, one by one, they would flip out from under the slippery plastic hooks and spring up to the open position again.

"You bitch! You rotten miserable bitch! I'll show you... you..."

"You must be hot in there, Mrs. Wellington. I thought you could use some ventilation."

She turned her back to me in her clumsy contortions and I saw her firm buttcheeks, the lower third of them or so, bulging out of the open hatch. How the hell had she ever gotten it closed, I wondered, even with hands? I let out a low whistle.

"Prove to me you're not an idiot who's gotten herself trapped in her own costume. Prove to me you wouldn't have had to go from door to door, asking your neighbors to rescue you. Why, there's Mrs. Nixon next door—that old pervert—that would have been humiliating, wouldn't it? Then there's those slutty young Sycamore girls across the street who'd have laughed at you. Now, unless you're nice to me, you'll have to do all that with your pussy open to the world."

She turned back to me and advanced, menacing with her hooks. "Damn you, insolent hussy!"

The very archaic nature of her insult made me laugh outright. "Hussy? You're the one in the fetish gear flashing her cunt all over the place." She turned her ant face to me and I could hear her draw her breath in as if to protest, but I pressed my unjust insinuation ruthlessly. "You have a daughter the same age as me, Mrs. W., surely you know how horny we young chicks are. And surely you must know that that costume you're trapped in isn't without its, shall we say, fetishistic elements?"

She was too angry and confused to articulate the obvious objection to this insinuation: that she had had no way of knowing I was even going to be there that morning. Flustered thus, she failed to prevent what had just been her weak spot from becoming her weak spot again. I jumped out of my chair and pretended to back up a little as she advanced, then lunged and grabbed a big fistful of fur with my right hand.

"Yowk!" she cried. "My pussy! Unh! You beast!" She struggled, doing a little dance on her heels, starting to moan. With my hand still on her snatch, I grabbed her with the left hand around the waist and pulled her in toward me.

I slipped my hand down and into her fanny crack.

"Oh! Betty! Goodness! Oh! Are you sure you...?"

Her arms went from pushing me to slipping around my own waist, running up and down my back in a confused action. It was as if, trapped in an ant costume, she was compelled to imitate some sort of primal ant ritual, some ancient insect sexual motion....

I let my middle finger find its way to the rim of her anus. I played about, slowly, gently, without entering.

We did a kind of slow dance, human and bug, with her trying to articulate her confusion. Her ass was dead tight, but the rest of her did not resist. I still had a good grip on her fur.

I backed her toward the little table on which I had put the kitchen tray, and throwing off the concealing tea towel, grabbed the K-Y tube (which I had gotten from the bathroom) underneath with my left hand. Popping the cap, I poured some down the deep crack of her abundant ass, to her surprise.

"I'm going in, Mrs. Wellington. Any objections?"

I peered through the dark glass of the bug eye, and from this close distance I could indeed vaguely see her face. There was a frightened, dreamy look to the eye, and heavy, husky breathing....

She whispered, "No girl ever dared..."

I slowly forced my finger in and she groaned a little, her ass sashaying more widely for a moment, then winding quickly into a brief, frenetic wiggle before surrendering to the slower rhythm of our strange little dance as my imperious finger established its dominance in depth.

I let go of her pubic hair. But I still had her by the anus, on the end of my left middle finger. She had a grip of steel, scared as she was. I wondered if my finger could get stuck in there and we'd have to walk this way to the nearest hospital. "What I have here," I said, "is a great ant perched on a little twig. Let's see if we can't anchor you a little more firmly."

Beneath where the tea towel had been there was not only the K-Y but two handsome zucchinis. Yes, I had taken them from the kitchen. Turning her head toward the table, she saw them.

"Wh-what are you going to do with those?" She slowly

pulled away a little from me, but her ass was clenched so tight on my finger she didn't get far.

I spun her a little, so her back was toward me, to get to the zucchinis. I greased them with my right hand, took one.

"Spread your legs, ant queen."

She did so, her head turning back toward me as if to ask a question or to ask me to be gentle, and slowly, but firmly and steadily, I pushed the zucchini up her snatch, inching in slowly as she groaned.

"Oh god!" she said, "zucchini! Stan would never have..."

"Shut up about that stupid man, will you? He's gone. Pay attention. I'm filling your thing with zucchini. How does that feel? Nice and tight?" I pushed it in nice and tight but left quite a bit of it sticking out. "Ah, very good. A meat sandwich with fresh veggies." I continued to hold the veggie while I eased my finger out of her asshole. "That's quite a grip you have there, Mrs. W., both ends. I think what's coming up next will be especially difficult so just relax, let all thought leave your buggy little head, and don't resist me."

I reached now with my left hand for the second zucchini and started to push it home, slowly, up the poop chute.

"Oh! Betty! Do you think you should, I mean..."

"Shhhh, relax queenie, relax that tight asshole, that's a girl, it's going in, yes it is, so you may as well not resist it. Yes, it's going in...."

"Uunnh! Oh! Ooooh, this is so filthy! You filthy bitch, I'm old enough to be your mother. You sneaky little thing, you you..."

Then they were both in, but I was careful to leave enough sticking out for safety's sake. I pumped them a little, fingered her clit, which was enormous, and watched it grow helplessly.

She did a strange thing with her arms, moving them around in a dancing fashion, then reaching back with them to touch me as best she could.

I stopped for a bit, and began to take more pics. I think she was so confused, her hooks hovering over the zucchinis deep within her, she didn't realize quite what I was doing.

"Next time you feel proud, Mrs. Wellington, just remember I COULD have done that even if you'd said no. I wouldn't, but I could have. Well, thanks for the pictures, but I really have to be going." I didn't mean it of course, but I was quite convincing.

"Huh? What the—"

"Surprised? You didn't think I was going to bring you off or anything, did you? That would have been too forward, I think."

"But you—"

"What would your daughter say? I mean really, Mrs. Wellington, have a sense of propriety. And even if I didn't oppose bringing you off on principle I'm still mightily pissed off by your haughtiness toward me not so long ago."

She exploded, testily, "You think you're so smart just because you—"

"What? Still not humbled? Even with your ass and pussy full of vegetables? Well, I'm off then." I prepared to leave. "I guess it'll be your daughter who finds you. Just tell her it was a masturbation accident—it could happen to anyone—because I'm sure she doesn't want to know her best friend's been boinking her mom."

She grappled ineffectively at the zucchinis. "The zucchinis. I can't get a grip on them. They're stuck."

"Not for human fingers, ant lady. Why don't you take those

hooks off? Oh that's right, Mrs. Out-of-Your-League, they're stuck too. Listen. I'd tell you to get stuffed, but it looks like somebody already did it to you."

"Betty! Please don't go. You've got me all hot... I was an idiot. I'm begging you, please do me. I haven't had it in ages and now...and I just can't be found like this. Not by anybody! You don't understand, the humiliation would—"

I turned to her. "Begging is best done on one's knees. Get on your knees and beg this chit of a girl for a thorough fucking, Mrs. Wellington, that's it, humble yourself."

Awkwardly, and leaning against some deck furniture, she stumbled onto her knees on the blankets and pillows poolside and groaned out her humble request, promising she would be mine "on any occasion" if I gave her relief now and rescued her from an intolerable public humiliation.

"Which you nonetheless so richly deserve, don't you, Audrey?"

"Oh yes, I've been, I've been an arrogant bitch. I deserve it, but please..."

"And you're not very bright, getting yourself into such a vulnerable position, are you?"

"No."

"Aren't you ashamed of yourself? Such a seemingly strong, proud woman? Shouldn't you be mastering me, rather than the other way around?"

"Oh, yes, yes to all that."

I pulled off my T-shirt and dropped my cutoffs to the deck, exposing the little black bathing suit I was wearing underneath, as one frequently wears when visiting the home of a friend who has a pool. I pulled the string on my bikini bottoms and let them drop. I walked right up to her, felt around her neck, forced my fingers between it and the tight opening of the bug helmet, and carefully began to work it off.

"What are you doing? Oh, you're giving me some air," she said hopefully.

It was like trying to get a cork out of a champagne bottle.

"Really Audrey, I think even with your own hands you couldn't have gotten out of this. You are rather a stupid bitch after all. 'Antwoman' indeed! You have the brains of an ant."

"Why, I—"

"Ever eaten pussy, dear?"

"Why no, I..." The helmet came off with a pop. I dropped it, clattering to the deck and it rolled and splashed into the pool. She had no makeup on. Her lovely triangular face dripped with sweat as she stared at what was before her. I turned her face up to mine, rubbed a thumb gently over her forehead below the bangs of her jet-black hair.

I bent down, grabbed both sides of her head, pressed my face into hers, and pushed my tongue into her mouth. She sucked my tongue in a hungry, imploring fashion, and in her eye I caught a look that said, *Please don't stop.*

"Seeing as you're the one with the fruit salad crammed up her cracks, you're going to service ME before you get any more. Get it, bitch?"

She nodded, fear in her eyes. I could see she didn't like the idea of pussy, except her own. But she was desperate for her turn. The zucchinis were talking to her, whispering up her big cunt and her little asshole all her desperate, unfulfilled, suburban housewife needs.

"You don't like pussy, do you? We'll soon fix that."

She nodded.

I shoved her face into my cunt. Her hooks flailed behind me, but eventually settled down on my ass. At my direction she sucked, nibbled, writhed her tongue.

I was on the verge of coming right away. Not that she was good at it. She was terrible and I told her so. But I had the haughty Antwoman, a proud, big-assed bitch, on her knees before me, humbly paying tribute, desperately trying to please me lest I deny her.

"Isn't your tongue longer than that? You can certainly talk with it...that's better, deeper now...that's it, work, you lazy, big-assed housewife...."

Finally, "Hold on tighter." I gripped her more firmly behind the head, pulling as if to shove it up my cunt. It occurred to me she might have trouble breathing, but I was coming wave on wave. It took all my strength just to remain standing, but even at that she was totally under my control.

"Shlurp, mmph," she protested, pulling back momentarily for a gulp of air. Then I pulled her home again and she squeezed my ass for all she was worth. I gasped, I groaned, I told her how wonderful it was, and it was.

I sat down to recover myself. Her mouth was wet and drooling. Still on her knees, she looked at me with an expression of humility, hope, admiration and fear.

"Not bad," I said laconically.

"That certainly was a new experience, I—"

"You talk too much. You're being mastered this morning in case that hadn't occurred to you, and I expect you to keep quiet until you're spoken to."

She began to open her lips in protest and I reached for the little apple I had on the tray and crammed it in her big mouth. Again with the thrashing hooks, lots of grunting sounds and muffled cries of indignation.

"You aren't quite thoroughly broken, it seems. On all fours, bitch." She complied, her legs wide, her ass arched high in the air. Kneeling beside her I began to pump. Oh I worked those vegetables, I can tell you, and made her nod her admission to my assertions of how good it was, and how degrading it was for her, too. I told her all the while how powerless she was, that I was thinking of leaving her this way once I was through with her, that I found older women such as herself mildly interesting but too full of themselves, that it was her daughter's best friend who was pumping her fore and aft, that she must be pretty desperate to turn pussy eater for this even though she didn't like pussy, that I had forced her to like pussy, that she would be eating my pussy whenever I told her to because I had conquered her proud will and she was now my bitch.

And what had she to say to all this? She nodded madly, she came ecstatically, maniacal ejaculator that she turned out to be.

It was the beginning of a beautiful friendship.

# TOP GIRL

Nan Rogue

I was lounging on the sofa in my bathrobe, applying a fresh coat of Violent Violet to my toenails, when my cell phone rang. The caller ID told me it was my boss, so I grabbed a pen and notepad before I answered. "This is Maya."

"Okay, you have a client in an hour and a half," Ann said. "First-time customer." She gave the name of a hotel and the room number, and I jotted down the information.

"So, what's the deal, Ann?" I asked. "Did he give you any idea what he wants? What do I need to bring?"

My boss paused for a moment, and I could practically see her pinching her left earlobe, the way she did when she was gearing up to tell me something I wasn't expecting. Finally she chuckled.

"It's a woman, actually. I don't know who referred her to us, but she knew the code. She said she would have everything you need." As a precaution, we used a code with our clients, so that any eavesdroppers would assume they were calling a restaurant. Dinner for two meant a fuck, cocktails meant a blow job, and a request for a large table meant you'd be servicing more than one customer. If they asked to special order something, it generally indicated some kind of fetish, so I'd pack my bag accordingly. The code was also a way to screen callers, and if anyone called and asked for sex in layman's terms, Ann would assume it was the LAPD and tell them indignantly that they had the wrong number.

"So what did she ask for?" I asked, leaning over to blow on my toes in hopes that the polish would dry faster.

"She said she wanted drinks, dinner, and dessert, and said money was no object. She requested the best table in the house. That's you, my dear."

"Oh Ann, you flatter me," I said, rolling my eyes, then hung up the phone to get ready.

Obviously, it hadn't been my life's ambition to go into the sex industry. Like so many other girls, I had taken off for Hollywood as soon as I graduated high school. I quickly learned that being the prettiest girl in my North Carolina class didn't amount to shit in L.A. and that my chances of being discovered as the next supermodel, actress, or whatever were about as good as the odds of finding a rent-controlled apartment. I had started waitressing at a reasonably upscale cafe, but as the money I had saved from graduation dwindled to nothing, I gradually sold out to make the rent.

At first I had taken a second job cocktail waitressing at a strip club, where I quickly realized that the agony of walking around in fishnets and stilettos and balancing trays of drinks wasn't worth it for the amount of money I was making. It was the dancers who made all the money in that place. So I had talked the manager into auditioning me on the pole, and the three years I had spent taking ballet lessons as a kid actually came in handy. So I started stripping, and I began bringing in enough cash to move into a slightly bigger studio, in a slightly safer neighborhood, with slightly fewer roaches.

I kind of enjoyed stripping. I had always been a flirt, and I knew I had a hot body, so I might as well be profiting from it, right? It was a kind of power trip for me, teasing these men, knowing that they would be thinking of me later while they got themselves off.

I had been dancing for about a year when I met Ann. It wasn't unusual for us to have female customers at the club, whether they came alone or with their boyfriends. Ann showed up one night near the end of my shift, and she watched me intently. She was wearing designer labels, so I paid her extra attention, and she stuck a twenty into my garter belt before she left. When she showed up again the next night, it was obvious that she had come back specifically to see me, so I went to her table and asked if she would like a lap dance. She smiled at me and said no, but that she would like me to join her for a drink, another fairly common request. I sat and talked to her for a while, and she finally revealed the real reason she had come to see me.

"You are very good at what you do, and I can tell that to some extent you enjoy it," she had said to me. "I can always tell the ones who get off on it."

I had shrugged; after all, she was right. She told me that if I was willing to perform more intimate services, I could easily make three times the amount of money I made stripping. The funny thing was, I wasn't even insulted, just speechless. In the end, I had given her my number and agreed to give it a try.

I was such an exhibitionist that I quickly became Ann's top girl, and I was bringing in so much money that I didn't even mind the commission Ann took for booking my clients. After all, she was keeping me safe, screening all the clients and making sure I never got hurt, and she was also smart enough to keep me from getting busted. I had regular clients, money invested in an IRA, and lived fairly luxuriously in exchange for sex. My parents thought I was the front desk manager at a hotel, and I certainly spent enough time in them to know the ins and outs in case they ever questioned me.

And yet as I knocked on the door of the woman's hotel room, I didn't really know what to expect. I had actually never had a female client before. Sure, sometimes couples would rent me out, but it was usually more for the purpose of two-on-one, with little or no contact between the woman and me. I figured this would make for a nice change, though. It had been a busy week, and my jaw was sore. This trick would probably be almost restful for me!

The woman who opened the door looked to be around thirty, with huge green eyes and short, dark hair. Her tank top showed off toned arms, and she eyed me suspiciously. I cleared my throat.

"I'm Maya," I said meaningfully. "Are you ready for dinner?" She looked me up and down and nodded, opening the door wider to let me pass. It was a pretty swanky hotel room, with a king-size bed. There were no personal articles that I could see, other than a shopping bag that sat on the table by the window. I smiled, recognizing the logo on the bag from the Pleasure Chest.

I waited expectantly to be told what to do. The woman seemed uncomfortable with my stare, strange considering she was the one in charge here. She seemed to realize that I was getting antsy, and she blushed a little. She pulled a small tray and a baggie out of the nightstand drawer, and started breaking up weed for a joint.

"I need to relax a little first," she said. "I don't usually have sex with strangers. Why don't you dance for me for a while, while I roll this?"

I knew that this particular hotel had all those satellite music channels on the TV, and I reached for the remote control. "What kind of music do you like?" I asked her. She gave me a smartass look that clearly said she didn't give a shit, so I chose some sensual, electronica-style stuff and got to work. I took off my dress and started swaying my hips to the music. She lit up the joint and settled back on the foot of the bed, watching me. I could see the appreciation in her eyes, and for good reason! I was wearing black lace and black stilettos. There was a mirror spanning the wall behind the headboard, so I could see my reflection behind her. Shiny red hair swept down to my shoulder blades. I kept it dyed this coppery shade, figuring L.A. already had too many blondes, and I had Brazilian waxes done frequently enough that none of my customers had any way of knowing I wasn't a natural redhead.

I peeled off my bra as I danced, cupping my breasts in my hands and squeezing them together. She offered me the joint and I took a long drag, exhaling as I handed it back to her. It was good shit, and I hoped no one in the neighboring rooms would smell it. I unhooked the thigh-high stockings from my garter belt, then turned around to give her an excellent view of my ass as I slid the garter and thong down my hips. I stepped out of them and left them on the floor, then turned back around, so that she could take in everything she was paying for.

Her eyes were heavy-lidded now, from the smoke and from lust as she gazed at me hungrily. She was definitely relaxed now.

"So," I asked huskily, "what is it you would like from me? You aren't paying all that money just to look."

Her jaw clenched for a moment, like whatever she was about to say was difficult for her. "I want from you what I can't ask my girlfriend for," she said finally. "I want you to top me." Seeing that this wasn't quite registering with me, she sighed and said, "It's a power thing, okay? I'm a top, always have been, and I can't bottom to my girl without swallowing a lot of pride. I'm not willing to do that. So I hired you. You will do what I tell you to do, and I'll get it out of my system. Got it?"

I was, until that day, blissfully ignorant of the top-and-bottom terminology, but I thought I understood what she was asking for. I knew all about power and pride, and I smiled, knowing I could strike the right balance to please her. She pulled off her tank top, revealing small firm breasts with lovely dark nipples. She stood to unbutton her pants and said, "Go get that bag off the table, and put on what's in it." The items in the bag turned out to be a black harness and a dildo that I estimated to be roughly ten inches long and three inches thick. I was accustomed to wearing all kinds of costumes in my line of work, but till now, none of them ever involved a gigantic rubber dick! It took me a few minutes to figure out how to put on the contraption properly, but I managed and returned to the bed, where she lay waiting. I found my reflection to be strangely erotic, the juxtaposition of the strap-on and my bald pussy underneath.

She was propped up against the pillows, with her legs straight out and barely parted. I stood there, feeling slightly ridiculous in my costume, and she said, "I didn't bring any lube. So you're going to have to eat me first." And she drew up her knees, spreading her thighs for me and displaying a neatly-trimmed cunt with a fat, pink clit. I had never gone down on a woman, and I wasn't about to ask her how to pleasure her. I knew what I liked, and I figured I would just let my instincts guide me.

My hair brushed her thighs as I lowered my head to her pussy. I had to stay crouched over the bed on my knees to keep the dildo from disemboweling me. I used my thumbs to separate her lips, and then belatedly thought about protection. I always had condoms with me, but that wasn't going to help me here. I knew I should ask her if she had saran wrap, or something, but I didn't quite know how to bring it up without killing the mood.

She sensed my hesitation, and looked at me wryly. "I promise you I'm clean. If you don't believe me, we can end this now, and I'll pay you for the dance." I knew better than to ever take a client's word for anything, and I knew that Ann would kill me if I caught something. But I could smell the juices emanating from her pussy, and they stirred a hunger in me that I didn't expect to feel for another woman. I had always liked my own scent, but I had attributed it to narcissism. I was surprised to realize I wanted to taste her, wanted to see what this was like. And even though I knew I was being stupid, I believed her.

I ran my tongue across her clit and she gave a jolt like I had touched her with a cattle prod. She tasted sweet and salty, and I lapped at her like a cat. She moaned and writhed, and I fought to keep at it, pinning her legs down with my arms. The ache in my jaw became more pronounced, but I didn't care—this was a matter of pride. I had a reputation for impeccable customer service to maintain, and I was determined to get it right on the first try. She was dripping now, soaking my face, and I could feel myself getting wet along with her. I pulled her clit into my mouth, sucking and nibbling on it, until she put a hand on my forehead to push me away. Gasping for breath, she said, "I want you to fuck me now."

I positioned myself between her legs and guided the head of the dick into her. I had figured that this would be a pretty mechanical act for me, since I would be fucking her with a piece of rubber and therefore wouldn't really feel anything. I hadn't counted on the pressure of the dildo on my already throbbing clit as I pushed inside of her. I also hadn't anticipated the thrill I felt as I watched her cunt stretch to accommodate what I was shoving into it. She gritted her teeth as I slid the dick all the way into her, grinding my hips so she could feel the soft leather of the harness against her sensitive clit. She looked up at me and I smiled, just a little, before pulling back out. I did so quickly, and the cock was so thick that her pussy made a *pop* sound, like it was a bottle of wine being uncorked.

For the first time in my life, I was not on the receiving end, and I was enjoying it more than I had ever expected to. Here was this woman who was so stone-minded she wouldn't let her own girlfriend fuck her, and she was totally in my power. Even though she was paying me, I felt like I *owned* her ass.

As I plunged into her again, I leaned down to bite her left nipple. When she yelped, I laughed. We found a good rhythm and she started lifting up to meet my thrusts, her eyes closed, grunting. I knew I was supposed to be following her orders, but I had the feeling I was in charge now, and decided to test the waters a little. I slowed down, and finally came to a halt with the dick still buried inside her. She opened her eyes and looked at me murderously, and I said sharply, "You said you wanted to be topped? Well, I'm going to fuck you so you won't forget it anytime soon." I pulled out of her and sat back on my heels. "Turn over," I ordered. She glared up at me, defiantly, and I smiled. This woman wasn't accustomed to taking orders in bed, but that was what she had hired me for, after all.

"If you want it," I teased maliciously, "you'll do what I tell you to do. Turn over, *now.*" Her angry eyes betrayed her, showed a flicker of appreciation and respect, and she rolled over. With her on her knees and elbows her ass pointed up to me like an offering, and I reached beneath her to tickle her clit with my fingernail, like I was strumming a guitar. She jerked, and I used my free hand to guide the head of the dick back inside of her. Then I grabbed her hips and pulled her down onto me, impaling her with a force that made her groan and lose her balance.

She put her hands flat on the bed, and pushed herself back so that she resembled a dog squatting on my lap. Her eyes met mine in the mirror, and she blushed at the image of herself at the mercy of a stranger. She looked away, but I grabbed her chin and jerked it back up to face her reflection.

"Don't look away," I whispered to her. "I want you to ride me like a good girl, and we are both gonna watch you get yourself off in the mirror." She bit down on her lower lip, but her eyes didn't stray from the mirror as she started to slide herself up and down in my lap. I could feel my own wetness seeping down my legs as her motions pressed the base of the dick against me, and I spread my legs just a bit further, relishing the pressure on my clit as she gained momentum.

I watched her in the mirror, her green eyes wild, her breasts bouncing, and a sheen of sweat glistening on her body. Her eyes were on me again, and I felt a rush at the thought of being the only one who got to see her like this, losing control with me the way she wouldn't let herself with her own girlfriend. She was panting as she got herself closer, closer...and then her entire body was shaking with spasms. She let out a bellow as she came, and I grabbed the base of the dick and moved it in a circular motion around my clit, until I was coming along with her, each of us staring at the other in the mirror.

She fell forward onto the bed, and I sprawled next to her. We were both quiet as our breathing returned to normal. I unstrapped the harness and set the contraption on the nightstand. My movements were clumsy—it was rare for me to get off with a client.

She rolled over and gave me a silly grin, embarrassed now that it was over. I smiled back at her, and forced myself to return to professional mode. Sitting up, I said, "Is there anything else I can do for you today?"

"Shit, no," she replied. "I think I'll need some time to recover from that." Still a little shaky at the knees, I got dressed. When I inspected the envelope of cash she handed me, I found almost double the going rate. I raised my eyebrows at her, and she said, "I'll call for you again. When I do, I'll expect you to be available." She nodded at the harness and dildo, still on the nightstand. "Take that with you, and bring it next time. And don't even think about using it on anyone else."

She had regained her veneer of control now, and I didn't say anything, merely smiled as I packed the goodies into my bag. I winked at her on the way out the door, and smiled through the entire cab ride home. I got out my cell phone to call Ann and let her know to put my newest client on the VIP list. When she answered, Ann said, "Hey, how's my top girl?" I chuckled at my title; Ann didn't know the half of it.

# AND THE STARS NEVER RISE

Missy Leach

Lee recognized the dented hood of her co-coworker's car and swerved into a spot directly in front of a fire hydrant to see what was going down. She jumped out of her pickup truck, bag in tow, and tried to look casual as she scanned for any meter maids. No parking enforcement was around, but she spotted the competition easily enough: her rival colleague, and five additional guys in various states of cleanliness from other firms. From behind a low wall circling a parking lot, her coworker was crouched uncomfortably near a pile of trash. Lee chuckled, remembering the shot she got last week of an angry woman bashing his hood in with the right half of a pair of Jimmy Choo heels. Yeah, Lee had photographic evidence of the perpetrator, but no way was she going to share it with that moron. She turned toward the restaurant, trying to spot the newest victim of his clumsy pestering.

Annabel sat at a small table on the porch at Urth, skimming the scant personals section of the *Weekly* and absentmindedly sipping a cup of black Manhattan Mudd. She touched up her lipstick, and then crossed one leg over the other, scratching under the pink bow on her left instep. It was cool in the shade, so she huddled in the late afternoon sun, trying to make her goose bumps go away. *What is wrong with me?* Annabel thought. Lost in contemplation, she jumped when the waiter brought her cheesecake out. She ate the strawberries off the top of the cheesecake and tried to dismiss the feeling that she was being watched.

"You're being hosed right now," said a low voice from the other side of her table.

Annabel dropped her paper in shock. Despite the oddness of the situation, Annabel looked at the person across from her the way she looked at any boy—shoes first. Satisfied with the pole climbers, she assessed Lee's hair. Short everywhere except for the top, a raffish mop looking like it was styled for a Smiths video.

"What did you say?"

"I said you're being hosed. They're taking your picture." At Annabel's confused expression, Lee threw a beauty pageant wave at her competition across the street. Without putting down his camera, Lee's coworker gave her a rude gesture and shouted something indecipherable.

Lee's smirk revealed a single dimple on her right cheek. "I suggest you head home before any of these assholes gets a close-up of you reading the Women Seeking Women ads."

Without thanking her, Annabel grabbed her purse and

jumped up, almost knocking her coffee over. She walked as quickly as she could to her car, trying to look like she wasn't running. She thought she heard clicking shutters behind her, but when she looked around, she didn't see anyone. Her hand shook as she jammed the button on her keychain to unlock her car door.

Annabel drove a block away and parked again, too upset to drive any farther. What the hell was going on? Should she call the cops? After a few minutes of listening to her radio, she calmed down considerably, and actually giggled to herself. What was she thinking? No one was there to photograph her. It was probably just some line that cute dyke used to pick up girls. Yeah, there were photographers, but of course there were, this was West Hollywood. There was probably someone famous sitting next to her at lunch. Damn it! Annabel could be so dense. Why didn't she flirt back instead of being skittish? She drove home in a considerably worse mood.

Lee sat on Annabel's front steps and rooted through her bag. What was taking that girl so long to get home? Lee carefully removed her borrowed white Canon telephoto lens and switched it with the kit lens that came with her camera. Maybe this exclusive would get her the cash to buy her own telephoto lens, possibly a cheaper Tamron.

Annabel's emotions clashed when she saw Lee sitting on her steps. Suddenly, she didn't want the thing she'd been pining for.

"Who are you?" Annabel hissed. "What the fuck are you doing here?"

Lee stood up. This wasn't going quite as easily as she had planned it.

"My name is Lee. I'm...well, I guess you could say I'm one of the paparazzi."

Annabel glared up at her and repeated her last question. "What the fuck are you doing here?"

Lee decided that for once honesty might be the best approach. "Listen, just let me get this exclusive, just one shot of you in your apartment, and I'll explain everything and I promise to never inconvenience you again."

Annabel pushed past Lee in shock. She wasn't exactly afraid of this cute butch in cuffed Levi's and boots, but she wasn't sure what she should do in this odd situation, either.

"Please," Lee asked quietly. She looked into Annabel's eyes and tried to appear as meek as possible.

"Fine, come in, no pictures unless I say, though. I just want to know what this is all about," Annabel said.

Lee picked up her bag, hung her camera around her neck, and followed Annabel into the apartment. She took a seat on the knockoff Eames sofa and looked around the small living room, trying to find an interesting backdrop.

"Stay there," Annabel warned her, and went into the kitchen and returned with two Anchor Steams. Lee was fidgeting intently with her camera. She looked surprised at the proffered beer, but then grinned and quaffed it.

"Now, what is going on? Are you a stalker or something?" Annabel asked, not believing it could be true.

"No. I told you. I take pictures of famous people," Lee replied.

"Ha. I'm not famous. So what's really going on?"

"Okay," Lee drew a deep breath. "You aren't famous. Yet. But you will be once the news comes out about your girlfriend. Your girlfriend is named Angel, right? Listen, you know that reality show she went away to do last month? You haven't heard from her yet, have you? Rumor is from some idiot camera guy that she's going to win it. And once that final episode airs, Angel is going to be famous. And so are you. Because the tabloids know all about you two. We know about the types of clubs you go to together and what goes on in those clubs, and since we got the tip, we've been following you. Because everyone in the world is going to want to know about Angel and her kinky lover."

Annabel's mouth opened and she inhaled sharply. This wasn't happening. It wasn't. She was being stalked every moment? They knew where she lived? She looked down at the cotton polka dot dress she was wearing. She looked at her chipped nail polish. She was being photographed? Wait. Back up. Angel was going to come back a millionaire?

Lee watched the emotions play on Annabel's face. Oh god, she really hadn't known, had she? Or else what was she doing sitting outside at Urth, looking so cute, putting on lipstick using the reflection in the lid of the saltshaker? Lee wanted to escape the situation she had created, but there was nowhere to go, and she didn't even have one picture. She took another gulp of beer.

"Bathroom?" she asked.

Dazed, Annabel pointed down the hall.

Lee crept into the bathroom and shut the door softly. She stood looking in the mirror, wondering what she should do next. Annabel's pink satin robe hung on the back of the door. She ran her finger gently down the sash, and contemplated what a lucky girl Angel was to have a girlfriend like Annabel. She leaned in close, and she could smell Annabel's perfume—something sweet, with lilies—on the robe. *What the hell am I doing?* Lee thought. *I need to get some shots and get out of here.* As quietly as possible, she unlatched the door to

Annabel's medicine cabinet and peered at the makeup and medicine bottles inside.

With no warning, the door crashed open, just as Lee was considering whether she was desperate enough to take a picture of an innocuous bottle of prescription cough syrup.

"What are you doing?" Annabel growled.

Lee let her camera fall around her neck, and a blush pinked the tops of her ears and her cheeks.

Annabel grabbed Lee by the shoulders and spun her around. In her heels, she was face-to-face with Lee. She pushed up against her like a drill sergeant and screamed in Lee's face.

"I heard you open my cabinet. I thought you came in here to use the bathroom! You filthy fucking maggot! You're going through my stuff like some sick pervert!"

Lee tried to back away in the tiny space, and stammered, "Wait, it isn't like that! I came to use the bathroom! I swear! I don't know what made me snoop!"

Annabel used all her force to shove Lee painfully against the wall. "Did you go yet? Did you? If that's what you came in here to do, you'd better do it." Pushing her full weight against Lee, her hands darted down and scrabbled at Lee's belt. The hateful camera pressed awkwardly into Annabel's stomach. She got past Lee's belt and yanked apart the button fly.

Annabel choked out a mocking laugh when she got to Lee's white Calvin Klein boy briefs. "If you're going to piss, then do it," she whispered against Lee's ear. Lee let out a strangled grunt when Annabel yanked down her Levi's and briefs and spun her around, pushing her down on the chilly white toilet seat. Annabel wasn't strong, but her fervor made up for it. Lee was paralyzed with shock, and didn't resist when Annabel yanked the camera from around her neck and thumbed it on.

"What, are you pee shy?" Annabel pointed the camera at Lee and snapped off a few frames in quick succession. "Mmm, very nice," she said as she got on her knees in front of Lee. Lee's blush raced down her neck and her lower lip trembled as Annabel snapped a few more pictures from the new angle. Seeing Lee's blush, Annabel's nipples tightened under her dress. Lee folded her arms across her lap, trying to hide from the camera.

Annabel looked up into Lee's eyes and said menacingly, "You'd better go now, baby, because you aren't going to get a chance later." Lee broke down in terror, not knowing what this deranged girl was going to do next, and let out a gush of shameful piss. A single tear escaped down her hot cheek. Annabel leapt up and gleefully snapped a shot of the tear, and hauled Lee off the toilet before she had a chance to grab any toilet paper.

Lee was off balance, and Annabel twisted Lee's arm up behind her back and steered her into the bedroom. Lee waddled in front of her, pants pooled disgracefully around her ankles. Lee stumbled as Annabel let go of her arm with a shove.

"Take off your pants and briefs. Leave the boots," Annabel commanded. Lee sat on the edge of the bed, and awkwardly pulled her pants over her boots. Her crying had stopped, but her shoulders were trembling and her eyelashes clumped together with tears. She wouldn't look up as Annabel took more pictures.

"Get off my bed," Annabel hissed. Lee slid off the low bed to the floor. "You're revolting. I don't want to look at you. Turn around."

The wool rug scratched Lee's knees as she turned her back to Annabel. Annabel kicked Lee's feet apart and knelt behind her. Lee could feel Annabel's warm breath on her nape. Annabel licked the short hairs on the back of Lee's neck, sending goose bumps up Lee's thighs.

"Do you think you know all about me, Lee? I know all about you, too. I can practically read your mind right now. I know all the nasty things that you want." Annabel pressed her stiff nipples against Lee's back and continued, "I should send you home now; I've got the pictures I want. But that would ruin your day. Because you like this, don't you? You and me, we like the same things, don't we?"

Annabel pushed Lee over at the waist, causing Lee to fall facedown on the bed, pinning her hands under her own body weight. With no warning, Annabel thrust her hand between Lee's legs. She rubbed her fingers harshly on the sides of Lee's clit. Lee was sticky and sodden, and Annabel laughed as Lee immediately arched her back and tried to open her legs more.

"Dirty, dirty, little boy," Annabel scolded. She leaned forward and jammed her fingers into Lee's mouth, and was rewarded with Lee greedily licking her own juices and piss off of Annabel's fingers.

Annabel snatched her hand away and stood up. She was ready to see just what Lee knew. She grabbed a wooden-handled hairbrush off of the vanity and struck Lee's upturned behind. Before Lee could even draw a breath, the hairbrush came down cruelly on her other cheek. Lee choked out a sob.

"Count out, you fucking maggot, don't you have any manners? I guess not, because you like to pry around in ladies' bathrooms, you nasty little panty-sniffer!"

Lee buried her head in the prickly down comforter. "Two, Ma'am," she mumbled. Annabel's cunt twitched at those words, and she faltered, her next hit hard enough to birth a bruise.

Trying to recover her poise, Annabel paused to snap a picture of the three distinct red ovals. The blow after the flash came unexpectedly, near the crease of Lee's right cheek, close to her thigh. Lee counted it loudly and stuck her ass higher into the air, anticipating the next crack of the hairbrush. Instead, Annabel turned the brush over and raked the boar-hair bristles over Lee's entire back. Lee yelped and tried to edge away. Annabel just grinned, and continued with solid wallops, scrapes from the bristles, and the occasional flash of the camera, until Lee began alternating between counting and begging, pressing her hips hard into the edge of the bed, trying to avoid the next strike.

"Please, oh please, Ma'am, I'm sorry, I'm sorry, I'm sorry," Lee sobbed, crying freely into the comforter. There was a large wet spot under her face, and another one where she was grinding her hips against the blanket.

"Now you're in my house, and you are going to feel just as vulnerable as you made me feel. Do you understand?" Annabel sneered. "Spread your ass open. I want to see everything."

Lee shuddered and reached back, her asscheeks blazing against her cool hands. Using both hands, she did what Annabel demanded, hiccupping into the blanket as she saw the staccato bursts of flash through her closed eyes. Annabel paused long enough to reach for something under her bed, and Lee was shocked by the cold glob of Probe that hit her between flashes. Lee made a mewling noise and spread wider. She heard the snap of a glove, and humped her clit against the bed as best as she could.

With one hand, Annabel took an off-balance macro shot of the gossamer hairs between Lee's cheeks, and used her other hand to push the tips of two fingers into Lee's asshole. Lee strained back against Annabel.

"Please," Lee murmured, and Annabel advanced past the second knuckles.

"Please, Ma'am," Lee gasped, and was rewarded with Annabel thrusting all the way in, stretching her ass wide. She held utterly still, hearing the camera auto-focus, and seeing the flash go off again behind her in the dimming light.

Annabel put the camera down and slowly twisted her fingers in Lee's ass. She used her other hand to lay sharp pinches along the bottom of Lee's flushed backside.

"I want to see you jack off. Now," Annabel said quietly.

Lee let go of her asscheek with one of her hands and reached in front to put her hand between her legs. She groaned as she used three fingers to rub arrhythmic circles on her clit hood. Lee began to shake, pushing back against Annabel's hand.

"You'd better ask, damn it," Annabel threatened.

"Please, please, please, Ma'am, please let me come," Lee sobbed.

"You're disgusting, but if you have to, go ahead," Annabel said, swiveling her fingers faster inside Lee. Lee's hips rotated in a tight circle and the prickling in her thighs grew, encompassing her stomach. When Annabel slammed a third finger in, Lee came, bellowing into the blanket. Her ass sucked in Annabel's fingers, clenching them over and over.

When Lee gave a final jerk and her hand stopped grinding against her clit, Annabel carefully pulled her fingers out and dumped the glove on the floor. She hopped on the bed, and pulled Lee up into her arms, pushing her disarrayed hair out of her eyes and kissing her for the first time, hard. Lee kissed her back ferociously, and ran her hands down the front of Annabel's dress.

"Oh, Lee, you've been such a good boy. But I still haven't forgiven you yet."

Lee nuzzled her face in Annabel's cleavage and looked up at her.

"Listen," said Lee, "I am so sorry. I don't know what I was thinking in the bathroom, I've never done anything like that. I was just curious, and I know it was awful, and I'm really, really sorry."

"Are you good at anything besides snooping?" Annabel asked, with an edge in her voice.

"Oh, yes, Ma'am," Lee smirked up at her, showing her single dimple to great advantage.

Annabel threaded her fingers through Lee's hair and yanked. "Don't be a smart-ass, just prove it," she snarled.

Lee slid down the bed and kissed both of the little bows on the tops of Annabel's frothy pink shoes before removing them. She delicately kissed each of Annabel's arches. When Lee looked up, Annabel's head was back in a sea of pillows, her eyes closed. She mouthed one of Annabel's pinky toes and then slid up her body, lifting the scalloped hem of Annabel's dress.

Annabel lifted her hips, and Lee obliged, pulling the drenched lace panties down and off. She reached up, pushing Annabel's dress straps down around her arms, exposing Annabel's full breasts to the chill of the darkened room. Annabel breathed deeply as Lee sucked first on her right nipple, and then the left. When Lee felt Annabel begin to wriggle, she responded by biting one of Annabel's nipples and twisting the other, eliciting a gasp. Moving beneath the dress bunched around Annabel's waist, she used her left hand to spread Annabel's lips wide and began to wash her clit with deliberate, flat strokes. Annabel's hips jerked in response, and her knees opened farther.

"More!" Annabel cried, combining a commandment with a plea. Lee pinched her fingers and thumb together, and started to push her right hand into Annabel. She persisted with steady, hard licks on Annabel's clit. Annabel continued her chant, squirming to bear down on Lee's hand.

Just as Lee thrust the largest part of her hand into Annabel, Annabel howled and her pussy began to spasm, crushing Lee's knuckles. Lee forcefully sucked Annabel's swollen clit into her mouth, and Annabel bucked against Lee's face, sending cascading juices over Lee's wrist.

Lee waited until Annabel stopped shaking to gently remove her hand, savoring the final internal tremors that Annabel involuntarily offered. She crawled on top of Annabel, impulsively covering her face in kisses, awed by Annabel's openness.

"I have to tell you something," Annabel whispered hoarsely. "Angel isn't my girlfriend. She's my best friend. We've known each other since we were eleven. So, could you call off your pack of wolves? Because I think I have room in my life for only one member of the paparazzi at a time."

Lee smiled into Annabel's neck. "Anything you want, Annabel. But can I still take pictures of you sometime? You know, just for my own private enjoyment?"

Annabel laughed, and gave Lee a hard pinch on her bruised backside.

# ANGIE'S DADDY

A. Lizbeth Babcock

I've never really had one. A Daddy, that is.
What I mean is, I've never had a real one, or one
that was really mine. But I have had the same
dream almost every night. It's about someone
else's Daddy. It's about Angie's Daddy.

In the dream, Angie's Daddy gives me what I
always want but never get. Angie's Daddy gives
me *me*, and makes everything okay just by saying that it is. He perverts and absolves me. He
adds to me and subtracts from me. He divides
me. And I hate the times in between when I
have to wait for him to come, and I have to try
to piece it all together myself. I hate those times
when I have to stand there, holding on to my
perversion like a bag of doggie doo, because no
one else knows what to do with it, or how to
make it good. And what I really want is to just

bring it all into focus, because what I really need is to see the whole picture.

When the dream is over, I feel this sense of renewal that fills me up and bottoms me out because I need him to renew me again and again, and it's never really enough and it's never really over, but it's still good and always worth it. Sometimes I wish the dream was my life and my life was the dream, and then I realize that the only thing that would change is what I believe to be real. And it's hard to figure out what to believe, and it's hard to figure out what's really real. Sometimes my thoughts get lost in the hardness of that.

Angie's Daddy is the kind of Daddy who gets what he wants because he takes it, and because he convinces you that you want to give it. And believe me, you do. Or at least I do, in the dream. But part of why I want to give it is because of Angie. It's because I want to be with her. And because I want to be in this experience with her. And because it's *her* Daddy. Sometimes I wake up with the whisper of her name on my lips, and then I feel the harsh impression of a hand around my face, correcting me, collecting me, like I'm a thousand marbles on the floor.

It's set in different places, the dream. Because what matters is where we're going, and not where we are or where we've been. And where we're going is to another world. Sometimes we take Angie's Daddy's rocket ship to the moon, and the man on the moon is our only spectator. Other times, it happens at the local fair.

This time, we're sitting on the couch in Angie's Daddy's living room. Angie and me are on either side of him. And we're giggly and cuddly, and soft like kittens. The television is on but there is no sound, because it doesn't really matter anyway. And sometimes when we're in the living room, people walk right by us like we're just playing board games, and sometimes we are. But sometimes there are too many games and I'm all played out because every game has rules, and sometimes the rules are red and they're written in blood. And rules aren't made to be broken, you know. You can't bend the rules.

Angie's Daddy is bigger than us, but then again Daddies often are. And there's something comforting about his bulk. I peer at Angie from around his thick chest. Angie is so beautiful. And I love her so, so much. In the dream, my love for her is overwhelming. Sometimes I try to tell her that I love her, but I can only mouth the words and she thinks I'm saying *elephant shoe*. And even in the dream, I sometimes question that it might all be a dream, and I try really hard to stay there, to stay sleeping, to get my beauty sleep, to be Sleeping Beauty, because there are special things for special girls and what I really want is to be kissed by her.

Something about being there feels important. Something about being there feels life changing. And despite the gravity attached to the experience, something about being there feels really comfortable, and really real. It's like coming home and being familiar. But there's this ache that goes with it. The kind of ache you feel when you just can't be with someone you want for whatever reason. And there's that need you have that you know is never going to be met. It's the same ache I feel when I walk around in real life. That terrible ache that I just can't shake because I can't take the dream back. And I'm afraid that if I talk about it out loud, words will fall from my mouth in red letters like rules that can't be changed. I feel that ache every day. And I wish Angie's Daddy could make *that* okay just by saying that it is.

The dream is sometimes like looking at puzzle pieces but

never seeing the full picture. And sometimes it's like tunnel vision, and there's no periphery and there's no context. Other times it's like looking through a kaleidoscope of images when I try to remember. And the light behind the images is so bright that I have to close my eyes because they're too bright, and they're shifting too fast. And sometimes the fastness of the shifting makes me feel dizzy, and the details get blurred and hazy, and it's like I'm looking at them through smoke.

But every time I catch Angie's eye, she smiles at me. And I reach my arm way across Angie's Daddy's chest and touch her with an affection I would normally reserve for sick or dying animals. And I have this feeling, this feeling that I need to tattoo her image on my memory because somehow this wonderful thing is going to be ripped away from me. And it's not because we're sick or dying. It's because of something else. So I try really hard to capture the details of her image...her fairy tale-long hair, her chocolate-drop eyes, and those big girlie lashes that sometimes tickle my cheek and neck. Only the details are isolated and abstract, like features cut from a picture that do not add up to a solid whole.

Still, I can't imagine her doing anything other than being right there in the dream. I can't imagine her looking any way other than how she looks when I'm dreaming of her. And I start to wonder how I look to her, but I remind myself that I need to put my energy into remembering. Only I don't know why I need to do that. So I ask the question right out loud in the dream. I ask, *Why do I have to work so hard to remember this?* Only there's no sound, and there's no answer. And I wonder if part of the reason is that they're trying so hard to forget. I wonder if some things are better left unsaid, even in the dream.

I feel Angie's Daddy's hand start to creep up my leg. His fingers are light like a spider at first, and they're tickly like Angie's lashes. I keep looking at her. And I have butterflies in my stomach, fluttering and flapping and determined to escape. If I open my mouth they will fly out in droves, all dotted and speckled and brilliant in color. And despite my apprehension, I feel really good all over. Angie's Daddy makes me feel good, but Angie makes me feel good, too. She's still smiling at me. And I feel my pussy start to get wet, like there's a sea inside of me. I feel a conflict too, but Angie's Daddy murmurs something encouraging in my ear. Something like, *It's okay. It's all happened before*. But it really doesn't matter what he says because what I want is to know that it's him, and not me, doing the encouraging. And I'm not sure why that's important, but I know that it is. It becomes important to me later, during those times in between the dream.

I want him to touch me there where it's wet, and I know that he will because it's all happened before. His fingers get heavier as they reach my thigh and crawl under my dress. He grabs handfuls of my skin and now my panties are wet, too. I'm amazed by how easily it happens and how wonderful it feels, this process of becoming saturated, this process of being taken by him. His hand finds its way around my hip, and it slides under my ass and under the edge of my panties. He easily lifts me with that one mighty hand and places me firmly on his lap, and I'm facing him. His hand is still on my ass and he's gripping me hard, gripping me like I might slip off of his hook and flop away. I lean into his chest and stay still for a moment, play dead for a moment. And in that brief moment of death, I feel that his breasts are bigger than mine. I experience the fullness of his breasts against me, and the firmness of his hand on my ass. I experience the sensation of Angie's fingers twisting and twirling in my hair as it hangs in her face. And I feel like I could fall asleep like this, and then I realize that I am sleeping.

I wait patiently as he moves Angie with the same technique and precision, like it was broken down step by step in some sort of instruction manual, like it's been repeated a thousand times before. Now she and I are side by side, straddling each of his massive legs. We are leaning into him because the angle of his legs forces us slightly forward. I feel Angie's warmth against me. Her warmth makes me feel even closer to her because she fills my senses, and she feels really real, even if it's just a dream. I want her to kiss me on the lips, and Angie's Daddy tells us it's okay to kiss. *It's okay.* And he says it with this authenticity, like it hasn't happened a thousand times before. *Show me,* he urges. And we do. It's like…waking up from a long sleep. It's like waking up and…

And I feel his fingers start to slide around my eager pussy, making me drip. He turns his whole hand to the side and glides it back and forth like he's sawing me in half. His slick fingers separate and reunite, and my compliant lips stretch and form around his changing shape. He grins at me like we're doing something right and like we're doing something wrong, only I sometimes find it hard to tell the difference between right and wrong, and right and left. His fingers push and poke at my tight openings, and swim recklessly around my swollen clit. He feels too big to fit inside of me, but I know that he will because it's all happened before. I let my mouth fall against his ear and my vision relaxes into his dusky hair, and it stays that way for a while. Everything's all out of focus.

I quietly gasp as his middle finger finds its way inside my cunt: partway in, halfway up. I writhe with it and against it, and my pussy opens up like a butterfly spreading its wings. I feel Angie's legs stirring against mine. And I feel the roughness of Angie's Daddy's scratchy face against my cheek and neck. Sometimes I look in the mirror to see if I can notice little scrapes from his stubble, but it turns out to be a fun house mirror and I can't see anything because my image is so distorted and I look so silly, and it's so hard to tell how old you are in one of those things.

I lean back, fighting the gravitational pull. I place one hand behind me on Angie's Daddy's knee, and one hand behind Angie on his other knee. His knees feel like basketballs in my hands. I hoist myself up and let his long meaty finger fill my cunt, completely. I ride it with a certain kind of deliberateness. I ride it like it's going to save me from a certain kind of elimination. And I let my breath entrust and commit to this experience. I breathe heavy breaths, in and out. And something about all of the breathing makes me feel mature.

I look at Angie's hair. It's draped along her back like a blanket. I carry that image with me as my eyes climb the wall and find a resting spot on the ceiling. I imagine being blanketed by her, hidden in the underworld of her hair. I imagine lots of things as Angie's Daddy gets me off. And I hear him grunt as he drives a second finger inside of me. When I look down, I see my creamy wetness glistening on his knuckles and collecting in his big palm. And it looks like gleaming glossy moondust. His eyes become fixed like he isn't really there, and his cock is hard beneath his pants. I feel a sweat building on my forehead as my pussy gushes and shakes inside his hand. I let myself collapse against his full chest, let myself feel little in the comfort of his bosom. And Angie rises, placing her hand on my shoulder, for balance. I can hear how wet her pussy is in his hand. He's got the whole world there; I can hear it. And I want to feel it, but instead I feel that ache. It's a sinking sort of feeling, a sinking shrinking feeling in the pit of my stomach. *That's right*, he assures, *you feel that?* And I want to look right at her, but there's this undercurrent of pretending that happens in the dream. And I think it's just part of the game we're all playing. I think it's like going to jail without passing go.

Sometimes Angie's Daddy gives one of us a task to do so that he can have private time with the other. These are the times when he undoes his zipper and pulls out his huge cock, first through the hole in his underwear and then through the center of his pants. This time he sends Angie to do something upstairs, only my fingers are entwined in hers and I have to untangle them one by one to let her go, and then she's gone. Angie's Daddy squeezes my face with one giant hand and pulls it close to his. His hot breath blasts me like an automatic dryer in a public bathroom. And my cheeks are hot and scrunched and blushing. I can't close my mouth because of the harshness of his grasp. And a teeny weenie marble spills out from the space between my lips, spills out and bounce-bounce-bounces its way down the hall and out through the keyhole of the front door—a piece of myself that will never come home. He stares me down until I soften and relent, my eyes plunging to the ground like little skydivers without parachutes. I could probably outstare him if I really wanted to, except I feel like I've gotten caught with my hand in the cookie jar and I'm not sure what the penalty is for that. But there aren't any cookies to be had here. There aren't any cookies, just Angie's Daddy's cock.

He spins me around so that I am facing outward and my feet are planted firmly on the floor. Only I don't like standing on the floor because I worry that something under the couch is going to reach out and grab my ankle, and that might make me scream. And my panties are around my knees but I don't know how they got that way. He says, *Special things for special girls*, and maybe that's all I need to know.

He reels me in by the material of my dress like a fisherman reeling in his catch, only he didn't need any bait, and he didn't need any worms. And when I'm close enough he wraps his hands around my waist. His hands reach almost the whole way around my center. He holds me tight, and I am not slippery and I will not flop away. I can feel the round head of his cock bulging and pressing against my needy little fuck-hole. I can feel his desire. And I can feel mine. I bend my knees up onto the surface of the couch, still looking out, and I rest them on both sides of his large thighs. I am spread wide open; my red slit parted in two. I lean forward, placing both hands on the cluttered coffee table, for balance. He tugs on my feet to hurry this process of positioning. Now my panties have completely disappeared and they never do come back.

He secures my hips and guides me toward him. I feel the fat bulb of his cock launching its way inside of me. And I am flooded with images; they roll over me like waves...Angie's tickly lashes, her hand on my shoulder, the kiss, our tangled fingers, and Angie's Daddy's rock-hard cock...his rock-hard cock splitting me open and filling me full. His cock is deep inside of me now, and it feels like real rubber. It feels like a ride at the local fair and I'm going to stand in line to do it again. I catch my image in the television between the commercials when the screen goes black, and I watch my hair bounce back and forth against my shoulders. I watch my tits jiggle underneath the thin fabric of my dress. It's the only clear image I have of myself in the whole dream. And even though Angie's

Daddy makes me feel like a little girl, the reflection I see is that of a woman getting fucked. And the proof is on TV just like the proof is in the pudding. Sometimes I see that image when I'm not even dreaming. I see it in those brief seconds when my television screen goes black. And Angie's Daddy's white shirt and big head make him look like a spaceman floating around in the background.

His thrusts become faster and deeper and the coffee table starts to slide forward as he pushes me harder and harder. If he doesn't do something soon, I will fall right on the floor, right between the couch and the coffee table. My arms start stretching out really far so that the tips of my fingers can still reach the edge of the surface. My body starts stretching too, and I feel like that image of myself in the fun house mirror—all drawn out and contorted. The edge slips away from me and I have no choice but to let myself go, to let myself fall. I land with my head right between his feet, and I can see clear under the couch. And what I see among the dust balls are puzzle pieces. Only I couldn't reach them even if I tried. And nothing's reaching out for me, and there's nothing to scream about.

Angie's Daddy shoots his load like the blast of a rifle, right down the center of my ass. The thick lather drips down along my narrow crack, glazing my pussy like a doughnut. He forces my arm behind my back and makes me smear his come all over my skin, hand over hand. And it feels like real lotion.

There's a clunking noise as Angie makes her way back down the stairs. And it sounds like she's wearing high heels, only they're too big for her. I stand on wobbly legs even though I'm not wearing high heels, and Angie's Daddy zips up his pants and clears his throat like there's soot stuck inside. *C'mon girls*, he says with a contrived authority. And the three of us maneuver our way back into our original positions on the couch. I feel that sense of renewal, and I don't want it to bottom out. I revel in the feeling of having a Daddy, even though it's Angie's Daddy. I revel in the feeling of being the apple of his eye, and the apple is clean and pure and there are no worms. I am full with my love for Angie. And it feels really real, even if it's just a dream.

But sometimes, I want to send Angie's Daddy upstairs. Sometimes I want to press a button and make him mute. Press a button and turn him off. And I want for me and Angie to be together without him. I want to play a new game with new rules. And the new game doesn't have any room for silly Daddies, silly rabbits. Sometimes I try to change the dream, but I know that it won't change because it's never happened before. And I wonder if a new game would just be too much for everyone. I wonder if it would make the world explode.

Angie's Daddy lights a cigarette and slowly fills the room with a thick gray haze. And he's there like a big boulder that I can't move, like a big boulder that crashes into me from time to time. I peek around that vast chest of his and look at Angie. I lean into him, stretching my elastic arm across his body to hold her hand. I try to tell her that I love her. *Elephant shoe! Elephant shoe!* And Angie's Daddy gazes vacantly at the hushed images on the screen. I keep looking at Angie. Every few seconds that bright light is flashing against her, affecting and disrupting her appearance. Eventually, the smoke will blur her features entirely, and it will be like looking through a hazy, shifting cloud. *Remember this*, I say to myself. *You have to try really hard to remember.*

# DOMME'S GAMES

Rachel Kramer Bussel

When Dana told me she was a dominatrix, I almost spit out my rum and Coke. We were on a first date at a classy French restaurant, both of us dressed in elegant outfits; she had on a sheer white blouse, black velvet pants and heels while I wore a low-cut white shirt, deep purple silk skirt, and killer heels. We'd been set up by my friend Eliza, who figured that femmes looking for other femmes were so rare, we'd surely hit it off, but Eliza had told me Dana was a trainer at a local high-end gym.

"Well, I am a trainer, in addition to being a domme, and the two jobs are kind of similar; I get to yell at people and watch them squirm. It's a total power trip, and I get off on both of them. But my real passion is women; with the guys, it's like a warm-up," she said, her almost black eyes glinting. She was gorgeous but had a danger-ous vibe, not like she might hurt me, but like she knew things about me and could see inside me in ways even my longtime friends couldn't. It didn't seem like an act, either, the way she shone her gaze on me so intently, like we were the only two people in the whole city, let alone the whole restaurant. I felt my face flush and my body twitch slightly as I waited for her to continue. Her hand reached for me under the table, strok-ing my bare knee beneath my skirt. The delicious warmth of her fingers traveled up my leg. She massaged just my knee, but with such intensity I could barely breathe. "Do you like to be dominated, Julie?"

"I don't know," I answered, only semihonestly. Nobody had ever actually so much as laid a hand on me or spoken in a harsh voice in bed...except in my head. In my head, I'd been naked in a room full of powerful women, crawling around as ordered, bending over so they could spank me and spread my asscheeks and order me to do all kinds of depraved acts that made me blush there at the table just thinking about them. In my head, I'd taken a fist in my cunt and a butt plug in my ass, all at the same time. In my head, I'd been shared by two women, tossed between them like a rag doll, "made" to have orgasm after or-gasm while clamps set off heat waves in my nipples. But fantasy and reality were very different creatures. They were about to meet, and I wasn't totally sure how I felt about that.

Dana's grip tightened, then she pinched my inner thigh be-fore replacing her fingers with the sole of her foot. She'd slipped it out of the heel and it was flush against my pussy, with none of our fellow diners any the wiser. "Really? You have no idea how you'd feel about being stripped down, tied up, and told exactly what you could and couldn't do?" She smiled at me, a victorious grin, her lushly painted lips curling up at the sides. "Open your mouth," she said, the sensual tone gone in favor of a clipped, brisk command, made even more imperious by her faintly British accent. She'd been living in the States since she was a teenager, and had actually lived in more of them than I had, both of us winding up in New York in the last year or so. My lips parted slightly, just enough to make me feel my breath slowly seeping out…and allow her fingers to slip inside.

Her nails were short, polished to a gleaming bright red that had glinted throughout the restaurant, teasing me with its brightness, and I felt their shiny surface against my tongue as she turned her fingers this way and that. She curled them against my teeth, claiming me in the process. My nipples hardened as I felt her possess me, fantasy giving way to an even hotter reality than I could ever have conjured. I gave myself over to her in those moments as my tongue melted against her. I wanted to do anything she wanted me to; pleasing her was suddenly all that mattered.

"For the rest of the night, you're not going to talk unless I tell you to. You will follow my orders and you will not protest. I'm going to show you what a real dirty girl you are and you're going to love it, I can just tell," Dana said as she pulled her wet fingers from my mouth. I missed them the moment they were gone, but they soon found their way to my lips, toying with the fat bottom one as I wet my panties with pussy juice. I had no sooner thought about the state of my underwear than Dana said, "Give me your panties, Julie." She sensed the words about to come out of my mouth. "No, not in the bathroom, right here, and hurry up about it." Before I could stop to think or worry or look around, I was discreetly slipping my hands down below and pulling them off, trying to pass them off to her under the table.

"No," she said, her voice short, clipped, and efficient. "Roll them into a ball and pass them to me across the table, like you were giving me your napkin." My cheeks were flaming and I started to wonder if this was a very good idea. It was fun, and totally hot, but what if we somehow got caught? I'd be mortified if anyone else at the restaurant knew that I had instantly become Dana's slave, that I would've practically walked around the restaurant naked if she told me to. I attempted to ball the black lace into my palm and pass it off to her between our plates. As our fingers met, though, she made sure that my delicate underwear shook loose from our grasp. The black lace was gone in an instant but I grabbed my water glass and drained it in a futile attempt to quell my beating heart and flushed face. I couldn't bear to look around and see if anyone had caught on.

I looked down at my plate, knowing I'd never be able to finish what was on it. I wasn't queasy, but I craved something more than food. I looked up at her, expecting us to exit quickly, so she could continue to order me around. Would she make me bend over and get spanked? Wear certain kinds of embarrassing clothes? Order me to masturbate? My mind swirled with naughty possibilities, but Dana managed to flip me around without us ever leaving the table. "Eat up, Julie. You won't get any dessert if you don't finish your dinner...and I know you want your dessert. It's your favorite," she said, transforming into Mean Mommy before my eyes. Her tone was gentle but had an undercurrent of force, like if I didn't do as she said she'd walk up behind me and shove my face into the plate—and make me like it. I still wasn't hungry, but with a shaky hand I picked up my fork. Each bite, no matter what was on the end of the tines, tasted like sex. That's the only way I can describe it; the food melted on my tongue and seemed to plunge me into another world.

I ate each bite while staring back at her, my cheeks red, my pussy getting wetter and wetter. "Very good," she said, leaning across the table to pat my head. The gesture was so completely condescending, clearly designed to put me in my place even though we were the same age, that just as I was about to get indignant, I realized that I was still soaking wet—I wasn't sure I'd be able to stand up without it being obvious. Dana must have sensed something was amiss because she smiled at me sweetly. "Julie, would you be a dear and get up and go ask the waiter for some decaf?"

I was amazed at how her requests and commands, though seemingly nonsexual in nature, were making me feel like I was going to come right then and there, like she had some invisible pointer aimed at my pussy and was ready to shove it inside me. I could feel my skirt sticking to my body, but hoped my arousal wasn't too visible. I was trembling when I found the waiter, feebly tapping him on the shoulder then haltingly getting out my request. In less than an hour, Dana had transformed me from my usual assured self to a simpering nitwit, but I didn't mind. I wanted to see what was going to happen next.

"Thank you, Julie. You follow orders very well," she said, giving me an appraising look. "What if I ordered you to get down on the ground next to me and put your head in my lap? Would you do it?" she asked, staring at me intently.

I stared back at her, wondering for a moment what I'd gotten myself into. Could I really do it? Should I? I had no one to ask, no help lines to call, but I followed the source of all my biggest dating decisions: my pussy. It was telling me to do it, diners be damned, so I slid gracefully to the floor and rested my head against her silken thigh, doing my best to arrange my skirt around me so not too much skin showed. She sipped her coffee and gazed down at me, a now-wicked grin gleaming from her face as she entwined her fingers in my long, sleek brown hair and gave short, subtle tugs. I gasped, then shut my mouth, not wanting to call even more attention to us.

Dana calmly finished her coffee, then loudly flagged down the waiter, calling out and even snapping her fingers. The spectacle unnerved and aroused me simultaneously. I could tell that people were starting to wonder what was going on, but Dana calmly kept her grip on my hair, sending sparks of arousal straight down to my cunt. When the waiter walked away, she leaned down, her lips brushing my ear, and said, "Are you ready for me to fuck you yet, Julie?" Then she tugged hard on my hair, making me gasp loudly. She let go immediately, and I stared up at her in awe. "What are you waiting for? Get up, we're leaving!" she barked, her tone morphing from seductive to stern in seconds, her voice certainly loud enough for others to hear.

I popped up, grabbed my coat, and was ready to go. By then, my skirt was really glued to my cunt, which was sticky with need. Dana pushed me ahead of her as she steered me toward her car. "We'll leave yours here," she said, and by then, there was no arguing with her. I'd do whatever it took to get her to fuck me. As it turned out, that didn't technically happen, but I'm getting ahead of myself.

She drove, keeping one hand on the wheel and one hand on me the whole time. I was so turned on I was tempted to fidget, but I made myself sit still. She made conversation even as her fingers crept up my leg, but when I tried to clamp them together and trap her hand next to my pussy, she immediately pulled it away, making a tsking noise.

"If you try to get me to touch you, I won't. Wait your turn, little girl," she said. And it was those two words—"little girl"—that really set me off. I waited, seething not with anger but with pure, raw lust. We got to her place but she didn't let me out of the car. "I think I want you right here," she said, her voice trailing off as she seemed to get a vision of what she wanted. "Strip!"

This was something else entirely. Her street was fairly deserted but still. "I don't think I can," I said, my voice trembling not with fear but with the underlying knowledge that I was really getting off on her orders.

She reached between my legs and fondled my wet pussy, pressing the already-damp fabric of my skirt against my sex. "Oh, really? It seems like maybe you protest too much, my dear." I knew she was right even as I shuddered half in horror, half in pleasure. But still, I began to remove my few items of clothing, taking my shoes off, then lifting the shirt over my head and wriggling out of my skirt, while heat suffused my cheeks. I pretended I really had no choice, even though I already knew Dana well enough to know that she'd respect my wishes should I politely request we go inside. I also knew I could "blame" her if anything went awry.

I settled down wearing just my bra, having already given her my panties, then turned to Dana expectantly, but she looked like I'd bundled up instead of stripping down. She cleared her throat, the noise loud in the confines of the car. "The rest..." she demanded impatiently, and I squirmed as I unhooked my bra, letting my large breasts with their hardened nipples fall forward to face her.

"Now I want you to come for me," she said, her voice gentle and seductive. "And I'm even going to help you." With that, she reached into the glove compartment and pulled out a pocket rocket vibrator. By then, I was too far gone to protest against anything she wanted me to try; I'd have pressed my breasts up against the windows for passersby to ogle, I was *that* horny. This request was more intimate, though and more arousing. Performing for Dana's eyes alone gave a new nuance to my exhibitionism. Instead of worrying what anyone else thought about what I was doing, I simply wanted to please her with my pussy. I turned on the vibe, which had a much lower intensity than what I was used to, but I was so turned on, it didn't matter. I sank back against the window as best I could, spreading my legs so she could see exactly how aroused she'd made me, then went to town. Whenever I had the urge to close my eyes, I reminded myself that not only was I displaying myself for her, but I could watch Dana as well, soaking up the pleasure of her eyes taking in my wanton state. Soon I was soaking her car seat as I shoved three fingers into my pussy while the vibe hummed against my clit, my hips rocking back and forth.

I let the shudders subside as I turned off the toy and looked up at her, suddenly embarrassed. We barely knew each other and she'd managed to strip me, in more ways than one, removing any armor I might have been wearing to reveal the girl who just wanted to be told what to do. "Come here," she said, pulling my head into her lap and stroking my hair. I was naked, but I wasn't cold or embarrassed with her arm around me, holding me in her embrace. She stroked my head, her fingers darting along my scalp until I felt that heat inside me begin to rise once again. Whereas normally I'd have been quick to let my lover know that I was ready to go again, this time I just nestled deeper into Dana's lap. She'd let me know when it was time for sex, and I had no doubt it would be explosive when she did.

# THE 231ST ANDERSON VAMPIRE FAMILY REUNION IS A THRALL-FREE ZONE

Alicia E. Goranson

The blood juices from the family tables were absolutely electrifying. I mean, the stuff at the guest tables was decent, but Poobah sneaked me a glass and I almost died again in her arms. I knew the reunion was going to be so boring I came close to bringing my own coffin, but Poobah insisted the blood would be worth it. And by god, she was right. The stuff burned my mouth with pricks and tingles and didn't stop as it ran down my throat and pooled around in my pussy. It drizzled me in this pleasure softness and I could barely stand in my heels. I licked my glass because it was so good to put my tongue against something. Poobah was sparkling at me. I looked up at her and I pressed my tongue on hers. Her mouth was thick with juice and her lips pumped with the stuff. I scraped the insides of her cheeks for every drop I could and she stole it right back. I was going to drag her into any room, even the linen closet, if it meant I could taste what the juice must had done to her cunt.

Which was when her mother interrupted us; her living mother, from when she was alive. Guilt goes beyond the grave, and when her mom asked to be invited, Poobah didn't say no, like I said she should have.

"Oh, there you are," her mom said, in a rayon cocktail dress that would have blinded Wayne Newton. "You gave me a heart attack, as late as you were. I thought something had happened to you on the freeway and you were too proud to call. Look at you. I thought that by not eating, you would have lost a few pounds. Shows what I know. Come give your poor mother a hug."

Poobah wrenched my hands still when she noticed I was about to spill the rest of my drink on her mom. I said goodbye and went off to socialize for the many hours it would take before her mom let her free.

The few drops left in the glass weren't enough for me. I wanted more.

The reunion was held at an old Connecticut manor with so many additions, it had swelled to the size of a Kennebunkport enclave. My problem was, the blood juice was on a table, the table was behind the velvet rope, and the rope was behind a pack of bored tuxedoed thugs who knew I wasn't family.

My chance came when one of the bartenders left her station with her coat slung over her shoulder. She was a buxom Italian beauty with coarse black hair and a compact living body like a plum hanging from a branch. I said "Excuse me," and she spun around.

"Sorry, I'm off duty," she said.

We're not supposed to turn on our thrall at these sorts of functions, but really, who cares?

I gazed into the corners of the bartender's soul. It was gold with a touch of green, like a mint julep. I said, "You made the best blood juice I've ever had. If it wouldn't be awkward, could I ask for the recipe?"

She burst out laughing. I blinked.

"It's just a honey fruit daiquiri with three ounces of blood, stirred," she said. "The way you guys act about it, it might as well be the second coming."

I had a very nasty idea. "Are you doing anything now?" I said. "Could you show me how to make it?"

"Well, I'm kind in the mood to crash."

I swept behind her, dug my fingers into her shoulders and squeezed two knots in her back until they popped. She gasped and slumped forward. "I'm a trained shiatsu masseuse," I said. "And you are so wound up, you could snap any minute."

Her head rolled back as I stroked the tender muscles under her flesh. Her neck's pulsing slowed. "On second thought," she said, "I could make an exception for this."

I gave her my room number and a little money for the ingredients. "I'll take care of finding the blood," I said. She didn't ask any questions.

I couldn't be seen with her but I was afraid my thrall would wear off before she made it to our guest quarters. I tried to make it more erotic by taking down the paintings of Poobah's dead relatives, and throwing a sheet over the rolltop desk. I hid the washbasin under the bed and counted seconds on my cell phone. My legs danced the waiting-for-sex tango on the bed, floor, bathroom, and back on the bed.

She knocked and shook the two bottles at me when I let her in. "Oh, you got the old servants' quarters," she said. "They must really like you."

"Eh, my girlfriend dragged me here," I said. "She's out with her own date right now."

The bartender put her bottles on the sheet and began to un-button her top. "That's fortunate for you. Do I get to know your name?"

I sat on the bed and smoothed out the covers beside me. "Do you want to know it?"

"Maybe. I can throw some business your way. If you're good."

I stretched out my legs and rolled down each stocking. "I'm Grackle. And who is the lovely lady who's about to have her world rocked?"

She turned her back to me as she slid her top off and plucked her bra free. Her plump skin had a few claw marks healing over. "I'm Philistine. Or if that's too long, you can call me Phil."

I lifted my dress over my head. "Well, Phil, why don't you take those pants off so I can work you over properly?"

I wish live people could smell pussy the way I can. I myself never wear any underwear at gatherings like this; she slipped her thumbs around the edges of her thong, and her musk bowled me over. If I could pant, I would have. If there's one thing I can say for living people, they're so liquid on their own.

She lay chest down on the pillows I had prepared, and I mounted her thighs. I oiled up my fingers with peppermint and began massaging the muscles from her neck down to her scapula. Her hips rose with every breath and I followed her pulse down each arm to her fingers. Her poor neglected back called to me and I worked it down to her succulent butt. I had to slide off and massage her calves before I started jonesing to stick my teeth in her. I could smell my own juice mixed in with the peppermint while I loosened her legs. She was a rock when I found her but near the end of our session, I had churned her into creamery butter.

She lay quivering with a small puddle between her legs that I had to bite my tongue to keep from tasting.

"Do you ever wonder what us vamps see in that drink?" I said.

"It's a biological reaction to nutrients your bodies lack," she said. "Like sugar for me."

She groaned as I pressed into the cove with her foot. "I mean," I said, "do you want to taste it the way we do?"

"Without the dying?"

"Without the dying. Though it may be hell on your roots."

I rolled her on her back while she drew slow breaths and gazed through space to me. She lifted her arms to examine how weightless they had become, and ran them down her olive chest. She stroked her palms with the tip of a hardened nipple and understood that, with the tension gone, her body was finally awake and wanting touch. I kissed her and she pulled me close to keep herself from floating away.

I pressed the shower cap into her fingers. I whispered, "Put this on, tight."

Her hair had been spread as streaks converging on her head. I missed it when she sat up and shook it in a twist, tucking it under the floral print. I lifted the basin behind her and took her in my arms while I laid her into it. I licked the salt from her shoulder and reached for the bottles she had brought. "How much of each?" I said.

"Nine, six, three," she said. "Juice, daiquiri, blood."

I found a glass candleholder and measured out the proportions into the basin. I poured the juice and daiquiri close to her ear, so she could hear the liquid spill and settle around her head.

I leaned in close, stroking her neck to her nipple and back again. I spread myself on her, pushing my pussy into her thigh, and held her arms against the sheets. I spread my mouth over her lips and swallowed her cry. I whispered, "You always knew you'd be providing the red stuff, didn't you?"

She nodded. I traced her shoulders for the best path for her to bleed, without getting any on her face. Her body quivered as I held it still and licked the flesh over her breasts clean. She was delicious. She was trying to tense up but couldn't, like water running through gauze, unable to find a place to soak. She was her own river and try as she might, she couldn't thrash within herself. She was at peace against her will. Her nervousness and doubt were nothing but sweat and rush and she breathed faster, holding on to her body through her lungs.

Then I bit her. Her entire body bled through, as if I was swept in the best damned hangover she ever had. We flew into each other while the red drops trickled over her, into the basin. Her jaw swung and she clicked her teeth together. A cut in one spot hurts, but when the pain is spread out everywhere, it's so wonderfully intense.

I slipped a finger into her pussy lips and she swayed her head back and forth in response. I followed her thoughts. She was straining to make sense of where the pleasure was coming from, in the midst of her rush. I followed the trail inside her to confuse her more. Her hips began to remember they could move. Her neck began to thrash. She mixed her own blood into the liquid around her head. I pinched her nipple to slow her down. I slid another finger inside her to speed her up.

My tasty Cuisinart and I ran the edge of our explosion as long as we could take it. I licked her wound to seal it shut and my tongue burst into pleasure flame. I couldn't stop licking up her chin around the underside of her breast and the inside of her elbow. She squeezed at my fingers inside her and I knew she was almost done. "Do you want it?" I said.

"Yes," she squeaked.

I pumped my hand into her pussy, but the fingers spread over her clit. I dipped my mouth in the bowl as her body arched up and she gripped my arms. The blood juice was sweet as liquid orgasm and I drained half of it in a single gulp. I swallowed most and dribbled the rest into her lips. She lapped it up hungrily, and her head rose up demanding more. She traded blood juice with me while our tongues locked together until our mouths were clean. I lifted the basin over our heads and poured the rest over our bodies. She went to clean it from my neck, while I caught puddles of it from her belly in my cupped palms and drank all I could. She pushed me down to have at me, but I couldn't stay there for long before I forced her over to lick her. We fought over and over until our tongues went down each other's cunts, and locked together as magnets. Her musk added a fourth ingredient to the blood juice, surpassing anything I had tasted before and I could not have my fill. I'm not ashamed to say that I climaxed from drinking her.

We were ravenous little beasties and it didn't take long before all the juice was gone.

"You're right," she moaned. "This stuff is damned good."

I searched the sheets for a drop of juice, but we had soaked them enough to drown any taste left.

We lay together until the buzz wore off. She had to go home and I had to rescue Poobah. We separated out our clothes from the pile and pulled them on.

"Thanks for showing me the drink," she said. "If any of my friends ever end up in your neck of the woods, I'll tell them to look you up."

"No problem," I said. "Thanks for being the drink. If I can send any of my friends your way, let me know."

We locked the room and I kissed her on our way to the lobby. Her hair was well-sexed but she wasn't the only one. We traded email addresses before we split up.

I found Poobah still listening to her mother in the ballroom, and I bent over between them. "Excuse me," I said, and put my arm around Poobah's shoulder. "I have to go fuck your daughter now. I'm sorry, it's not personal."

Her mom's mouth fell open and for once, nothing came out.

Poobah shrugged. "Bye, Mom. See you next year," she said, and hurried back to our room with me. She sniffed my fingers.

"You always have more fun at these events," she said. "I don't know why I bring you."

# A NEW YORK STORY

D. L. King

Elaine had been living in the top floor of the
brownstone on Washington Square North for,
well, for a long time. She moved into the floor-
through her freshman year at New York University and just stayed.

The brownstone was old, probably from
the mid-nineteenth century, and the landlady
warned her that it had a reputation for being
haunted but Elaine fell in love with its charm
and felt a ghost would only add to the ambi-
ence. Besides, she'd never seen a ghost before
and didn't really believe in them anyway.

Her inheritance from a dead aunt left her
quite well off and able to easily afford the rent.
She'd fallen in love with The Village and its bo-
hemian atmosphere. It felt like the home she'd
always wanted to have, was meant to have.

Everything was so free. People could be whoever they wanted to be in this comfortable, insulated existence. Artists set up their easels on the street and painted. Poets and philosophers stood in Washington Square Park and proclaimed their manifestos to the world. Lovers wandered hand and hand through the park, as well as on the streets, heedless of the outside world.

Elaine was too busy, while in school, for any affairs of the heart; at least that's what she told herself. Instead, she carried on love affairs with the likes of Mata Hari, the beautiful temptress, and the dashing Amelia Earhart.

She knew from an early age that she wasn't interested in men. But a woman—one with a mix of intelligence, power, and a beautiful, ethereal grace, could cause her heart to quicken and take her breath away. It was better not to think of such things. She knew others were able to carry on relationships like that, but she would never be able to, certainly not in public. If her mother ever found out...well, she'd never approve. After all, it was against nature, wasn't it?

The '70s were a much more sexually open decade, following in the footsteps of the "free love" of the '60s, but still it wasn't for old-fashioned Elaine. Although every time she saw two women sitting close together or holding hands in the park...oh, but she just couldn't bring herself to be like them. And anyway, she really didn't need anyone else. She was fine on her own.

When she studied though, she often found herself daydreaming about her favorite women from history. Amelia would offer to take her upstairs for a quick hop. Once up and away from everyone and everything, she would slide her hand under Elaine's skirt and caress her knee. She'd move her hand up to Elaine's thigh, then very slowly bring it between her legs.

Elaine would sigh and spread her legs wider as Amelia felt the damp underwear covering her pussy. Amelia's middle finger would press against the white cotton, pushing it into her widening slit, occasionally taking her eyes away from the sky to glance at Elaine and smile. As Elaine's legs parted, Amelia used the tip of her finger to stroke back and forth, pushing the fabric even farther up into her opening.

"Do you want to feel me inside of you, sweet girl?" Amelia would ask.

"Oh yes, oh god yes!" she'd say as Amelia, eyes watching the sky and one hand on the yoke, would push the crotch of her panties aside and insert first one finger and then a second into Elaine's pussy.

Elaine's eyes closed as she felt the fingers pump in and out of her sopping opening, thumb playing against her clit. As the fingers sped up Elaine became lost to the ecstasy of feeling, and finally with a deep moan she came, opening her eyes to her books scattered across the bed and her hand inside her still convulsing sex.

Sybil watched from the foot of the bed with the intensity and yearning of the starved. Why couldn't this girl feel her? Others had felt her presence. She had managed to make a few run screaming from the house, and return only in daylight, to retrieve their belongings and move out. She wasn't really trying to get rid of the tenants; although it had been fun to watch the men dash out of the room, scared out of their wits. Heaven knows if she could have worked that particular trick on her husband, when she'd been alive, she would have!

No such luck. She had had to suffer through years of his unwanted advances, as well as four pregnancies. She really wasn't cut out to be a wife and mother but what else was there for a lady of her position? But she loved this house that he'd built for her—loved it so much that when her time came, she hadn't wanted to leave. Interestingly enough, that was all it took: not wanting to leave.

How happy she was to realize that she could interact with the living, or at least some of the living. Yes, she was enjoying her afterlife much more than her life. Now, she could do as she pleased and take pleasure as she pleased. If only this pretty little Elaine girl could feel her.

Others were able to feel her, if they were sensitive enough. She had watched the bodies of several women through the years react to her touch. She loved playing with them while they slept. As a spirit, she could reach inside their clothes to caress them, and she so loved watching their bodies react to her touch. She took pleasure in opening their nightclothes, as they slept, to gaze upon their bodies. She watched their nipples get erect as she ran her hands over their breasts.

Initially, it had been difficult for her to do more than cause a sensation of cold, but after long years of experimentation and concentration, she could make them feel pressure when she cupped their breasts and even delicious pain when she pinched their nipples. And, in turn, she was able to truly feel the bodies of those she caressed. She could cup and hold and pinch. She could even taste and smell.

Right before this new girl moved in, another young university student had lived in the apartment and reveled in Sybil's touch. This had been the first time, to Sybil's knowledge, a tenant had known of her presence and welcomed it. Every night, this young woman would invite her, not only by her actions but verbally, into her bed.

"Hello," she would call, tentatively. "Hello spirit. I'm here. I'm ready for you. Please come to me."

She lay on the bed, nude and completely open with her arms and legs spread, waiting for the caress of Sybil's mouth and hands. Her body was so responsive. Sybil felt such power, watching the girl's nipples crinkle and harden as she passed her hands over them. Listening to her moan as Sybil rolled them between her cold white fingers. Watching as goose bumps formed everywhere her hands went.

Sybil gloried in the continuous weeping of the girl's pussy until she could watch no longer and felt a pull to place her mouth over the girl's slit and lap at the wetness dripping from within. Drinking from her opening and stabbing her erect bud with her tongue, she enjoyed kneading and squeezing the girl's ripe breasts at the same time until the girl vibrated and rocked under her, finally gushing her climax.

Although the girl looked right at her, she couldn't touch her or make contact on her own. Sybil watched the girl's hand pass right through her, leaving a trail of silver mist in its wake.

Yes, it was obvious that she could see Sybil. But it became clear that she could see little more than the outline of a body when she begged Sybil to stick her "beautiful, cold, silver cock" into her.

After that, Sybil began to lose interest in her. Somehow, all that year, Sybil had just assumed that the tenant knew she was a woman.

Weeks passed and Sybil would watch with contempt from the foot of the bed as the girl would entreat and plead with her to take her once more. Finally, in the early summer, the girl moved out and the apartment was empty again.

Sybil had no real knowledge of the passing of time. She

watched other tenants come and go, but none of them interested her. She still played with them occasionally, but she felt herself becoming more and more lonely. She was beginning to fade when Elaine moved into the apartment on a bright fall morning. Sybil was interested in the new tenant, but she couldn't seem to get this girl to notice her.

Elaine tended to talk in her sleep and Sybil was overjoyed to learn that she seemed to be more interested in women than men. She enjoyed watching Elaine pleasure herself. She loved watching the play of emotions and feeling cross her face until a final expression of contentment and joy overcame her in the end.

Sybil played with Elaine almost nightly for several months with no response. Well, no response other than the purely physical and autonomic. It seemed Elaine was completely unaware of Sybil's presence.

Sybil watched closely as she pushed the T-shirt up past Elaine's breasts and saw no response from the sleeping girl. She passed her hand over her smooth and flattened nipples and watched them crinkle and erect from her cold touch, but still saw no response on Elaine's face. Kneading the lovely breasts and sucking on them brought Sybil lots of pleasure but nothing from the sleeping girl.

Sybil peeled the panties down past the girl's sleeping pussy. She managed to slide them over her pert bottom and down her thighs to just above her knees. As she blew her cold breath across Elaine's pussy, she watched the dark brown hairs move. Not being able to wait any longer, she pried the girl's legs apart enough to get her mouth on that beautiful slit. As she licked and sucked at the opening, a normal, physical response took place. Elaine began to produce her own moisture as her body responded to Sybil's stimulation.

Sybil enjoyed sliding her hands under Elaine's bottom to squeeze her cheeks and finally, slowly, insert a finger into the girl's anus. More and more wetness would flow from Elaine's pussy when Sybil played this game, but still there would be no response from Elaine.

Sybil noticed that, on those occasions when she left Elaine's panties down around her knees, eventually Elaine would move her own hand down and pleasure herself in her sleep. At those times, Sybil saw expressions of emotion pass over the girl's face.

It really bothered Sybil that she was unable to elicit those expressions. It made her want to work harder and all the more intensely to achieve her goal.

This routine went on for years with no change. Sybil tried everything she could think of, even biting and slapping, although she was afraid this might wake Elaine up. Unfortunately, Elaine never seemed to take any notice of Sybil.

Elaine graduated from NYU and, although she didn't need the money, took a job teaching history to high school students at a private school in Brooklyn Heights. She loved her students and most of her fellow teachers.

Occasionally she would go out with a group, but she could never bring herself to date. She watched the sexual mores change through the years. She loved watching the growth of the Gay Pride Parade. It had gotten so large that she almost couldn't stand long enough to watch the whole thing, yet she had let the parade pass her by.

It was okay; she got what she needed from occasional masturbation, but mostly from the ghostly encounters, which had been occurring since she first moved into the apartment. That was one of the reasons she couldn't bring herself to move out of the floor-through. Of course living in the heart of Greenwich Village, right on the park, didn't hurt either. She had been considering buying the brownstone; real estate prices were pretty good and she had the money.

Ah, but back to thoughts of the ghost...she loved the ghost. Elaine had gotten a very brief glimpse of her one night. She could tell the ghost was definitely a woman, young and beautiful. She had her hair up in a bun with tendrils hanging down and clinging to her neck. She wore a long satin dress with a very low-cut neckline. It hugged her torso tightly then flared out at the hips. It was obvious she wore a corset, as Elaine could see the beautiful swell of her breasts threatening to overspill the bodice. She could also detect several layers of petticoats under the skirt. Elaine wished she could run her hands down the woman's torso and around her hourglass waist, feeling the tightness of the fabric that appeared to hold the ghost prisoner; she wanted to have a look under the petticoats, unfasten the underwear she found there and explore the woman's contours and interior.

It was thoughts like these that made it impossible for Elaine not to masturbate. All in all, she preferred the ghost to make love to her, but if she thought about those sensations, she became so wet she just couldn't help herself. Once, while masturbating, with her eyes opened to slits, she saw the ghost again, standing at the foot of the bed watching her intently and smiling.

Elaine placed the ghost as having lived around the late–middle 1800s. Her dress looked very fine and expensive. She wished she could see her in color, but the ghost appeared only as a fairly substantial silver mist, preventing her from detecting any colors at all.

Elaine thought a great deal about the ghost over the years. Due to the richness of the clothing, she thought the woman might have been the first owner of the house or, if not her, some male member of her family must have been.

She lived for the ghost's amazing sexual caresses. All along, she had been afraid that if she responded, the ghost would leave or stop playing with her. She had convinced herself of this and it was the last thing she wanted. She longed to look at the ghost, respond to her and talk to her. She already thought of this woman as her lover; she wished she could be a companion, as well.

It was so difficult, not responding to the ghost's ministrations, as she was so adept at bringing Elaine to orgasm. She wanted, more than anything, to let herself go, to see if she could touch the ghost. She wanted to hold her and pleasure her; to reciprocate for all the joy the ghost had given her.

Years passed and things continued as they had since Elaine had first moved into the house. For some reason, she never got around to buying it when the rates were low and now, at the turn of the century, with the rates as high as they were and rents having gone up so much, she really wished she had. Well, no matter. She had a good broker who had invested her money well. She had made a killing in tech stocks and he had managed to get her out before they took their inevitable nosedive. She could afford the rent but she could kick herself when she thought of how low prices and interest rates had been before.

*If I put it off any longer, I'll never buy the house,* she thought as she left to meet with her broker one beautiful, bright morning in September. Yes, she would go ahead and buy it, she thought, getting out of the cab in front of the World Trade Center.

Looking up, she smiled, thinking about how much she loved

this ridiculous building and its twin. About how happy it made her whenever she visited her broker, way up on the eighty-third floor. She didn't care about the prices going down; she had enough money. It would be good to be a property owner in New York, instead of a renter. She'd ask her broker what he thought of the idea.

Elaine awoke on her bed, in the dark. She felt a little disoriented. It was strange, but she didn't remember coming home and taking a nap. Well, she must have done, she thought, as she sat up.

Her eyes quickly became accustomed to the darkness and, with a start, she realized that things seemed much clearer. Colors seemed sharper. Her bedspread even looked brighter. She ran her hand over it. The nerve endings in her hand responded like never before. They seemed ultrasensitive. It reminded her of descriptions she'd read of acid trips in the late '60s and early '70s. As she looked up, she saw the ghost standing by the foot of her bed. As usual, Elaine acted like she hadn't seen her, and looked past her toward the bathroom.

Her head snapped back around and she stared at the ghost. "Why can I see you in color?" she asked aloud, before clamping a hand over her own mouth.

The woman standing at the foot of the bed frowned. "Are you implying that you can not only see me now, but that you've seen me before? Can this be true?" Words tumbled from Sybil as she released her anger and frustration. "Have you always known of my presence? Were you able to feel me? And if this is true, why did you ignore me? Did you think I'd go away if you ignored me? You answer my questions right now, then perhaps I'll answer yours!"

Elaine looked down. "I didn't know you could speak," she whispered. "What's your name?"

"Never you mind my name, my girl! Answer my questions! I've always cared so much for you but I must confess, I'm rather angry just now. Don't toy with me!"

"O-oh, I'm sorry; I'm not toying with you, I promise. Yes, I've known about you since I first moved in. I saw you a few times but tried not to look. I always felt you; oh god, how I felt you. I just didn't want you to go away!" Elaine said.

"I was sure somehow that if you knew that I knew, you'd stop making love to me and you'd go away. I fell in love with you and couldn't bear the thought of your leaving. Now I've made you angry. Please, please don't go away. Don't leave me," Elaine said, beginning to cry.

As the tears ran down Elaine's face, Sybil's heart melted. She sat on the bed next to Elaine and put her arms around her shoulders, hugging her tightly. "Don't worry my dear, I've no intention of leaving you. Don't you know I love you too?" she asked, kissing Elaine deeply.

Pulling away, she said, "My name is Sybil Forsythe. My husband bought this house for me in 1867, as a wedding present. I loved it too much to leave when I died. I'm so glad you came back here; it means you love it too. Well, either that or you love me too much to leave," she said, giving Elaine a squeeze.

"I do love it," Elaine said. "I'm going to buy it." Sybil seemed sad, as she moved back and looked at Elaine.

"Look, I told you, I do love you; it's not just the house that I want, it's you too!" Elaine said. Her words didn't seem to change Sybil's expression.

"It's okay, I won't buy the house if you don't want me to. I can keep renting. I'm sorry. It's your house; I know it's yours.

I promise I won't take it away from you," Elaine rambled on, apologizing to Sybil. She couldn't stand to see the ghost so sad. Great, she finally started talking to Sybil and she had managed to immediately mess everything up.

"Oh my dear, my dear. You won't be buying the house. No, don't look at me that way; I'm not mad at you. You asked a question earlier; do you remember? About seeing me in color."

"Yes, I remember. Why?" Elaine asked.

"Why do you think you can see me in color now, when you couldn't before? Take my hand, my love." Elaine reached out and grasped Sybil's hand. It felt solid.

"You see, my beautiful Elaine, you've died now, too. That's why you can see me in color, that's why we can chat with each other."

"And that's why you feel so much more solid to me?" Elaine asked. Strange, but she didn't seem to be upset about dying. She was much more afraid of Sybil not wanting her anymore.

"Can you feel how solid I am? You feel just as solid to me. All your sensations are heightened, aren't they? Just think what lovemaking will be like now," Sybil said, her lips curling into a "cat that ate the canary" grin.

They watched the young woman lying on the bed. She was naked and beautiful. The two specters at the end of the bed embraced and lingered over a long, deep kiss.

"Shall we?" Sybil asked.

"Oh yes, let's!" Elaine replied.

Sybil took the right side of the bed and began sucking on the girl's right breast while moving her hand down to finger her clit. Elaine took the left side of the bed, but lower down. She pushed her tongue into the girl's pussy while pinching her left nipple. As the sleeping tenant began to moan, the ghosts' ministrations became more zealous and insistent.

# NATIVE TONGUE

Shanna Germain

Everything on the menu is foreign to me. The
waiter, who's wearing a blue T-shirt with a
bunch of words on it that I don't know, don't
want to know, waits for me to order. The menu
has a few words I know, too many for my liking—*ceviche* and *coca light* and *burrito*—but
I skip those, pretend I haven't seen them, and
point only to the ones I don't know.

When the waiter leaves, I look out over the
ocean and listen to the other diners talking in
a language I don't know. Their conversation
washes past my ears, no different than ocean
waves. There's only one other white person in
the place, and his Spanish carries the same mu-
sical roll and lilt of those sitting at the table
with him.

I love being in a place where I have no

language. Sitting here at this open-air restaurant, waiting for Margret and not understanding a damn word, it's heaven. There was a time when I thought I wanted to know every language in the world. That's why I started working as a translator eight years ago. But now, I wish I could take that desire back. That's the funny thing about languages, like learning to read. You can't take it back. A word that you know can never become a mystery again.

Believe it or not, of all the languages I know, one that I don't know is Spanish. When you translate for a living Spanish is the least requested, because everyone knows it, so I never bothered to learn. And that's why I've allegedly come to the least tourist-ridden beach in Costa Rica, to immerse myself in the Spanish language for three weeks.

But in truth, I have come to meet my lover. Margret's plane landed at noon, and barring unexpected delays or bad roads, she should arrive just in time to join me in the feast of whatever it is I just ordered. I'm dressed in a bikini swimsuit—black, to match my hair which I'm wearing in one long braid down my back—and a black and red sarong that's wrapped around me like a strapless dress. It's a sarong that Margret bought me last time I saw her, and I could tell from the light in her eyes that she liked the way I looked in it.

The waiter sets down the beers I asked for—that was one thing I knew how to say. Brand names are surprisingly and sadly universal.

He gestures to the empty seat with a flat palm. I don't know if he's questioning where the other half of my party is or if he's asking if he can join me.

"Soon," I say, and I'm struck by my own desire to communicate even as I'm trying to leave all communication behind.

When he leaves, I sip my beer and lean back in my chair with a sigh. I'm jet-lagged, but only a little, and the peace that the beer and the breeze and the lack of conscious understanding brings is amazing. I watch the ocean break across the sand. Out near the water, a woman in a swimsuit races the waves. She is the color of dark honey, tanned and toned against her off-white bikini. I am lost in pictures. I will my brain to shut off, to stop finding words for every color and movement and object.

My bottle of beer is nearly gone before I feel hands tugging at my braid. The hands climb up the back of my head, and then down over my eyes. I bring my hand up to feel Margret's thin wrist, layered over with tiny metal bracelets. They jangle when she pulls on my ear. And then she is slipping her arms around me, nearly choking me, to hug me from behind. She doesn't care who sees, and wrapped in her car-cooled arms and her turpentine and lavender scent, I don't either.

Margret lets me out of her backward bear hug and sits across from me. She is long-limbed and reedy, with big blue eyes and shoulder-length curls the ruddy tint of cedar shavings. She grins at me, showing the little space between her front teeth that I love, and then tips the top of her beer bottle toward me. We click glasses, and then drink.

"Margret," I say.

It is the only word, other than my own name, that can pass between us. Margret speaks only her native Dutch. Nothing else. That's how we met earlier this year. She needed an interpreter in the States when her artwork was showing around town. Because she lived in Italy, I assumed she spoke Italian or French or even a bit of English. But no. As it turned out, she'd lived all over the world, but only spoke Dutch. A dying language, and one I didn't speak a word of.

Still, she was gorgeous. And her paintings were the same—landscapes so infused with emotion and light that you forgot they were just paintings of trees and clouds. She didn't seem to think in words, only images. I found her another translator from our company, but not before I'd fallen for her. Hard. It wasn't just her curls or that gap-toothed smile. It was the language, or lack of it.

My partner, Helen, is a dictionary writer. Woman of all words, always the right word. In our house, every word has meaning, every word has weight, has to be picked over and examined, dead or alive, until it can be stored and measured and accounted for. "Good night," is never just good night. It might be "Good night, I hate you" or "Good night, why won't you feed the cat?" or "Good night, let's fuck." But it is never, ever just good night.

Helen will say things like, "Did you know there is no word in the English language that is commonly used to describe a woman's private parts?" even as I have my tongue or fingers in her private parts. Even as I bring those private parts to places that have words: wet and shudder and moan and orgasm.

With Margret, there is no good night. There are no private parts. Well, there are private parts, but there is no worry over what to call them. There is just the way she puts her fingers to her lips and parts them for me. The way I dip my fingers in her as though she is the ocean. And there is the way she's looking at me right now, blue eyes narrowed, her soft bare foot beneath the table, wrapped around the back of my calf.

The waiter brings us plates of food: some kind of fish with crackers, little crab legs and calamari-like rings in a red sauce. When he has filled our table and pointed at our beers and we nod yes, Margret lets her hand rest on his arm for a brief second before he turns away. She says something in Dutch.

I shake my head, but I can't hide my smile, or the way her words made my insides feel. Only Margret would say something to a Costa-Rican waiter in Dutch and expect him to understand.

After we stuff ourselves silly, feeding each other bits of seafood and slices of fruit, we go down to the beach. Margret shimmies out of her sundress, and for a few seconds, I open my mouth to tell her it's not a nude beach. Which is a silly instinct, considering. And it doesn't matter anyway, because she's wearing a tiny bikini under the dress. Dark blue, only slightly darker than the ocean and the same color as her eyes. It covers her small round breasts in two triangles. Her nipples point in the triangles' direct centers. I want to drag my tongue across the fabric like a cat.

She takes my hand and tugs me toward the ocean. I drop my sarong to the ground on the way. We walk through the waves to the point where the water evens out. It is nearly up to our chins, but so calm that we can touch the sand at the bottom on our tiptoes and don't get knocked over.

Her sigh as she leans back into the warm water is one I recognize. It's a sigh of pleasure. I join her as we lean back and float, our faces to the sky. There is no sound but the surf and, far off, the chatter of birds or people. It is hard to tell which is which, and so I tell myself they are birds.

Floating like this, I wonder at how this can be, so many ways to love and I'm thankful there are no words to describe this kind of love or that one. It isn't as though I don't love Helen. I do. It's just that there are too many words now. In the beginning, the words were stones we dropped into the water to walk on, to go the same places together. Now the words are stones that we carry in our fists, our arms always drawn back, ready to fling.

Margret's hand finds mine beneath the water, and I curl my fingers over hers. Already our skin is salt-sucked and wrinkled. Even so, I swear she's the softest thing I've ever felt. I slide my hand up her arm, pull her closer to me. She laughs, and grabs my belly. The water pushes us closer, pulls us apart, and still, her lips find mine. Her silent tongue enters my mouth, touches all the places where we make words and soothes them as easily as the sea.

When we are sandy and salty and wet as we can stand, we stand under the simple outdoor shower until the cold water makes us shiver. Then I lead Margret on the path up from the beach. Soon, we're at the edge of the rainforest. They're that close to each other, forest and beach and ocean, as though they're siblings, sisters that couldn't bear to live together, but couldn't bear to be too far apart.

Beneath the canopy of trees, we follow the path up and up. The sunlight makes stained-glass patterns as it passes through the leaves and vines and lands at our feet. Small brown and white monkeys swing from tree to tree above our heads, making *oo-oo* noises as they go. Margret reaches back and takes my hand and we walk like that, our footsteps crackling twigs, our breath puffing without sound.

Tucked back in the woods, the hut I rented for us is just that—a hut. Open to the air around the top, with a plain hammock on the front porch. Inside, there is only the bed, and a tiny table. Margret doesn't seem to care. She runs and throws herself on the bed so that the mattress shoots her back up in the air, sends her damp curls flying out in all directions around her. She pats the blanket next to her. *Come*, no matter what language you don't speak.

I start to lie down next to her on the bed, but she shakes her head. She makes a shimmying motion, her hips moving back and forth across the simple blanket. I tuck my thumbs into the sides of my bikini bottoms, wiggling my hips. Like this?

She puts her hands to her lips and nods. I slide my bikini bottoms down, half inch by half inch, shaking my body with it. Compared to Margret, I'm curvy. My belly slides in above my round hips, accentuates the curvy ass that I can only keep in shape with daily bike rides. She seems to delight in my curves as much as I delight in her angularity.

There is no "Am I skinny enough?" or "Are you sure you should be eating that?" There is only me, sliding my bikini bottom down over the wet and salty curves of me. There is only Margret watching from the bed, her lips parted, her own damp body soaking into the blanket.

I slide the bottoms down all the way, step out of them. Margret runs her tongue across her bottom lip and waits. I unhook the back of my bikini top. There isn't as much here to shimmy out of, so I just let it fall away. I've had my nipples pierced since I last saw her: two tiny blue stones hanging from each peak. Tiny blue stones that match her eyes.

Her eyes get big when she sees them, and she puts her hand over her mouth. Then she rolls over on all fours and crawls across the bed toward me. She takes my hand and pulls me down, until I'm kneeling on the bed. When she leans forward, the smell of saltwater is everywhere. Then her tongue is on my nipple, round and round the nipple and the jewelry. Her warm mouth sucks. The piercings are newly healed, sensitive, but in a good way. Margret catches one between her teeth, and pulls up. My body reacts like she's pulling on a string tied to my belly, the inside of my thighs. Everything pulls up with her mouth.

"Margret," I breathe. She smiles at her name, and then runs her mouth lower, down the flat expanse of my belly. When she hits my thighs, she rolls on her back and scoots herself under me. She uses her tongue to paint pictures up the inside of my thighs. Of what, I can't imagine, but I close my eyes and see them as long, wide streaks of blue paint.

I have shaved for her and for the ocean, short enough that when she runs her tongue along the hairs I know it must prickle her. She uses her tongue on my labia, then parts them, wiggles her way inside, slippery as a fish. Her tongue is a flat brush sweeping the inside of me until she hits my clit. Dot, dot, dabbing me. Her tongue there speaks to me without language. It is a promise of things to come, a press and release that feels as quietly natural as anything that has come before it. There was a time when Helen and I used our tongues like this, on our bodies, instead of against each other....

I brush the thought away. Don't want to think about that right now. Don't want to have to find the words for it.

I fold my body down until I can nestle my own tongue against Margret's bikini bottom. She's still working her tongue against my clit, but I try to focus. I slide her tiny bikini to the side to allow me access. I tuck my finger inside her labia. She is wet already, smelling of sea salt and musk.

I slide two fingers inside her, loving the wet clutch of her, the way she moans into me. My thumb rubbing across her clit, I slide a third finger in. I fuck her like that, pushing so hard her tongue slides back and forth across my clit with the movement of her body. Through the wet fabric of her suit, her hard nipples rub my belly with the movement.

Margret arches her back. Her tongue becomes frantic across my clit, and then she gives up and sucks me, hard, into her mouth. We don't come together; she goes first, moaning as I dive into her with my fingers. It is this sound, the meaningless vibrations of her throat as she sucks my clit, that lets me follow her.

The place we bring each other to, there are no words for that. No words at all.

It is dark when the sound wakes me. Long and loud, like big trucks are driving over the roof of the hut. It takes me a second before I realize what it is. Howler monkeys.

Margret lies awake next to me, her body rigid in my arms.

"Was de hell?" she whispers. At first I think she's speaking English, but then I realize it's just one of those phrases that sound like its English equivalent. It still amazes me sometimes how similar languages are, even after hundreds of years and thousands of miles apart. Languages are a species like any other, I guess, each adapting to their environment, but most still keeping their roots. Some even growing more and more alike over the passing years, despite every hypothesis that says they shouldn't.

I could say, "Howler monkeys," but I know she won't understand, so instead I pull her close to me. I say with my body, "It's safe," and then I kiss her so she'll know for sure.

But her mouth is set flat against mine, and her lips don't open. She is letting me hold her, but she is not relaxed. The moon peeks through the open slats around the top of the hut, and I can see her eyes, big and wide.

The sound comes again, closer this time, a big low howl that fills the hut and echoes all around us. If I didn't know what it was, if I hadn't heard howlers before, I'd be going out of my fucking mind too.

"What is it?" Margret says again, and this time when I understand her, I think that I have suddenly absorbed a new language, like osmosis, while we slept. And then, in another heartbeat, I realize she is speaking English.

She seems to realize it at the same time, covers her mouth with her fingertips. I let go of her, sit up on the bed.

"Shit," she says through her fingers. "I am so very sorry, Lilla. It was meant to be a surprise that I learn English. I ruin the...surprise."

Hearing her speak makes me feel like I am farther from home than just in another country. I am on another planet, an alternative universe where everything you thought you understood is reversed, a book that is read from right to left, bottom to top.

For once, I can't say anything. All those languages in my head, and I don't have a word. Not one. She meant to surprise me, I see that now. It is a gift she has tried to give me, learning this language, something to bring us closer.

But all I can see are her lips moving. Her tongue is forming words that I do not want to understand. I turn away. She comes behind me and puts her arms around me, but already her fists are closed tight, filled with words.

# THE STORM CHASERS

Peggy Munson

*Rumspringa*

I've thought about kissing a girl for a while, but I don't expect it to happen here.

The Amish kids go bowling at this place in Pennsylvania, where Ohio stands yawning at its border. A girl is smoking cigarettes outside like she hates everything. Her hair is in braids that she has twisted up into odd coils against her head. She stares at the balcony of clouds that watches a flat horizon dreaming of steel. I can tell she's one of the Amish kids on *Rumspringa*, partying like it's 1999. *Rumspringa* ("running around") is the window of time when they can break the Amish rules before deciding if they want to get baptized.

She sits there like an old house equalizing pressure after a draft blows in. I'm just sucked in her direction, and she looks like she's used to it. I plop next to her on the concrete stoop and she doesn't glance my way. "Yeah, I'm Amish, so what's your second question?" she says before I speak. It should be mentioned that I hate my new haircut and I tried to fix it earlier but ended up chopping off another three inches and now it's as rancid as a wet dog limping hopelessly through the world's unbalance. So I've got my hood up on my black hoodie and these fucked-up bits of hair peeking out. All I do at home is prune myself and masturbate.

"Sorry to hear that," I finally mutter, not knowing what else to say.

"You're *sorry?*" she says with hostility. "You're the one living the Apocalypse, English." She stubs out her cigarette on the ground and now it's dark, Midwest-dark, the kind of dark with coal dust in it. She is pretty—maybe sixteen with yeast-risen cheeks. Still, about the same age as me so I don't know why I'm talking about her like we're different. A car's headlights do a swoop around as someone parks and that's when I see the etchings on her inner forearm: unmistakable cut marks all up and down. "Oh my god," I say, grabbing her wrist, which she quickly yanks away. "What the fuck?" she exclaims. "That's fucking rude." She starts to throw shit in her bag to wobble upright. I feel a jolt through my cunt from touching her.

"I didn't mean to freak you out. I—" I say, my hand reaching up, and then my hood falls back and she notices my hair and starts to laugh at me. Her laugh grows into a plume of smoke, and then she's coughing on her own laugh.

"I'm just uneven," I say defensively.

"That's for sure," she replies. Her lips are some kind of bad candy, something laced with something illegal and maybe even deadly. Probably Ecstasy.

There's a spasm of air between us, traveling up my legs. Then she casts me this look that is pure sex, so unexpected it makes me blush.

Some guy named Jacob drove her here in a borrowed car. And I've got a boy inside the bowling alley, a friend named David who wants to be more. Now that this girl and I have an animal look between us we know (just know) that we have to make out with the boys to overcompensate for the way the world is gathering into a funnel cloud to spill us on the ground and the horses are undoing earth with their hooves. We end up on the edge of this field that is so lonely it keeps trying to hoard the moonlight, and the boys have beer. Everyone loves a drunk Amish girl on *Rumspringa* so the boys make sure she gets the first bottle and I find out her name is Ellie.

Later I am dizzy and have lost sight of her and David pushes his hands up my shirt. His fingers on my breasts do a drowsy massage. He kisses my neck. He pushes me backward and I'm initially relieved to be lying down but then I feel his hard-on in his pants. "Jesus, David," I say to him. I need air. I say it over and over like a halftime cheer. "Air air air air air." It's one of those moments of pep rally incongruity I've felt before when I can't seem to smile for the same reasons as everyone else.

"What'd you do to your hair?" David asks. He looks elated to have kissed me. He has a dopey smile on his pimple-ridged face. "No, it looks good," he adds, and he means it.

There's something ominous in the orchestral score of crickets and that unspeakable dark motor within boys of a certain age. Sometimes the only way out is through. I keep looking around for her and we kiss and he presses his bulge against my leg. I don't let him fuck me though.

The voice across the field is reciting something from a German opera. "And the English are all dead!" he exclaims at the end. It's her boy, Jacob, and he has her by the wrist. They drag across the field in our direction and she looks ill. The clouds have all been shredded into little pieces and they are nuzzling against stars. Everything is above us pressing down. I tell the boys to go get more beer so they'll leave us alone.

"How can we do that?" Jacob asks. He's already drunk with anger in the corners of his eyes.

"That gas station," I retort. "We passed it up the road."

"Will you be okay?" David asks me, like he's my boyfriend or like he cares. They know that getting beer is boys' work, and that's the only good thing about them.

We have maybe forty minutes, and she tells me that her mouth tastes like him and she needs a goddamn cigarette. She keeps saying it but she can't find her pack of Camels. "A goddamn cigarette," she repeats. It takes me a while to figure out she sucked his dick and I'm about to ask her if she liked it when her eyes get all saturnine and ringed and she stops my question dead. "I don't want to talk about it," she says.

"Did he make you?" I ask, but I am positive he did.

"I just want this fucking taste out of my mouth," is all she says. Finally, somewhere deep in my pocket, I find a wadded piece of wrapper that contains one breath mint, and that one mint cools down the core temperature of the night. "Thank god," she says, rubbing her fingers unconsciously on the marks on her forearm. "That's better."

There is a thick choking shame wending its way from the water table below this field. It's just like any other place around here, strewn with litter from kids who got drunk and pretended to strangle cornstalks with their fists. Her breath comes out in accelerating minty puffs and then, suddenly, she puts the tip of her sneaker over mine, rubbing the rubber together. *Burn*, I think. *Burn rubber.* I'm thinking about masturbating in my bedroom with the plastic handle of this big pink makeup brush I fuck myself with, listening to albums she has never heard: I want to bring her into my world. But we just stay there, poured into molds of ourselves hardening, our breathing startled by its perpetuity.

"I can't fool around with you," she says finally. "It's too finite." But for the first time in my life, I feel like I could go on forever. I know she feels it too, the infinity braiding its way between us.

She is the one starting it with her hand on my knee, with pent-up pride like the bow of an iron, smoothing me down in front of her.

She rubs her hand down the outside of my jeans to the crease where my thigh meets my bush, and she just holds it there. She just presses the edge of it down, karate-chop-like, into that bit of human give. It is one pinhead of nothing that is everything, all angels. There's a pulsation—some rocket between the edge of her hand and my hole. To the whole of me. It's an incredible rush.

I reach for her chicken-scratched arm. That arm is like a foreign language, an unbound scroll.

She tries to pull away but I am surprisingly rough and say, "Don't." I kick up from the bottom of some murk, trying to get air. *Air.* I hold down her thighs with both palms and look at her. She takes my face in her hands and kisses me all over my cheeks and lips so perfectly. I smooth her shifting hairs back

from her eyes and she keeps diving further into me, whimpering. Then our hands are grappling for everything as quickly
as possible: inner thighs, breasts, ass. I feel it everywhere, fast
and spreading out: heat lightning. We only have a few more
minutes before the glare of headlights, and that's when I do it,
slide my hand past her waistband to stroke her wet hole. "Oh
god," I say. "You feel so amazing, Ellie." We pull away when
we see the boys. Soon enough the angry boy is throwing bottles
on the ground trying to smash them. "It's a christening," he
says drunkenly. "A christening."

On the drive home with drunk Jacob at the wheel I think
tonight is the night we are probably dying in a DUI. Ellie and
I sit together in the backseat and her knee knocks against mine
and she steals slight touches on my arm when she can. Because
David on my other side is so drunk anyway, she takes a moment to nuzzle against my neck and rub her lips on my ear
and whisper, "I want you." I know we are never going to kiss
again. *Never*: that cataclysm.

*Never never* in the timber framing.

*Never never* and we are probably dying.

But no: drunks spill back into the slurred world. Ellie and
I look longingly at each other—the restless dead. We're in the
parking lot: David returned to his abandoned car. We stop to
watch Jacob kiss her: it's torture. "She's minty fresh," Jacob
says to my face, and he steers her shoulders toward the car. She
makes a tipsy trip, and he loses his hold, so I lunge and grab
her arm.

"Whoa," she giggles. Her eyes go from lamplight to electricity, and we carelessly lean into a drunken kiss, and I feel the
slick danger between my legs. "What the *hell* do you think
you're doing?" David snarls abrasively. "Are you asking for

*Meidung* you crazy bitch?" I feel the eggshell air. I know the boys will come after us with timbers, with brush and switch. But this is how adults choose their baptisms. "I'm running around," she hisses. "Get used to it."

*Electricity*

She needs me: she needs electricity. If I could pedal fast enough, I would generate enough of it. At the dinky cemetery past her house, I cram my hand down my pants and rub my clit and think about her varnished eyes. I remove the plastic makeup brush from my bag and slide it into my hole, moaning quietly. I think about her careful quilting hands on every stitch of me. I want to undress her: how many layers? What made me fall for Ellie wasn't just how slick and wet my cunt was when I went to pee after she kissed me that night, how many wads of tissue it took to wipe her off of me, but those violently etched arms. I want to make her feel something worth the shunning of life in those razor cuts.

I stick a note in the post at the edge of the farm. *Please, Ellie, let me touch you,* it says.

She finally writes back that she has been "bundling" with Jacob: it's a *Rumspringa* tradition where a teenage boy sleeps in a girl's bed and they are encouraged to talk, fondle and grope. They're not supposed to fuck, but the Amish are pragmatists, and sometimes girls get pregnant. "It's awful," she writes. "He keeps making me feel his dick. I just want to have an orgasm." Her nerve endings are too overshot for her to cum by her own hand. "I mean with you," she adds. "An orgasm with you." She needs electricity.

So I go stealthily into Target and buy a plug-in "massager" to make her cum. I want to stroke her skin in the milkweed-tossed air. Everyone can do the other thing: go into raw mercy. Everyone can scrape with fingernails the inside of the oyster shell. It's only rare, repressed, broken people who can coax an elusive sensation from someone as fucked up as Ellie and I. I practice when I'm home alone: the massager and the makeup brush and David Bowie and that exquisite bowed time before my body explodes. I think of white bonnets.

We bundle in a fleabag motel, beneath two scratchy blankets. "You look pretty," I say, giving her a pack of Camels. I'm high on the scent of her hair: simple and buttery with a hint of burned kerosene. Her hand kneads my leg and then something desperate and thundering takes over us, and as soon as I put her smoke in an ashtray we are tumbling under the blanket, kissing and trying to get our hands to each other's tits. She changed into street clothes before meeting me but underneath are cotton wares: a sweet undershirt and plain panties. As soon as I touch her nipple over her shirt, giving it a squeeze, I know exactly where the technological world went wrong, putting wires between sensualists.

"I'm freaked out," she says suddenly. "Will you burn me?" I pull back, but my fingers keep exploring her tits.

"No way, Ellie. I can't." I'm confused by the request. "You mean with a cigarette?"

"I'll feel calmer." She reaches for the ashtray.

I'm skeptical. "Where?" She has marks all over her.

She pulls up her undershirt, then she points to three spots from her navel to her clit. "Make buttons," she says. The Amish can't have buttons, or other markers of vanity.

She covers her face a little while I make buttons of singed skin. I focus completely, and she digs her hands into my scalp and pulls at my hair. Each time she moans, I get a deep throb in my cunt. I like burning her with the cigarette. When I'm done, she has three button-burns trailing to her bush. "Fuck, Ellie, I want to make you cum," I say, grabbing her scarred wrists. "Show me," she says. I nudge her shirt with my nose and take the pearly button of her nipple in my mouth, then kiss down the button trail, bite and pull at her underwear, and finally put my mouth on her sweet juices while her head thrashes a little on the pillow and then she holds my skull in place. Down on her.

"Check out the electric sorcerer," I say, holding the vibrator like a sword after I plug it in. I lift her head up a little with my hand and kiss her cheeks and lips while I press the vibrations on her clit, tease her hole, smell the sweet rising of the lazy minutes before her noises get loud and she grabs on to me, screaming "Oh fuck" and jerking and shaking and curling her limbs. Right as she cums I stick two fingers inside of her so I can feel her hole pulse against me.

"It's just a little lightning and a key," I say. "Electricity."

"It's definitely you and me," she replies. "Not a key."

*Bolt*

"The night falls like a bolt of cloth. Look at it—it makes a velvet thud upon the plain," says Ellie. I wrap my hands around her and kiss her: she always feels like velvet to me. We have scraped together just enough money to live. Ellie still has a month or two before she has to tell the Amish if she's coming back.

Ellie presses her ear to the tracks and then hobbles over on her knees and presses her other ear against my belly stud. "It could be the Lake Shore Limited," she says, then reaches around and cups her hands on my ass, kissing the skin above my belt buckle. She shoves me back against a tree by the time the train rolls by, clanging and blowing its horn. She fucks me with her knuckles sliding in and out while I feel the vibrations of the train in my body. She whispers, "Open up, English," and holds the smoothness of my back like I'm a flattened penny.

We hang out at the train yard at night. It is splintered from the town—with old, sturdy containers of runaway echoes. Without fatty Amish food, Ellie has a body like a tent post and her hair falls around her in a stilled centrifugal swing ride. She perches on the rails like a bird of prey and waits for the night to produce a scared animal.

The train yard is where our new friend Spade sleeps in a dirty Lands End sleeping bag in a boxcar. Spade is a gender-queer boi who left the Amish after hallucinogens twisted his head around. He and Ellie speak the same Pennsylvania Dutch and she calls him Bu for boy. He makes drawings with colored pencils and tacks them to utility poles at night. His drawings appear to be from a tortured, maniacal child in art therapy: red with the brutality of flat figurines. He often tells us he can't wait to bolt from this town, but he knows he's too crazy to ride the rails. He tells Ellie and me to join him on the other side of this Grimm fairy tale.

"Don't be silly," says Ellie. "You're the story, Spade. We're your bookends."

We leave for work in the tie-dyed light, and put on white aprons with scalloped edges. Ellie fills the coffee machine and I screw lids off the salt. She has slight curves that remind men of highways, so we make good tips but not enough. This is a sleepy town of horny, frustrated men who walk around with coffee steam crimping bowed beards. Sometimes guys give us a few bucks to watch us kiss on our breaks. Ellie's lips are terse, friendly postcards then. She holds my shoulder blades like they're decorative plates. In our apartment, Ellie eats like a bear with a honey jar. She likes foods she can scoop out—kiwifruits cut in half, hard-boiled eggs she hollows out of their shells, peanut butter she eats from the jar. Ellie marvels at the simplest things about living independently. We give Spade change for the truck stop showers and take him clothes we pick up at the secondhand shop and keep him groomed, like a pet. He's the second boi we have ever met.

"Take my order, miss," Ellie commands me, flopping me down on the bed, biting my nipples through my shirt. She pulls my polyester uniform off, wrapping the apron strings around my wrists. She grabs my panties with her teeth. She runs her tongue between my pussy lips like she is scooping the flavor out. She stops right as I'm about to cum. "Wait, my English Breakfast," she says. "I have to check out your bum."

She grabs the paddle we got at an antique store where the woman said "corporeal" and "punishment" so many times I had to fuck Ellie on the way home. It's an old schoolhouse paddle. Ellie gives me a few whaps on the ass. She wants to make sure that today is forgotten and tomorrow's dress digressed. I chew the edge of the sheet to blot my sounds until she makes me cum.

Then I flip her over. Sometimes she looks like a drowned thing, so kittenish and waiting for resurrection. Because she has not decided about baptism, they have not shunned her: she meets them and their sad beards as the elders try to talk her back home. When I slide my fingers into her and run my tongue over her clit and make her moan, I feel like I am chasing a storm.

Spade—who reads voraciously—talks about Allen Ginsberg. "The girl Beats got so shafted," I reply, and then realize Ellie has no idea what we're talking about with her eighth-grade education. We melt chocolate in a can and dip leftover diner flapjacks in. Ellie teases my hem, rippling the edge of it up and down and brushing her nails against my skin until Spade looks blue-balled. I love the telekinetic energy of one thing influencing another thing.

"I really need to get a cock. I'm a war amp," Spade laments, looking at the denim folds of his crotch. He's drinking the last slurps from a bottle of Jack Daniels. We've been working extra when we can, saving up to buy the Click Dick for Spade. The Click Dick comes with this casting material dentists use. You wrap it around a man's dick and make an imprint, and then send it to the company to fill with silicone. We want to surprise Spade for his birthday with a realistic-looking, custom cock. We've been looking for a man to meet our size credentials, and we think we've spotted him—the Wooly Mammoth. The Wooly Mammoth is as hairy as a clogged drain, with a bulge as big as a burial mound: a real flannel man.

"You want a show, Spade?" Ellie asks coquettishly.

"What kind you got?" perks Spade.

"Barn-raising burlesque," says Ellie. So then we dance around and tongue-kiss and tease Spade and he rubs the bottle of Jack on his conjured boner. She grabs my hand when she notices I'm getting too friendly with her Amish comrade and says, "Tomorrow's the early shift." She knocks her knuckles on Spade's and says, "Keep the *Glaawe, Bu.*"

Half a mile away, Ellie throws me down between the tracks so hard I get rocks and tiny bits of coal in my teeth. She bends over my face. "Are you starting to want an Amish boi?" she asks. She holds the back of my neck. There is a strange low breeze building between the parallel lines. Her breath is jagged. Ellie yanks my head back by my hair. "You think an Amish girl can't fuck you hard enough?" She is agitated. She pulls a beer bottle out of her pocket that she was saving to recycle and shoves it under the side of my underpants. She straddles me, her knees on the ground, and fucks me with the bottle from behind. It's so rough that I can't stop myself from reacting. My hips pull toward her, suckling on the glass. The more I pull, the more nasty she gets, riding her own hand that's pushing the bottle into me. "You're my best friend, English," she says as she hammers the glass in. "You'd better give it up for me. Stop playing chicken on the tracks."

I'm about to cum when I hear the unmistakable rattle awakening like cold bones. Ellie doesn't stop until we see the light screaming toward us. I start to poke her belly, slap her arms, and push her off. I grab her by the neck and shove her backward. We roll onto the bank and she is coughing when the train passes. The quiet cargo slides by and moonlight stutters through the gaps. "Ellie, I love you more than anyone," I say sincerely, and then we melt into hot kissing and I start fingering her wet hole. "I'm so in love with you." I hear the beer bottle crunching under the weight of steel as I slide my fingers into her and listen to her squeal.

I'm still intrigued by Spade's gargoyle eyebrows. I get dizzy looking at him, like I'm staring up at spires. Ellie keeps a proprietary arm over his shoulder. The other boi we met, Clyde, was in the Army. He came up with the idea of an Amish pinup girl tattoo and asked Ellie if she would pose for him. He put some rouge on her cheeks and had her bend over an old butter churn wearing full Amish garb. After he sketched Ellie, he got the image inked on his calf. Three months later, Clyde came back with his legs blown off just above the knees, and went to college to become a meteorologist. The tattoo had been blown off too but he was glad to be out of the Army. Ellie had a phantom limb yearning for the tattoo. "Do you think my old life will turn into that," she asked me once. "Some blasted comic strip?"

The Wooly Mammoth asks me to look in Ellie's face, with my wrists tied to the reading sconces. I watch the meteor shower going on in her eyes, which should be dead but Ellie and I like new adventures. He pulls off my panties and asks Ellie to lick me out. He is polite, a public-service-announcement bear. He strokes his dick while she goes down on me. "We have to put the casting stuff on now," I tell him and he nods. I watch Ellie's fragile hands, little stick-dolls, making an imprint of his cock. I stroke my clit and moan because she looks so pretty. The next day, Clyde returns from college. He tells Ellie he has joined the Ohio Storm Chasers. I look at her glittery eyes and realize she couldn't care less about my yearning for Spade. Clyde likes her without a cartoon self.

We sing "Happy Birthday" and give Spade the lopsided-looking gift. We can't wait to hear his reaction. "Oh my god," says Spade. "You girls are perfect."

The sky looks like globs of clay and Ellie is malleably moody. "I hope it doesn't hit the farms," she says worriedly, gazing toward Amish country. This storm system has come with deadly warnings but our apartment building doesn't have a basement anyway, so we may as well ride with Clyde. Clyde is ebullient, pulling up in the van. It is amazing how prepositions shift around so fast: someone is under a car, or a tree has gone through a wall, the innocents are all grown up. Ellie scratches the scars on her arms. "We're so literally *under* the weather," says Ellie. "And it feels amazing."

A batting of gray clouds hovers above us. I can feel the rises and falls of barometric pressure like the heart-in-throat of a roller coaster. "Not in Kansas my ass," says Spade, jumping into the van. "Ohio is so tornado alley today." As we ride, Spade proudly strokes his bulge and Ellie chats with Clyde in the front. I want to get inside of Spade's zipper and nuzzle close to him but Clyde soon points out a funnel cloud touching down. "Oh my god," says Ellie, holding Clyde's video camera to the window. It's incredible. The big swirling beast is chewing up the ground. Clyde works the hand controls to accelerate and Ellie suctions against the window like a goldfish. We watch the vortex rip through someone's shed as mangled wood gathers into the swirl.

I've got my face pressed close to Spade's face and I start to cry a little from fear and he kisses my cheeks and forehead, and then he starts kissing me deep on the mouth. Ellie squeaks in this terrified voice, "It's coming." I lift my head and see the cyclone rushing in our direction as Clyde barrels toward an overpass where we can shelter the van. He parks on the edge of its concrete and we hurry him down into his wheelchair and then tumble into a low-lying ditch. Spade throws his whole body over me and the ground smells like straw. Clyde is not afraid: he has been to war. He has his video camera running the whole time. I hear a roaring sound and feel Spade's cock pressing against my leg and his heartbeat pounding into mine.

We are shaken afterward, and we stop at this steak house. "I'll put it all on Visa," says Clyde. We eat baked potatoes and iceberg lettuce dripping with too-sweet dressing and Ellie touches his thigh. The steak house adjoins a motel and we decide to crash there for the night since it's not safe for any of us to go back to our cheap housing anyway. Ellie wheels Clyde over the threshold and helps transfer him onto the bed and the next thing we know she's moaning as his hands rake her hair. Spade asks me if I want to go outside. We head under a stairwell beside some soda machines. I count in my head, *one one thousand, two one thousand*, waiting for the thunder to crack after the lightning flashes in the distance. "Come here," Spade says roughly, yanking me by the arm and flinging me against the wall. He feels up my tits and kisses me, but then a violent rain starts coming down, "Many hands make light work," says Spade. "Should we help Clyde with the Amish girl?" I rub his cock for a second. "Yeah," I reply.

Ellie is kneeling on the bed wearing only panties. Clyde gets in his chair and wheels over to talk with Spade in the bathroom, so I start kissing Ellie and squeezing her tits in my palms. She looks exquisitely gutted and fresh. "God you're gorgeous," I tell her. When the bois come out they are stroking the bulges in their pants. "We've got a pressure front moving in," says Clyde. Spade is gentle with Clyde, helping him out of his wheelchair and laying him on the bed with his flaccid trouser legs and huge cock jutting out. Ellie goes over to him and starts rubbing his cock but Spade says, "No, let English have a snack," and pushes me toward the bed. "Go on, suck my brother off," says Spade. Ellie tucks her legs under her butt as I undo Clyde's zipper and tentatively take the cock out. I've never sucked a boi-cock before. I bend down to kiss it and wrap my mouth around it as Spade grabs me from behind and starts pressing his bulge into my ass. "That's it, baby," Spade says. "Help out a veteran."

The TV is on behind us, talking about the storm. I hear the sound of breaking glass and human distress. Clyde shoves my head down on his cock and I feel it ramming the back of my throat and I am trying not to gag. The bedcovers have that odd, neutral, over-trodden smell. Ellie slides her hand down the back of my pants to feel if I am wet. Then Clyde pulls me off and says, "Get your girlfriend's panties off. I miss my tattoo." So I yank Ellie's panties off roughly, and watch her climb on top of Clyde and start sliding her pussy down his cock. I flick her clit a little with my fingers, and then get up to get her vibrator from my bag and plug it in. Then I pinch Ellie's nipples hard until she is bouncing up and down on Clyde and Spade pulls at my arm. My pussy is dripping from sucking Clyde's dick and watching Ellie ride. She moans and grabs Clyde's shoulders as he holds her cheek. Spade throws me facedown on the bed next to Clyde, pulls my hips back, and shoves a couple of pillows under my tummy. Then he starts working his cock into my pussy. "Go on, *Bu,*" says Ellie. "Hammer her." Spade holds my shirt hem in his fist and grinds the heel of his hand against my nipple, grunting.

Then we all hear a thundering crack of lightning that is a little too close, striking down: the kind that leaves an imprint of light in the eyes and flickers the lights and makes the heart skip a beat. When it happens, Spade pushes into me so deep my lower lip slides up the sheet as I moan. I grapple for the vibrator and Spade puts the edge of the vibe on her clit. "Come on, Ellie, a group effort," says Spade. "A barn raising. Let's hear you hum like artificial light." First she makes little whimpers that knit us all closer. Clyde coaxes her with his fingers circling the button-burns down to her hole. "Who's got the button," Clyde teases, as Spade pulls the vibe away to squeeze Ellie's clit in his fingers and I grab her nipples. Then we get rough with the Amish girl, pinching harder while Spade buzzes her clit again and Clyde digs his hands into her ass. She squirms and moans and finally her face just breaks open, thunderclap-angry and cumulus-soft, and she starts gasping "Oh! Oh my god," while we swirl collectively into a spinning mass of vertiginous lust. I start to cum when I hear Ellie cum, then Spade grunts and grabs the base of his dick and shakes it into me. We want to make Ellie so dirty she can't go back.

The TV keeps replaying the roaring cyclone, the sounds of shattered structures ripped asunder by winds. Tomorrow the Amish will be the first responders as they always are in tornado alley: helping the English rebuild roofs and pick up glass. But prepositions have shifted. What the Amish call the outside will be their charity recipients for now. What's inside of Ellie belongs to outsiders now. We each keep a finger or two on or inside of her, and she's still whimpering with pleasure as we ride her fits and storms. We all feel so perfect cloistered in the spun winds of her sweet noises. "*Gelassenheit* to the storm," says Spade. "Submission to the storm."

# ABOUT THE AUTHORS

VALERIE ALEXANDER is a freelance writer who divides her time between California and Arizona. She is currently at work on her second novel.

D. ALEXANDRIA (d-alexandria.com), "Boughetto Princess," a Jamaican descendant, hails from Boston, has been published in *Best Lesbian Erotica* (2005, 2006, 2007), *Ultimate Lesbian Erotica 2006* and under the pseudonym Glitter, published in *Queer Ramblings Magazine*, *Gay Black Female Magazine* and Kuma2.net. She is currently penning her first novel and a collection of black lesbian erotica.

JACQUELINE APPLEBEE is a black British woman who enjoys writing erotica at inopportune moments. She is a library assistant by day, but has also earned a living making sex toys and silver jewelry. One of her fondest memories is of serving tea at S/M Pride, to an admiring crowd. Jacqueline has appeared in Clean Sheets, *Iridescence: Sensuous Shades of Lesbian Erotica* and *Travelrotica 2*. "Shine" is dedicated to a sweet chubby boi-dyke named Jad.

A. LIZBETH BABCOCK lives in Toronto and has done extensive work in the queer community, including counseling queer youth in an alternative school setting, and managing a supportive housing program for people with HIV/AIDS. She likes peach pie and is a chronic daydreamer with a slant toward the perverse and bizarre. Her writing appears in *Best Lesbian Erotica 2007*, *Best Lesbian Bondage Erotica* and *The Queer & Catholic Anthology*.

L. ELISE BLAND (lelisebland.com) never travels without her diary. Dominatrix, stripper, pervy actress—she's done it all and has lived to write about it in both fact and fiction. Her most recent publications include *Secret Slaves: Erotic Stories of Bondage* (The Fetish Chest), *Naughty Spanking Stories from A to Z: 2* (Pretty Things Press), *The Best American Erotica 2006* (Fireside/Touchstone) and *First-Timers: True Stories of Lesbian Awakening* (Alyson).

When not writing smutty stories about desert girls, BETTY BLUE spends her spare time raising a teenage son, editing corporate web copy, and learning Russian. Her stories can be found in *Best Bisexual Erotica*, *Best Women's Erotica*, *Best Lesbian Love Stories*, *Tough Girls*, *Best Lesbian Erotica*, *Best of Best Lesbian Erotica*, *Hot Lesbian Erotica*, and *Blood Sisters: Les-*

*bian Vampire Stories.* Betty lives in San Francisco with her partner, writer Jack Random.

RACHEL KRAMER BUSSEL (rachelkramerbussel.com) is senior editor at *Penthouse Variations* and hosts NYC's In the Flesh Erotic Reading Series. Her anthologies include *Up All Night*; *Glamour Girls: Femme/Femme Erotica* (both Lammy finalists); *First-Timers*; *He's on Top*; *She's on Top*; *Yes, Sir*; *Yes, Ma'am*; *Caught Looking*; *Hide and Seek*; *Crossdressing*; *Ultimate Undies*; *Sexiest Soles*; *Sex and Candy*; *Naughty Spanking Stories from A to Z: 1* and *2* and *Best Sex Writing 2008.*

CHANDRA S. CLARK lives in Chicago. This is her first fiction publication.

ISA COFFEY (aka, elizabeth): It's dark. I'm driving fast; way up high. With you, baby, always with you. History: thirty years under my belt, still helping young, middle and ancient women/ men discover the mystery-power of our sexuality. Recent history: growing wild, native medicinal herbs; healing my post-surgical wild brain. And to Gerry Gomez Pearlberg, especially: keeping bees. They're making honey; piercing our feet; fanning the heat from their hive.

SHANNA GERMAIN (shannagermain.com) is a connoisseur of anything that can be put into her mouth: chocolate, beer, coffee, various body parts, silky fabrics and nasturtiums. You can read more of her work in books like *Best American Erotica 2007, Best Bondage Erotica 2, Best Gay Romance 2008* and *The Mammoth Book of Best New Erotica,* as well as on her website.

ALICIA E. GORANSON (alicia-goranson.com) wrote a Lambda Literary Award finalist novel called *Supervillainz* that has hot trannyguy sex in it. And superheroes. And serious dyke drama over this little sublet in Jamaica Plain. And a girl sells out her girlfriend's roommate for a PDA. And it ends in a big old queer rally where shit totally goes down. It won the first Project QueerLit award, too. She has more messed-up stuff on her website.

ROXY KATT (roxykatt.com) lives in Canada. She got started composing erotic stories in the genre of "VHF" (Vaudevillian Humiliation Fetishism) because of being traumatized by certain supposedly normal cartoons as a child. Damn that Popeye and the hapless Olive Oyl! Within her troubled soul resides the never-ending battle between good and evil (or, as she likes to put it, the war between Batgirl and Catwoman).

D. L. KING (dlkingerotica.com) lives somewhere between the Big Wheel at Coney Island and the Chrysler Building and has a passion for roasted chestnuts sold on the street. She edits a literary erotica book review website, Erotica Revealed, and has written two novels, *The Melinoe Project* and *The Art of Melinoe*, both published by Renaissance E Books.

TAMAI KOBAYASHI is the author of *Quixotic Erotic* (Arsenal Pulp Press). She lives in Toronto.

MISSY LEACH (missy.com) is passionate about dolls, lip gloss, books, missy.com, photography, antiques, cotton candy and the Oxford comma. She will spare you biographical details on pets, partners and cities of residence. "And the Stars Never

Rise" marks her first time being published, and she is quite pleased to be here.

CATHERINE LUNDOFF is a computer geek who lives in Minneapolis with her fabulous partner. She is the author of two collections of lesbian erotica: *Crave: Tales of Lust, Love and Longing* (Lethe Press, 2007) and *Night's Kiss* (Torquere Press, 2005). Her short stories have appeared in such anthologies as *Caught Looking, The Mammoth Book of Best New Erotica 6, Garden of the Perverse, Amazons, Best Fantastic Erotica Vol. 1, Lust for Life* and *Best Lesbian Erotica 2006*.

PEGGY MUNSON (peggymunson.com) is the author of the Project QueerLit–winning, Lambda Literary Award finalist novel *Origami Striptease*. Her erotica has been published in numerous publications including *Best American Erotica* (2006 and 2007), *On Our Backs* and *Best Lesbian Erotica* (1998–2007). Peggy's first book of poetry, *Pathogenesis*, is forthcoming in early 2008 from Switchback Books.

AIMEE PEARL is the nom de plume of a kinky bisexual femme who resides in sex-positive San Francisco. She is deeply in love with her girlfriend—and heavily in lust with a couple of other people. She and her partner have a delightful, committed open relationship, so she is able to explore her desire for others, like the one who inspired her story. Like the third sentence says, every word in it is true.

RADCLYFFE is the author of numerous lesbian novels and anthologies including the Lambda and GCLS Literary Award–winners *Erotic Interludes 2* and *4*, edited with Stacia Seaman;

*Distant Shores, Silent Thunder* and *Promising Hearts*. She has selections in *Best Lesbian Erotica* (2006 and 2007), *A Is for Amour, Caught Looking: Erotic Tales of Voyeurs and Exhibitionists* and *Ultimate Undies: Erotic Stories about Lingerie and Underwear*, among others. She is also the president of Bold Strokes Books, an independent LGBT publishing company.

NAN ROGUE considers her sense of humor and vulgarity her best features, and is thrilled to have the opportunity to share both with a wider audience. Nan currently resides with her hot musician girlfriend and their large, spoiled iguana in coastal North Carolina, where she works as a bartender/in-house therapist in a predominantly queer pub. This is her first published work.

MIEL ROSE is a chubby, rural, low-income, queer femme witch of various European ancestry. She is currently living in the Northeast Kingdom of Vermont healing and dealing with undiagnosed chronic illness, childhood trauma and past life bullshit. She looks forward to making it through her Saturn return and finding a group of queers and outlaws to spend the rest of her life with. Her first accepted porno story will eventually be found in *Tough Girls 2: Down and Dirty Dyke Erotica*.

ANNA WATSON is an old-school femme living in the Boston area with her two sons and her butch Beau. Her work has been published in *Best Lesbian Erotica 2007*, *Erotic Tales II* (under the pen name Cate Shea), and is forthcoming in *Fantasy: Untrue Stories of Lesbian Passion*, Suspect Thoughts Press's anthology on drag kings, and on the Steamy Audio website. As Cate Shea, she writes for customeroticasource.com.

# ABOUT THE EDITORS

ALI LIEBEGOTT is the author of the following books: *The Beautifully Worthless, The IHOP Papers* and *Cha-Ching!* She currently lives in Los Angeles and is a staff writer for the Amazon TV show *Transparent.*

TRISTAN TAORMINO (tristantaormino.com) is an award-winning author, radio host, speaker, sex educator and feminist pornographer. She is the author of eight books, including *50 Shades of Kink: An Introduction to BDSM, The Secrets of Great G-Spot Orgasms and Female Ejaculation,* and *Opening Up: A Guide to Creating and Sustaining Open Relationships.* She has edited twenty-five anthologies and was the founding editor of the Lambda Literary Award–winning anthology series *Best Lesbian*

*Erotica.* She runs Smart Ass Productions, and has directed and produced more than twenty-five adult films, from sex education to reality porn. She's written for a multitude of publications from *Yale Journal of Law and Feminism* to *Penthouse,* is a former editor of *On Our Backs,* and a former syndicated columnist for *The Village Voice.* She has appeared in hundreds of publications and on radio and television. She lectures at top colleges and universities and teaches sex and relationship workshops around the world. She is the host of *Sex Out Loud,* a weekly radio show on the VoiceAmerica Network (sexout-loudradio.com).